This book is for the ones who got away.

ISBN 978-1-304-64866-2

Edited by Mark Henry Bloom

Cover photo by Vincent Skeltis

# Not Lost For Lookin'

A fly-fishing romance ghost-story

adventure of the high Sierras!

**Mokelumne** (muh-KUH-lum-nee) *n.* People of the fishnet. [Miwok].

# Ghost

*May 13*

Ghost in the corner. Have you ever held the gaze of someone you can't see? It's very strange.

6:30 and I slept on the couch again. I lay and watch him lean casually against the wall, just behind the growing light of morning. He nods his chin and smiles as I get up and head to the tub to draw a bath. He follows me in and slides down to sit against the wall. He kicks his long legs across the floor, crosses his heavy work boots and takes off his Smith and Wesson hat, resting it in his lap. His black hair falls and curls across his forehead.

The water begins to sound as steam rises from the tub. I undress in front of the old and carved oval mirror, dropping clothes in a circle at my feet. In the mirror he watches me. Wedged between the glass and the ornate frame is a faded black-and-white photograph of my grandmother. She is sitting by a river, my lanky grandfather standing beside her. They are fishing, the bank still white with snow. I'm about the same age as she was then. I look carefully over this picture, my face surrounding it in the glass. I look for traces of me. All my life I've been told what a dead ringer I am for this woman. A compliment. In the photo her smile is gleaming, her posture confident. I focus on my reflection beyond hers. Our leaf green eyes just beginning to show the fine lines of age at the corners. Our fine hair still dull brown from winter's seclusion, awaiting the long days of summer sun that will turn it a dirty gold. I take a step back and survey this family body. Strong. Balanced. No longer softened by layers of youthful flesh but yet to be carved and lined by age. It is, I realize, in its intended expression. Ghost gives an appreciative whistle from his spot on the floor.

> You know, Rose, I used to think you couldn't get any more beautiful, but you keep doing it.

> You just can't see very well through the steam, honey.

I smile and step into the tub, sinking down until my chin touches the waterline.

> If you get more lovely every year, what are you going to be like when you're eighty?

> Who wants to know?

> You know I do, Rose.

He says as he puts his hat back on and looks out the window at the rising sun. From the kitchen I hear the door slam and footfalls coming down the hallway. Leo pushes the door back against the tub and steps in. He moves to the sink, grabs his toothbrush and turns the water on full.

Ghost holds my gaze and says nothing. He lifts the hat off his head and offers it to me. I take it with wet hands and turn it round and round looking inside the brim. It's stained with dirt, and sweat forms a salty line around the band. I pull the hat to my face, burying myself in its darkness, and breathe in as deep as I can. He is all around me. I breathe him out and turn the hat around, settle it snug onto my head and sink as deep as I can into the water. Leo spits and shuts off the faucet. He turns around to leave and sees me sunk down in the tub. He looks tired. He looks decided.

I wish you'd stop wearing that dirty old hat.

He says over his shoulder as he strides out the door.

# Opening Day
## Slab Creek
*May 14*

My Dad was born in Hangtown, California, on opening day of trout season, 1943. California Fish and Game always opens its Sierra trout streams around the second week of May. His birthday happened to fall on Mother's Day that year — and though my grandmother saw that as an auspicious sign — the pride that my Papa and his fishing partner Jack Grant felt at having to miss opening day for my Dad's arrival was tenfold. Everyone knew how birthdays would be spent from then on. This year my Dad turned seventy. We've spent the last decade or two fishing opening day together. It's not a forced tradition; it's just the way it is. We always fish opening day and we always fish opening day in Slab Creek. It would have been a trip to Slab Creek that my Papa and Jack had to miss that spring day seventy years ago. So today Dad and I gather our gear to see if we can catch up with those two. My Papa died when I was nine, so Slab Creek is really one of the only opportunities I have to fish with him anymore. And at that he's not always there. But on opening day? They're all there on opening day. Always.

Jesus Christ, Dad, come on! It's getting late.

Well now, Rose, just hold on. I just have one thing I have to check on at the winery.

Dad!

Did you make the lunch yet?

11

Yeah. It's all packed and the—

Got the gear?

Yes, Dad. I got it all packed and ready to go.

Beers? Did you get a couple beers? I think the cooler's up on the shelf somewh—

I got it all. For Christ's sake, how long have we been doin' this? Let's g— Wait! Where are you going now?

But he's gone before I can finish. Fishing is traditions. And in my family, with Dad, it's more than just traditions: it's routines, habits. Our Modus Operandi. Unchanging and unfailing. Predictable. The rods and gear always get staged at the back door. The mini-cooler always gets four beers, one coke and lots of ice. Dad always wears a plaid long-sleeve, jeans and the same work boots he wears every day. I always wear whatever I want except I have to wear jeans and boots; otherwise, Dad won't go with me. You see, where we go fishing, things can get a little brushy.

The routines today are as they always are. Not the least of which is the obligatory struggle to pry my father out of this place like a tick out of the rump of an old dog. Which is just what it is. The winery is his old dog and it's going to do what it's going to do regardless of whether or not some tick is irritating its nether regions. *The dog's been trained, Dad!* I want to yell. *I'll tell you what's going to happen if you leave and go fishing. Nothing! Except you might have a good time in the mountains.* But I'd be saying it to the dust cloud he just kicked up from the driveway after speeding off toward the winery. I really have no idea why it's so hard to get him to leave for fishing. But it is. It always has been and it always will be. We are already fishing.

I follow him down and observe him from the Jeep. He's scurrying around the winery tanks. He's a quick man, not big. Strong and lithe. Others consider him a handsome and charming man, a pleasure to be around and do business with. But those people don't have to chase him around like I do. He almost walks into me as he drags a hose from one tank to another.

Well, guess we better get out there. Geez, Rose, it's late! Isn't this thing packed up yet?

It's opening day. It's never very smooth. For the rest of the season everything will be staged and ready all the time. But not the first day. The first day is for remembering. I settle in and await the conversations to come. It's the same drive, every time, every year. The same stories at the same bend in the road and at the same spots on the creek, every time, every year. But it's a comfort. One that I need. With the edges of my life beginning to fray, I need the few things I can always count on. I need to hear Dad absently ponder whether or not we should drop in and say hello to Bob Slate as we drive past his vineyard. Need to hear the ins and outs of how Dave Wright almost landed a 25-inch Brown who'd glommed on to a 9-inch Rainbow as we stand at the tail end of the Big Hole. Need to see Dad shake his head in silent admiration as we drive past the old barn that marks the edge of old Jack Grant's place, long since gone. Yes, especially this. Jack, my Papa's best friend. His fishing partner. I need, through my Dad's silence on that bend in the road, to understand how important their adventures were in forming his knowledge of what makes a worthwhile life. What makes a worthwhile person. And after we pass beyond the old farm, I need to hear him say to himself, "What a man." He doesn't say it to me because at this bend in the road, as he looks west over the distant pasture, he's twelve years old and sitting on a downed tree

13

above Silver Fork watching Jack scale a sheer rock face to get to the deep end of one of that river's epic holes.

This land is checker-boarded every square mile or so between private land, national forest and logging. So what you get is a wide dirt road, sometimes mud and sometimes choking dust depending on the season, crowded in from the sides with dense tall forest punctuated by expansive clear-cuts, barren and raw. I despise the clear-cuts. In the clear-cuts I'm reminded how hard people can be. How certain parts of our humanness can be catastrophic. There are gentler ways to harvest things. In the forestland that abuts the highways full of traveling tourists, they employ these methods. Because it looks good. Because people won't get upset. But back here in Slab Creek country, in scrubby foothill Forest Service land where sightseers would never go, they take it all down. Every bit. They take a sharp knife and peel back a big thick slice of Mother Nature's thigh. It'll grow back. But there will be scars. And as we drive through this clear-cut I'm reminded that there's a difference between the kind of scars that you get and the kind that are given to you.

We pass the cut and dive deeper into a fingerling canyon that will lead us down to Slab Creek. The forest is tall and shady, and we round the familiar bend that swings us around the edge of an old homestead. Some places have an enchantment that would be there if it was untouched wilderness or if you built a whole city on top of it. This is one of those spots. This place was abandoned by the turn of the century and hangs suspended half in and half out of this world. It's a little pillbox of a valley, studded with old twisting and crippled apple trees suspending masses of blackberry vines. Fences, cattle runs and barbed wire surround the north edge. The crumbling foundation is losing its battle with gravity and is sinking bit by bit into the soft dirt. Rusty cans with bullet holes decorate the fence line.

We slow down, stop. Sometimes we get out and look around. This time we don't. The place makes us uneasy but glad. Some thought about the effects that a powerful place can have on a person escapes me. I grab for the threads, as I always do here, but come up only with the impression that places remain and people do not.

But maybe it's just that I don't want to think about this homestead today. In seasons past I've gone through this little clearing and seen only the sun-dappled fruit trees. The strong foundation. I've imagined how perfect life must have been here. Today it's the parts that are missing that nag at me. The walls of that house, for one. The view, but no window to frame it. I turn my eyes back to the road and say nothing. Dad and I are both notoriously good chit-chatters, but not necessarily with each other. Aside from reciting these old notations of place and of men, we are quiet. My mind wanders back in on itself, to its messy countertop, to fuss and shuffle through the growing disaster of my carefully arranged life. It pulls at loose threads, starting runs despite my best efforts to keep it all together. But the homestead says, *No*. The homestead says, *It's coming*.

Rose! Did you hear me?

What?

I said the water looks good, don't you think?

Huh? Oh yeah. It looks perfect. Just perfect.

Dad has an impeccable sense of timing. He's not about to let me wander off anywhere except the actual woods. We're crossing the little stone bridge at the bottom of the canyon upstream from where we'll fish. You could fish here, I guess. If you are lazy, don't want to hike, are afraid of poison oak and only want to catch eight fish in a day. In my family we don't fish from bridges. It's downright cheating. The only exception my Dad has ever made to this rule was thirty-something years ago when he brought the family here. I was too small to walk very far so he dropped us in right at the bridge. And good thing he did because in a little hole up there underneath a big oak tree, I caught my first Rainbow. And not that it's important, but it happened to be the biggest fish caught that day, a fact my father tells with some pride. I have to laugh a little now at our refusal to fish here. It may be a bridge but it's a tiny bridge on an even tinier creek way out in the middle of nowhere in an elevation that doesn't attract much of anyone for anything. So in actuality, the fishing's probably pretty good. But cheatin's cheatin' so we drive on. We follow the little road out to its furthest point, overhanging the canyon, and cut the engine. It's all business now. Not necessarily in this order: Dad pees behind a tree, I pee behind a tree, we pull the rods out of their cases, attach reels, split up the lunch, check our fly boxes, roll up the windows and lock the doors. Dad looks around for a suitable place to hide the keys.

> I'm putting the keys under this rock here, ok? Here, I'll lean this branch over it so you'll recognize it, just in case.

Just in case he dies, he means. It may or may not be true to say that we have a slight bent toward the dramatic. But in our defense, you never know what could happen out in these places. We're never in range for cell phone reception (it's a proven fact that cell phone signals make for very poor fishing), we often go down treacherous canyons with no trails,

16

there's always rattlesnakes and I hate to state the obvious, but one of us could drown. Slab Creek, though, isn't very big and if you fell in probably the worst thing that would happen is you'd get clean. But then there's our own inevitable mortality. And this keeps tugging at the fringe of my thoughts as this is the first time I've been out hiking with Dad since he was diagnosed with an enlarged heart last year. Though he's able to maintain a pace that a mountain goat might begrudge following, we all kind of watch him warily, wondering if at any point he's just going to drop dead. Or at least I do. I shake my head at the injustice of a heart that the bigger it gets, the more likely it is to kill you.

If Dad is thinking about these things, he doesn't show it. He's already over the drop-off. All there is to show where he went are a couple of rustling pine boughs and some deep footprints in the pine needle crust of the canyon wall. I put my arms up across my face, close my eyes and push through the dense wall of young saplings and buck brush. I immediately lose my footing, slide ten feet, land on a ledge and manage to stand up just long enough to jump down the next drop. You have to take this slope like a skier. Jump and land on the left edge of your boot, digging into foot-deep pine needles, then jump, turn mid-air and land on your right boot, sliding a few feet, throwing a wave of needles and oak leaves in your wake. Ahead of me I can see my Dad literally striding down this vertical slope, two steps ahead of his own momentum. There is only one way to keep up and that is to just let go. Fishing with Dad means you jump off the wall. You hop across the rocks, not thinking about if they are wet or slippery or if you're going to fall. No one who thinks about those things can fish with my Dad. No. To fish with my Dad you have to *know*. You have to be able to walk on water. You have to be able to walk on air. You don't think about it and you sure as hell don't talk about it.

We careen down the steep half-mile that is the entrance to Slab Creek and land in a soft avalanche of our own debris at the edge of a little spring creek. We bounce up and over this and follow it down to the first singing pool of Slab Creek. It ain't much if you're looking for water. Maybe twelve feet across on average. But this place is not about the obvious. Most fishermen would take one look at this and laugh their asses off. The thing about it, though, is it's jam-packed with trout. This little creek is so full of trout, in fact, that they are just about looking for any excuse to get out. So when Dad ties on a little green caddis, pulls about eight feet of line out, grabs the fly in one hand while he sneaks the tip of his rod through a veil of tangled branches over the creek and pulls the line tight, well, I know what's going to happen. He gives a preemptive satisfied smile, pulls the fly 'til the rod is bent taut and lets go. The fly shoots out like an arrow from a bow, laced perfectly between the thousand overhanging vines and branches and drops into a tiny pocket of water no bigger than your face. Then wham! Fish on. A bright healthy Rainbow pirouettes across the pool and Dad is chuckling.

> Would you look at that! Well, well… what do you know? I got one. Nice one. Have you got one yet, Rose?

> Jesus.

> What?
> Nothin'. Good one. I'm gunna go up here, ok? You finish this hole.

"Finishing the hole" means pulling out another three or four bright little fish from that hot-tub-sized pool. I get a little distance upstream, feet squishing on the sponge of moss that is the forest floor. Down here the sun comes in bits and pieces no bigger than your hand. The air breathes. There is no wind but everything stirs. Down in this canyon, the membrane between this world and the others is very thin. Salamanders lift gently off the floor of the stream, waving globed fingers at me. I sense my Papa nearby, though he's probably down watching Dad. It's all right. I've been alone a lot lately. And what I need to work out, I might just as well ask the salamanders or the banana slugs about. Or the ladybugs for that matter, though they don't seem to be out yet. Good thing. I'm not sure I could handle the ladybugs just yet. I sit down and open my fly box and start poking around for what to put on. Decisions just seem to get harder and harder. I see a fat red salamander with his nose pushing up out of the water's skin. He might know.

What do you think? Caddis? Stimulator?

He floats an inch or two, sticks an eye out. *Why ask me? You do what you want. You always do.* He says through a bubble. I throw a little stick at him and he doesn't move. I poke around touching this fly and that, but I just can't help it and grab a #12 Royal Wulff and close the box. Salamander laughs as I tie it on and walk up to the next pool. I don't mind if people, or critters for that matter, think I'm stubborn. There's a Royal Wulff on my line and there's a ghost of a Royal Wulff on my Papa's line downstream. There are old and tattered and rusted Wulffs all over this creek. Lodged under rocks, entombed in tree trunks whose bark has long since overtaken them. Held gently in the twisted underwater cages of Slab's Elephant Ear roots. They are the record and the history of Us. I pull my line out as I hop to a flat rock just downstream of a nice shaded and shimmer-coated pool. In keeping with my training, I start at the lowest point and cast a few loops out toward the undercut. I know it's going to be fast and I laugh before the fly hits the water. It hits the water right in the current above the undercut, catches and gets swept right along the edge. Whap! Brown trout. I play it to the shore, which takes about two seconds. A Slab Creek "big one" is all of eight inches.

Nice one, Rose. That a Brown?

A tall and handsome man in faded blue cotton shirt, heavy khaki work pants, boots and felt hat stands behind the sunlight, rod in hand, creel on his hip.

Oh! Yeah, yeah it is. I just pulled him out from under that bank.

I saw that. Tried to get him out of there myself last time but no luck.

Maybe you weren't using the right fly.

I try to manage a smile.

Whatever fly I use is the right fly, kid, you know that!

He laughs as he turns away, shifts the bulky creel behind his hip, pulls his hat snug against his brow and with long and graceful steps, hops across the massive entwined roots that hold the banks at bay. *I know that, Papa. You bet.*

I look back at the pool and wonder if I should try for those three trout up under the waterfall, but I feel there's been enough for this spot. I release the Brown and hook the now-christened Wulff onto the rod, reel in the slack and head upstream. The creek is, as always, beautiful. Every pool an emerald set in the ornate carvings of god. Tree trunks split a thousand times over, twisted over themselves and into the sinew of the forest. A vaulted canopy of light and leaves converse in whispers high above me, dropping their words into silence. I fish.

Time does not go on, as it tends not to when fishing, but it's been a while since I've seen Dad. Usually, always, we leapfrog each other upstream. Not crowding but within eyesight or at least within a short jaunt upstream. I know I've been fishing slowly and Dad hasn't passed me, at least not that I've noticed. Etiquette states that you give a nod as you pass or wait for the one being passed to finish fishing so you can let them know you're moving upstream. This is what we do. But it's been quite a while and I begin to get worried. I hate myself for thinking about it, but I start thinking about Dad's heart and then I start to worry if he's downstream somewhere in trouble. But he could just as easily be upstream and fine. Or upstream and in trouble. And if he's in trouble — i.e., had a heart attack; i.e., dying; i.e., dead already and needing CPR, which I don't know how to do, or a helicopter I can't call and which can't get in here anyhow, then what am I supposed to do?

You're supposed to carry him out.

Says my Papa, sitting in a fern grove on a stump. I turn around, surprised.

Carry him out? I know, I know. That's what I'm supposed to do. I've thought about it so many times. I've thought about if I get bit by a rattler, someone better haul my ass out. That's what we do. But Dad? Out of Slab Creek? Alder, sure. Caples, maybe. But this is straight up, Papa!

You have to carry him out.

I do?

You can.

I can. Yes, I know I can, Papa. If I have to carry him out, I will.

Carry my Dad out of Slab Creek Canyon. I turn around and start walking carefully downstream to look for him. Carry him out? I can. I will. It might kill us both, though. *Goddamn your heart, Dad! Jesus. I'm a chick. I'm way more out of shape than you. How am I supposed to do it?* Papa is gone. Ghosts are only good for advice and perspective, not for heavy labor. *Put him over my shoulder? Drag him from the armpits? Over both shoulders? Fuck.* I wonder where he is. I question whether I should have gone downstream. *Maybe he passed me already. Maybe he's dying right now. He better not be. If he passed me without signaling me and he's not having a heart attack, I'm going to drown him. This is not fun-fishing. This is sucks-fishing. He shouldn't say he's healthy enough to go fishing if he's actually just going to get all the way out here and die and make me haul him up out of the crack of Slab Creek. Damn. Damn damn damn! Where are you Dad?*

Where are you, Dad?

I yell and the creek mumbles something in response. Branches scrape and leaves rustle and centipedes click their thousand legs along the bark. *Somewhere*, they all say. *Somewhere, somewhere, somewhere.* I turn and march upstream. He must have passed me. I just didn't notice. I hike as fast as I can along the overgrown river's edge, scanning the slope, the bank and the water all as I pass. The forest floor is deep in ferns; he'd be hard to see lying down. But even if he were having a heart attack, I know he'd have the wits to get himself somewhere obvious. I'm looking over the rock slabs and walking as fast and as careful as I can and I come around a sharp bend with a sheer rock outcrop and nearly knock my father off a rock on the other side. But he's not curled up on it clutching his chest. He's leaning off a rock on one foot with his rod bent over and a little trout dancing across a pool that I'm just beginning to recognize. The Lunch Hole.

Whoa, Rose! Watch out! What the hell are you in such a hurry for? Aw shoot! He got away.

Dad's line floats up in a lofty arch above his head and winds around a branch of a live oak tree hanging over the cliff above.

Damn!

Aw! Sorry, Dad. I didn't mean to—

Why are you... aw, damn this thing.

I'm so relieved I can't even explain myself. I feel like a complete moron. Of course he's fine. He's always fine. He's not the one who dies of an enlarged heart. Not Frank Waters. Not my Dad. No. He fishes; that's what he does. Not dying, fishing. And he doesn't worry about it, we do. But we are foolish. He knows. It's his heart. He knows it better than anyone and if he's not worried, then we sure as hell have no business worrying. He wouldn't be touched, he'd be insulted if he knew. So I just manage an awkward smile and hope he doesn't think I'm acting any weirder than I usually do.

Hold on, Dad. I'll climb up there and get that. It's time for lunch anyhow.

The Lunch Hole is a beautiful long hole that runs deep and green through the middle, shelved on this side by an abbreviated cliff that lands on a shelf of smooth black granite that has come to define Slab Creek. It's on this little shelf that we sit, protected and hidden. The opposite shore is a green and tangled stage on the canyon floor with wild California grapevines making love to broad leaf oak saplings and towering pines. Center stage is an old and arching live oak in a veil of Spanish moss feigning heartbreak. Through the glint and glare, fish pulse, suspended. We say nothing.

We eat our lunch and feel thankful. Lunch on the creek is so much more important than lunch any other time. If only for the feeling — a pure and simple realization that you do not belong here. That it is neither a privilege nor a right. That no one or thing grants you passage. Not nature or god or any other lofty thing. You simply realize, between bites of delicious soggy bread, that you are only here and breathing because a gathousand-billion things are lined up and sustaining in order for you to be. It's just plain old good goddamn fortune is what it is. The molecules of the air are holding together at a consistency that your body, the organism, can breathe it in and pump blood to your normal or enlarged heart. Fortune that an earthquake doesn't send that cracked cliff down upon your head. That one of those sugarpine cones don't come screaming out of the tree and take your lights out. That gravity or oxygen doesn't suddenly change enough to kill us off. What do we know? What makes us think we can count on things as much as we do? Our constructed world does. But you get out here on the Lunch Hole and you realize you're lucky. Damn lucky.

We're damn lucky, Dad.

Yes we are.

I don't have to tell my Dad I'm worried about the molecules of air not staying together like they're supposed to. That kind of thing doesn't apply to him. He's lucky for other reasons that he keeps to himself.

You're looking pretty distracted today, Rose. What's going on in there?

Oh, nothing. Or everything. I don't know. I'm feeling nervous I suppose. You know when you jump on a rock and it moves just a little bit and you can't decide if jumping off is going to make it worse? That's how I feel about everything in my life right now. Frozen. And nervous.

You need something to focus on. How about the book you were writing about that mountain man who built the old cabin up in Mokelumne canyon? Haven't heard about that lately.

I can't make up fiction when my life is chaotic, Dad. It's just, I don't know, too much unpredictability. Seems like all I want to do lately is fish. Maybe that's an escape, though.

Why don't you write about something predictable then? Write about fishing. Nothing scary about that. It could be a guidebook or a journal.

That's not interesting. Who would want to read my fishing journal?

I would!

Well, *you* would. But you already know it by heart. Nothing ever changes in fishing.

Exactly. Here, you want one of these cigars? I got a Swisher
Sweet; it's a little broken. Hell, well here's half. Or I got this
vanilla-flavored one or—

Ah, gimme that half, it's fine.

I want to argue with him but I can't. Even the cigars are unwavering.
Having a selection of cigars is part of it, but you can only smoke Swisher
Sweets at The Lunch Hole and certainly only a Swisher on opening day.
We smoke quietly and send smoke signals up the cliff face and watch
them disperse into the layer of little no-see'ums hovering under the
overhanging branches. Dad smokes his half down then flicks it with his
middle finger out into the stream. Watches to see if any fish think it's a
snack. They never do but the thought amuses him every time. He lays
back on the rock, tucks his creel under his head and pulls his hat over his
eyes.

Just going to take a quick nap here.

Always.

I quietly hop upstream and look for my own place to rest. A green and
mossy hummock calls me from behind a grove of tall firs. I throw my
creel down, rest my head upon it and close my eyes to the only bit of sun
encroaching on this shy stretch of river. As I sink into the soft and grassy
embrace of the knoll, my thoughts dissipate and I do not chase them.
Sitting high up on the boughs above, I look closely at my hands,
becoming absorbed by their scaly skin, the sharp knobs of knuckle
wrapping clear around the branch. The claws that punctuate each finger
click distinctly against the fragile bark, dropping crumbs upon my sleeping
figure below. I stare at that, detached. The wind blows a ruffle of feathers

about my face and carries with it the distant sound of running. A deer, by the sound of it, thudding and crashing through the underbrush of the woods. I straighten up and with hard beats, rise up and away from the branch. With a wing dipping to the sound, I slip toward the upland rise. Footfalls crash and fall below me as I follow, the red hide of the deer showing in glimpses below me through the shaggy branches of pine. She bursts upon the clear-cut in the full spotlight of the sun and she runs. Dodging the stumps at full speed, cutting left then right, she looks back for whatever pursues her so doesn't see me coming. I drop upon her, wrap one talon around her shoulder and the other around her belly and pick her up off of the ground as she kicks her legs, twisting and wrenching to see me with her amber and fear-brightened eyes.

I awake with a start, the sound of hooves still beating in the woods around me. They fade away as I sit up and take stock of my surroundings. Creel, hummock, rod leaning casually against a sapling. I pick up my gear and slip away from this spot, feeling like a trespasser. The river's chatter and endless gossip comforts me. A few pools between me and the knoll put me back in a happy mood. The creek is, as always, restorative.

I work my way upstream and cast into a long run where every cast gets a strike. I throw them all back and start feeling a little guilty for their trouble. The day is waning and the bugs are out and this is what Slab Creek gives you. You'd have to be dead not to catch fish here. After ten or twenty more strikes I can't take any more torture so I take out my pliers and cut through the hook way up where the fly is tied and remove the hook's entire lower half. I hike around the bend and am surprised by the Big Hole. For a moment I stop and look back downstream and wonder if I should wait for Dad and let him fish first. But on this hole one person gets the tail and the other gets the top. You don't get both. This is The Big Hole. The top is deep and dark with a waterfall of tinkling diamonds raining down a scratched and chipped granite wall. The entire left side of the pool runs along a perfectly vertical wall of rock that extends up into the trees and down into the water. The right side is sequestered under a fallen oak that's hunkered over it's watery prey, holding itself off the water with one massive and gnarled arm on each bank, its bulbous trunk reaching toward the waterfall, twisted and glaring back over its shoulders. It mumbles, *Don't even try. What's here is mine.* No, the top of The Big Hole is practically impenetrable. So I'll fish the tail, which is wide open, and let Dad negotiate with the hungry oak beast up top.

I pull out my line with the hookless fly and lay it down where cliff meets water. I see a trout come up from the bottom in a slow and lazy spiral and slurp the fly in. I don't flinch to set the hook because there is none. The fish dives back to the bottom and the line pulls tight and then I feel a tug. Then two more tugs, the rod bends with it then springs back and the fly comes shooting up out of the water and into the trees behind me. I just smile.

> What's so funny, Rose? Looks like you lost one. You shouldn't be laughing about that.

> I never had it to begin with, Dad. It actually had me for a moment, if you want to know the truth.

I show him my hookless fly and he looks at it for a second, furrows his brow, then shakes the image out of his head.

You know, Dad, we don't remember the ones we've caught half as much as we remember the ones that got away.

You said it. Well, you going to fish the top of this?

No, you take it.

Dad pulls out his line, casts out a few times for distance then perfectly threads the fly-line between the tangled end branches of the heaping tree and the cliff, a space of about three inches thirty feet away, and lays the fly down perfectly in the popping bubbles where the waterfall mingles with the surface of the water.

Amazing.

Nothing.

Darn. Well, that's where they should be.

You know, Dad, in all our years fishing here, I've never seen anyone catch a fish in the top of this pool.

Nope. Me neither. But I did see Dave Wright almost land a 25-inch Brown after it tried to eat the 9-inch Rainbow he'd hooked down at the tail end there. Did I ever tell you that one? That's a good one. He played it right up to his feet then reached down to grab it and it flopped off and got away. Boy, that poor little Rainbow though. Just a pawn...

He chuckles as he clips his fly off and reels up his line. The oak tree huffs and shifts its weight. Drops a branched hand down into the water where a 24-inch Brown trout snuggles in between the wavering twigs and watches the current pick off the dead leaves and take them downstream. It's time to leave. It's fair enough. We break down our rods, return flies to tin boxes and look up, straight up: the supposed way out. The nearly impossible way out, as opposed to the truly impossible ways out flanking this hogback for a mile in each direction. It seems overwhelming from this point.

Well, if we're going to get there, we might as well start.

Dad says as he grabs for a low-hanging branch and pulls himself up the steep embankment that crowds the river. I follow him at a steady mountain goat pace as we dig in and pick our way out of the canyon. Exhausted, we make the road and catch our breath before walking the last half-mile to the jeep. The thought of two cold beers in an icy cooler ensure we don't dally. Reaching the jeep Dad locates the keys under the branch. Neither of us mentions the fact that he was here to retrieve them himself. It's a good day when no one drowns, falls in, gets eaten by a bear or has a heart attack, but that goes without saying. We open the tailgate and, so as not to be cheating, we put our gear away before we open the beers. That done we sit peacefully on the tailgate, drink our beer and survey the day in silence. It is, as I know it always will be.

Me and Dad drive away from Slab Creek Canyon and head toward home. I lean my head against the bumping window and close my eyes to the hum and rumble of the jeep over the washboard road. It is the end of opening day. I'm tired. I've thought, have been thinking about, everything everything everything and now, I don't think about anything. Dad thinks but he don't say. Or maybe he doesn't. I don't know. We roll along the dirt road, the wind in the windows and in my hair. Blowing. We round a bend, and the flat platter of the clear-cut, stacked with stumps, approaches at an even pace. The earth moves under our jeep and slows down.

Ravens.

All around us is a clearing and the pedestals of trees sawed off at the beginning. And all above a swarming tangle of squawking, flapping ravens. They expand and then tightly converge. They see us and settle. On every stump, they alight. Uncountable. Maybe twelve ravens on twenty-two stumps. Maybe a hundred ravens on a hundred stumps. It's hard to say.

On stumps surrounded by dry mud too hot for even weeds to grow are ravens. Some are preening. Some are shaking the dust out of their wings and craning their heads behind them. Some pin prey against the surface of the stump with their talons while they rip and rend the guts all about them.

Dad stops the car. He normally wouldn't do that. But he does and he stops it right beside the largest stump in the cut and on this largest stump is a giant raven. He is framed in the window. His feathered coat is ragged and dirty and full, sticking up all about him in contradiction. His head a mohawked crown of violent blue-black feathers. His talons the size of my own hands. He turns his head sideways to show us his one gleaming golden eye and he doesn't say.

But I know.

# Fly Away Home

*May 19*

Ghost folds another paper airplane out of old scribbled-on scrap paper. He regards it before deftly pinning corners and smoothing perfect edges. He hands it to me, starts in on another one. I pitch the airplane toward the ceiling from my cross-legged position on the couch. Lyla and Ace leap convulsively around the living room trying to catch it before it hits the floor. Lyla snatches it with a cackle, parading it around the couch.

> Throw this one low. It should sweep up and to the right. Then Ace can get it.

He hands me a square-shaped plane with a wink. I throw it low and it resists the floor, sweeping up and to the right. Nose straight up in the air, it pauses, then falls straight back down landing smack dab in Ace's eager hands. He turns to escape out of the room with his catch and runs hard into his daddy's legs.

> Hey bud! Watch it! Where are you going so quick?

Leo says as he rights Ace and turns him around. He looks to me on the couch.

> I'm going out to pick up some lumber in Stockton. I want to take the kids for the day.

> Oh. Sure. That's fine. I guess I'll find something else to do. Maybe I'll go back out to Slab Creek.

Again? You just went.

I know. But actually, I was thinking of starting a new project. Writing a fishing journal for the summer.

Seriously, Rose? You need one more project? You're distracted enough as it is. The kids need your attention.

You're taking the kids!

I don't mean now. There's everything else too. The mortgage is due.

I'm already working full-time at the winery, Leo. I don't know what else to do. I'm not going to kill myself when you're turning work away.

You're going to have to ask your parents for money again this month. We're not going to make it.

I can't. I just can't ask them one more time. We have to figure something else out.

They can help.

I know they can. But that doesn't mean they should. I'm going fishing. I'll be back in time to make dinner and put the kids to bed.

A comment crosses Leo's face but he doesn't voice it.

C'mon guys! Get your shoes on and get in the car.

I stay on the couch as they pull away. I fight the anger that tries to well up and out. I grip a couch pillow and just as it's about to choke and die, a paper airplane hits me in the forehead.

Snap out of it, Rose. There's nothing you can do. Just get your stuff and go fishing.

I throw the pillow through the ghost and walk back to the cedar-lined closet and pull out my fishing clothes. Tug on strong but faded old jeans and thin wool socks. Tuck a threadbare cotton button-up into the back of my pants for later. From the back of the closet I fetch my best boots. Packers, which after years of use will tolerate only my feet. I pull these on and admire the patina of the leather, dark black in spots where the laces constantly rub.

Good for another season or ten.

I say out loud with satisfaction. My grandmother always said you must never ever buy cheap shoes or bras. Dressed, I head out through the kitchen down to the Landcruiser waiting on the street. With every item I load into the back, I feel a weight lifted.

I get in and take the cut-off to Main Street. Main Street is not just the main street, it's the only street. Hangtown is essentially two rows of old, cracked and huddling Western fronts of brick and stone, climbing upon each other to loom over the little main drag that dissects them. Like fat-legged children squatting over a game of marbles, they crowd in on all sides. High up their foreheads are stamped with signs and symbols. The Oddfellows, the Masons, the Druids. I park by the Druid monument and hop out. Apparently it marks the spot of some ancient and powerful triangulation, but no one knows for certain. This area has long been an attraction for people with unusual motivations. Not just those who marked the buildings, but others. Practitioners of witchcraft and black magic moved into the south county back in the '70s and are there still, while hard-set rednecks refuse to come out of the woods in the north. But there is precedence for the independent-minded.

The town sits near the site where gold was first discovered in California, resulting in a mass migration of people that, to this day, is the largest in all of human history. And they came here. They made this town. I think about that as I look around the little street, busy with the morning regulars. I picture the asphalt gone and the streets caked in dirt with miners dry panning the ruts because in those days, gold was everywhere and easy to find. It's not so easy now. The miners and the hordes are gone, and all that's left are respectable business folk, farmers doing much the same as they always have, families, churches, PTA and city council members. They all call it Placerville, the official name, though I refuse. I long for the harsh and earnest times of the gold rush. Wild and thriving years without law yet without the chaos you'd expect. Abiding by the few rules that everyone knows and all agree to. I think about this as I walk past the Emigrant Jane, the old whorehouse. And it reminds me of Texas Sally. She was the only whore in camp in the early days, and when she was shot by a man, the miners and all the men in camp were so furious, they dragged the murderer to the center of town and hung him without a single protest. You see, they loved her, whore or not. And they needed her.

People greet me as I make my way down the street toward the corner coffee shop. Born and raised here, as I am, I know everyone and everyone knows me. It's "Hi Fred, and how's the shop?" and "Good morning, Jan. I saw your new grandson last week. What a big boy!" And so on and so forth. I love these folks and likewise, but of late I feel like I'm speaking through a bubble that has formed around me, and though it's clear and you can see me in it and all appears normal, on the inside I'm in my own atmosphere. And it stirs and moves with invisible machinations. I can chat and coexist with my friendly and civilized neighbors, but I'm always watching over their shoulders for the occasional vestige of Old Hangtown to appear. And they do. A jacked-up little pick-up truck with no doors and caked in mud will drive past amidst the sedans and minivans. The street blockades or no-parking signs the city continually puts up will disappear during the night. I have the distinct feeling that these souls are all around, still around. The people of Hangtown. And like me, they walk amidst this scene feeling like they are in exactly the right place, just at the wrong time.

I swing the door to the coffee shop in on screeching hinges. The owner and only employee of the place stands behind the counter, white hair in a thick wave matching a white apron stretched tightly across a substantial belly.

Hey Mac!

Morning, Rose! Haven't seen you in a while. What has you out so early?

Aw, just going fishing.

Great day for it. Where to?

You know better than that, honey.

Can't blame a guy for tryin'. The usual today?

Yeah, thanks.

Mac heads back to the long wall of griddles and fryers then returns directly with a black coffee and a side of bacon. He wraps it up as I push a few crinkled bills across the counter. He scoops them up and throws them in the till without counting them.

Say hello to the kids and family, all right?

Will do.

With more urgency than usual, I head out of town, needing to put some distance between me and the routines of my home and my town. As the miles unfold, everything around me loosens. The drive out to Slab Creek is as it always is. Hitting the high spots, avoiding the ruts and skimming the washboard at 35mph just like Dad taught me. It's not a bad road if you know how to handle it. I slow down past the old homestead just beginning to frost itself in apple blossoms. Around the bend is the clear-cut, and last week's encounter with the ravens edges in on my thoughts. I approach, tensing despite my best efforts to stay rational and calm. *Were they even there?* I have to wonder. Scanning the field of stumps, some movement catches my eye. Someone is walking along the edge of the road. *Nobody* walks around out here. This is miles from nowhere with nothing and no reason to be here. Unless you're growing redneck weed out in the manzanita. Or Mexican weed under the pines. One glance tells me it's not a hillbilly or a cartel thug. First off, it's a woman. Her hair is long and tangled and red as Indian paintbrush. She's got an old beat-up backpack on one shoulder and a fishing pole over the other. I pull up alongside her and slow down. She stops and turns a pale, freckled face toward me. Her cheeks are full and pretty. She is compact and small, but I can see through her scuffed jeans and plaid shirt that she's strong. She

drops her backpack in the dust and puts her hand casually on the door.
With amber eyes and a huge grin she says:

Howdy!

Howdy yourself. What are you doing way out here? Are you lost
or something?

Lost? I'm about as far as you can get from lost. I'm just walkin'.

Where you headed to?

She looks in the back of the Landcruiser, glances over the fishing gear
tossed around in the back.

Oh, I bet you'd like to know!

You want a ride?

No thanks, I'm going somewhere special and I'd just as well go
alone.

She picks up her pack and walks a bit in front of me. I gas the 'Cruiser
and roll up alongside her again. She keeps walking. I keep pace with her
for a few yards before she stops again. She takes a deep breath but doesn't
turn, so I say:

Looks like you're heading to Slab Creek.

Nope. What gives you that idea?

Your fly-rod. That and Slab is the only body of water for ten
miles.

She turns to face me at last, staring at me so cold my fingers start to feel numb. She waits a good long moment then says:

I'm not looking for company.

Me neither, I just want to make sure I know where you're going so I can either fish it first or go somewhere else. I'm assuming you're heading for the bridge?

Did you just accuse me of fishing from a bridge? Does this look like my first rodeo?

Well, you're out here in no-man's land on foot. I'm not sure what to think.

I'm heading to a secret spot. There's something there I want to check on.

That's ironic. *I'm* heading to a secret spot to check on something special too.

Now you're making fun of me.

No, I'm not. I'm actually going to a very special place to fish and check on something. Why don't you get in and I'll give you a ride.

She looks hard at me with clear eyes and then gives in with a laugh. She walks around to the back of the 'Cruiser. Shaking her head, she opens the tailgate and throws her stuff in a heap on top of the creels, rod-cases, boots and beers in the back. *What the hell,* she says getting in the front seat.

What's your name?

Glory. What's yours?

Rose.

We wind our way away from the ugly clear-cut ridge top and drop into the lush, steep canyon that swirls down to the creek bed below. We drive over the little stone bridge that neither one of us will fish from and can't suppress a smile.

What are you doing out here on foot? Don't you know this elevation is full of dope-growers? And not the nice hippy kind either. There's trip wires with A-K's and shit all over Rock Creek in the next watershed. I hope you weren't thinking of fishing there next.

Oh, I know all about those wires. I probably laid most of them myself.

I look at her the way you might look at a caterpillar wielding a pocketknife.

You serious? So you're out here growing weed?

No. My boyfriend is. I'm out here because I'm trying to get as far away from him and that scene as possible. A while ago, things got crazy and I split. I got nothin' and nowhere to go, but what I do have is my fishing pole, a bunch of beans I stole from the house and all the money of Jesse's I could find.

Jesse's your boyfriend? Won't he come looking for you out here?

No, he doesn't know about this place. I've decided to just spend as long as I can out here, 'til the weather turns or I run out of money. After that I have no plan, but I don't care to think about it right now. What brings you out here alone?

I'm just goin' fishing. Thinking of writing a fishing book.

Like an instruction manual?

More like a journal. Each outing as its own entry. I'll probably describe the river, its history, then whatever happens there on that day. I'll write it all down. I haven't developed the idea more than that. I figure it will become what it wants. But that's the work excuse for being here. Mostly I'm just getting away.

Well, you and me both then. What are you getting away from?

My life, I guess. Not all of it. I have two kids; they're wonderful. Hard work but good work, you know? Then there's my husband. It's just tough right now.

That all? Sounds like a pretty normal life.

I guess it is. Normal. There's a man who haunts me.

Affair?

Kind of. Not exactly.

We look at each other for a long moment, then she shrugs her shoulders and asks no more questions. A short stint brings us to the drop-off, where we hop out and get our gear together. Glory has an old fiberglass rod, scratched to hell and crudely mended in spots with epoxy and duct-tape. She sees me looking at it. She shrugs and smiles. She don't need much, I guess. It's a good way to be. I don't need much either, but I do need a good fly-rod. I take out my Sage and Glory gives out a little whistle. I shrug and smile, then say:

Key's in the tailpipe.

In case you drown?

Hey, you're right: it's not your first rodeo.

We laugh and head over the cliff. Careen down the steep pine needle canyon wall to the tangled green basket that holds the magical pools of Slab Creek. Glory walks right to the first pool and plops herself down on a big fallen cedar. I sit next to her. We open our fly boxes and start poking though them. She furrows her brow at this one and that. I wonder what her fly is; I can picture her with something sassy like a Stimulator. She fishes out an old elk hair caddis and holds it up. Part of its wing falls off onto the ground.

That's lookin' pretty rough, Glory.

She puts it in her hat and rummages around the box some more. She pulls out another caddis and holds it up.

The hook's all rusted! Give me that box.

I take the box and peer in. There are a small handful of the most abused-looking flies I've ever seen.

This is just unacceptable. Here, I'm going to give you some of my flies. Are you serious? You thought you were going to get through a whole summer on those? Didn't anyone ever teach you proper?

I do all right, thank you very much. But I will take that pretty orange one you got hiding up in the corner there. What is that?

She nods at a small, sparkling new orange Stimulator with tawdry rubber legs.

That's a Stimulator. You've never seen one? Girl, you need to get out more.

I tie on the usual. I nod toward the first hole and Glory hops up as if to say, *Don't mind if I do*. She threads through the tall ferns to the edge of the hole without making a sound and casts out. It lays out fair enough and instantly gets hit by a quick-flashing fish. Glory yanks back on the rod, causing line, fly and fish to come flying out of the water and up into the tree crowding in from behind.

Aw hell! Yells Glory.

The branch wiggles and dances with the flipping little fish swinging like a live piñata. I run over and grab the fish as she grabs the branch. I unhook it and toss it back in the water.

Catch and release? She asks.

Jesus.

I say, shaking my head.

I might think you're laughing at me. But I'll assume you're just jealous.

Why don't you try a roll-cast? It will keep you out of the bushes.

That's what I was trying to do.

Ok, here's a little trick my Dad taught me. Just put the fly at your feet with some slack, like this. Then hold the tip up tall. Now look where you want the fly to land and just point at it, real quick-like, with the tip of the rod. Like so.

The line lifts up off the surface of the water in a big gently rolling arc. Like a wheel moving across the surface of the pool with the fly rounding the top and landing gently near the pocket of the waterfall. We wait. Nothing strikes.

Well, it sure looks pretty anyhow.

Glory says with a smirk. I roll up my line without comment and head upstream to the next pool. I glance back to see Glory's line appear and disappear behind a vine-covered sapling. I make my way lazily through the fern-covered banks, stopping occasionally to watch the red salamanders in the shallow eddies. Papa isn't around today. He probably doesn't want to crowd us. He was always very careful not to ruin the fishing by bringing too many fishermen along.

There's a deep little run along the top edge of this hole that catches my attention. It's the only deep spot in the pool and certain to be holding the only big fish in here. It's blocked on the side closest to me by a protruding rock and on the other side, the entrance to the run, by overhanging branches dangling just inches above the water. I could cast into the middle of it, but everyone knows if the fly doesn't come floating down naturally from the top, it's not going to fool anybody. The whole situation is exacerbated by a wall of brush and trees behind me. Most fishermen would just forget it and move on to the next hole. The problem is, every hole on Slab Creek looks like this. It's a fly-fishing nightmare really. There's never a clear place to freely cast. The creek is choked with elephant ears growing out of the middle, ferns and vines dangling in on all sides and thick forest right up to the edge. The holes are small and the fish are spooky. Yes, it is most certainly a fisherman's nightmare, but if you can learn to cast on Slab Creek, you can cast anywhere. On Slab Creek, the trajectory of the fishing line needs to become three-dimensional. It needs to defy physics. It needs to move according to the rules of the magic in this hidden canyon. Going where you will it and moving like a live thing. Like a snake that strikes forward by moving side to side in opposite directions.

I take another good hard look at this deep little run and all the obstacles protecting it. *This can be done*, I think. It can always be done, in fact. The way just needs to be seen. And the way becomes obvious. I simply need to cast out enough line to reach the hole, without back-casting. It needs to land to the left of the rock even though I'm to the right of it. Then it needs to continue up the left side of the rock, making a sharp right turn so it doesn't hit the overhanging branches and the last four feet of line needs to head back to the left and lay directly in the current. The fly needs to land just at the edge of the bubbles from the waterfall so that it looks as if it just accidentally got washed over the falls. Just an average cast on my Papa's favorite creek.

I strip out some line, flick the tip of the rod straight up in a quick motion so the line extends vertically above me in the air, avoiding the trees behind. Then I flick the tip down and forward, generating speed, and at the very last second I make an abrupt pull to the left. This throws a left curve in the half of the line closest to me and loops it over the rock. The last half of the line continues forward, threads itself between the rock and the branches and pings the fly off the rock at the base of the waterfall, missing the bubbles. Not perfect, but I'll take it. The fly catches the current and gets swept under the dangling branches just as I hear a long appreciative whistle from the cliff above me. I look up to see Glory doffing her hat and smiling. Then she points and makes a gaping face. I look back just in time to see a big golden side rolling over my line and my fly bob back up from under the water.

Damn it!

I yell as I turn to scowl back at Glory, but she's gone on ahead. Leapfrogging. *At least she knows the etiquette,* I say to myself. *Except the part where you're not supposed to distract someone when they're waiting for a strike.* She's just getting me back for the tree-fish incident and that's fair enough. I fish alone peacefully for a good long while and then round the bend to the Lunch Hole. Glory is there with a fish on and another with its lights out on the bank at her feet.

What are you doin'? I ask.

Gettin' lunch. You want one?

Well, I have what most folks would consider lunch in my creel. But I do like a nice fresh trout now and then, I guess.

She lands the second fish, grabs it around the belly, turns it over and cracks the back of its skull against the rock with a loud *pop.* She reaches into her back pocket and produces an old pocketknife, flips it open and begins gutting the fish. The knife pulls and catches on the flesh as she saws at it.

Here. Give me that thing.

I say, taking my little elk-bone fishing knife from my creel. I turn the fish belly up and split it from tail to gill with a quick draw of the blade. I hand the fish back to Glory and she works on the entrails while I cut the second one.

> You're going to have to do something about your gear. You couldn't clean your fingernails with that knife.

> Yeah well, I'm workin' with what I got here.

She makes a little pile of sticks and pinecones on a big flat slab, digs around in her pack and produces a lighter and a little piece of chicken wire rolled up. In a matter of seconds she has a flame going and the fencing folded over it. She reaches into her shirt and produces a little leather pouch that hangs from a string around her neck. She loosens the tie, reaches in and pinches a bit of chunky salt crystals. Clearly from a natural salt spring somewhere, it's peppered with tiny bits of black granite. She salts both fish and sets them on the rack. They begin to cook and steam.

> That's some pretty salt, where'd you find it?

She just looks at me with a raised eyebrow then goes back to tending the fish. Guarding her secret places. I can respect that. I know a good place to harvest salt in these mountains too and I'd never tell a body where it is.

We make a spread of our food between us. Salami, nuts, fruit from home and two steaming fragrant trout. We eat in contented silence, watching the leaves float reflected down the river. Leaves rustle above. It is, as it always is.

> Pretty good trout, Glory.

There's nothing like trout right out of the stream. It tastes so clean. It takes like, I don't know, like life. It's that fresh.

Life tastes like fresh trout?

Yup.

Do you ever order trout at a restaurant or from the store?

Hell no! Those aren't trout. They're not trout unless you catch 'em and kill 'em and eat 'em right there. Those other things, they're something else. Old, gray, dead... or farmed things. They sure as hell don't qualify as trout in my book. They're only trout if they lived wild and had a proper death, like being caught on a fly or nabbed by a grizzly bear.

Glory takes the last bite of trout with a satisfied grin.

Say Rose, where did you learn to cast like that?

Like what?

Oh seriously. Don't play modest. I watched you down there.

Well all right. I learned right here. And I learned from my Dad. But I'm nowhere near as good a fisherman as he is.

He must be a fishing god.

No, he's Frank. But he can actually walk on water if it will get him closer to a fish he's going for. I've seen him do it, no joke. The man's got will. Did you learn to fish from your dad?

Oh god no. I taught myself. The only thing my dad taught me was how to mix a gin and tonic, how to avoid taxes and how to blend the perfect secondary colors. He was an artist and a world-class alcoholic.

So you didn't have the greatest growing-up?

I didn't say that. My dad was my closest friend growing up really. He was a genius painter and he loved me more than anything else on God's green earth. In fact, he had nothing but unchecked love for everything and everyone. But he had no defenses. He was so sensitive that the whole world and everything in it literally hurt him. I think that's why he had to be drunk all the time.

Where is he now?

He's dead. Drank himself to death a few years ago. Left me with a lot of good memories and a whole host of bad habits. He was a good man who couldn't do no good, you know? He used to get himself into these ridiculous situations. It was constant and tragic and funny as shit. Like the time he ran over his own leg with his van.

How the hell do you run over yourself with your own vehicle?

That's a good question.

Well?

Well maybe I'll try to explain it later. Isn't there something special in this canyon we were supposed to be checking on?

We simultaneously get up and pack up the lunch, grab our rods and kick the hot coals into the creek with a sizzle. There is something that needs checking on, and I know by now it's the same thing Glory's here for. We don't need to mention it; we just head upstream together. The place we're heading for is a huge grove of dead and decaying trees. Some standing and some toppled over each other, all rising from or falling into the deep green weave of vines and ferns that form the cloak draped intimately over this entire canyon. As we walk toward the bend that will take us to the grove, we hear a slight crunching underfoot. Here and there little red lights, like dizzy stars, zip through the periphery of our vision. Glory looks back and smiles. She knows it's here. The magic that lies in the bosom of Slab Creek. It's the heart of the canyon itself and it only shows itself once a year.

As we approach the bend, Glory's shoulders become dotted, then covered with little red gems. Ladybugs alight in her hair. They begin to fall all around us from the sky above. They crunch underfoot. We round the steep cliff face and there the dead grove rises before us. Every surface that isn't living — dead wood, stone, sand — is covered in a seething thick blanket of ladybugs. Two inches deep, they crawl over and under and around each other. A red and moving mass. In the center of the grove, a ring of old and forgotten trees curve up and together like the rib cage of some huge and ancient beast. Ribs covered in uncountable drops of living blood. Glory spreads her arms wide, closes her eyes and turns her face to the treetops. The ladybugs drop like rain onto her cheeks, her neck and her hands. She's smiling.

This is where my Papa lives. I say quietly.

This is where I want to live when I die. Maybe you can ask if he won't mind the company.

She says with her face still upturned to the treetops.

Is your man here too? The one who haunts you?

No. He can't get in here. Most people can't. You have to be either really alive or really dead to be permitted into this place. He's not living like he wants. He's just another uneasy ghost.

She drops her arms to her sides and picks her rod back up. We take a last long glance around the ladybug grove and then without further comment make our way hand over hand up the steep canyon wall. After a slow and arduous climb, we stumble through thick manzanita, sweaty and gasping, and spill out onto Slab Creek road. The road brings relief and we laugh easy as we pick pine needles and ladybugs out of our hair and clothing. Glory runs the last few yards to the Landcruiser, snatches the keys out of the tailpipe and opens the tailgate.

> I don't know you well, but I know you well enough to bet there's cold beer in here somewhere.

She dives into the back, tossing gear aside and eventually yanking out a small cooler sloshing in ice. We put rods and creels away, pop caps on the door-jam and pile in for the drive out. The rumble of the road below, ice-cold bottle against my thigh, quaking gearshift beneath my palm and warm dusty sunshine streaming through my open window is both memory and actuality. It is as it always is.

> So where am I taking you, Glory?

> I been camped out just up the road from where you got me this morning. I'll show you.

We wind uphill through the tall pines, then through the clear-cut. Around the bend, we approach the old homestead.

> Right here. Glory says with a nod to the homestead site.

> Well, I should've guessed. Is there a sacred spot of mine you don't know about?

Probably not, my friend. I been at it a long while. And what makes them yours anyhow?

I pull off into the grassy meadow that surrounds the homestead. Glory has her laundry drying on the fence of the old cattle run. I help her carry her gear to the foundation of the old house where she has tethered an old tarp from the chimney to the only remaining wall. Inside the chimney she has a small metal box serving as a wood stove with a thick iron plate for frying on top. To the side she assembled some foundation stones to make a shelf upon which there is a small kettle, a pan, a tin coffee cup and a spoon. Against the stone wall is a neatly arranged raised bed made from wood from the old split-rail fence along the road. On top of this frame she wove young pine-boughs together to form a soft mat and on top of that a woolen army blanket and a sleeping bag.

Somebody's been reading John Muir.

A girl's gotta make do.

She says as she hangs her denim jacket on one of several rusty nails sticking out of the wall. I watch her, then notice an old tin bowl half full of water.

Where are you getting your water from?

There's a spring down the end of the meadow there. The people who lived here actually had a springhouse built at some point. The cement bottom and walls are still there, just filled in with mud. I'm going to dig it out here soon and get a roof to cover it. It's on my list.

You don't even have a shovel! Listen, Glory. Why don't you come back to town with me? I just... well, I don't think you should stay here all summer. Rock Creek is not that far from here. What if your boyfriend or his people stumble across this?

What am I going to do in town? I don't have anyone or anywhere to go and I don't want to waste that money on rent.

I have an idea. You could stay at my folks' house for a while and come with me for my fishing and writing project. My plan was to fish once a week and write about it, but honestly, fishing alone just isn't really natural to me, and my Dad isn't really supposed to be out hiking too much. All I really want is some company and some help getting in and out of places — someone who can appreciate a little adventure. You're clearly qualified for that. In exchange you get a safe place to stay and a real good excuse to go fishing. What do you say?

Glory looks up as a red-tailed hawk swirls above. She takes a long moment to answer as she watches this bird, seeming not to have heard me. The hawk screeches down at us, flaps its wings and climbs higher.

You know, it was a red-tail that saved my life.

Glory says, still watching the bird.

What are you talking about?

When shit got crazy and I left. I don't really know what happened.

I'm not sure I follow.

It was a couple of weeks ago. I just woke up pinned against the wall of our bedroom by a pile of broken furniture. I don't know how long I was out. There was a coffee table overturned on top of my leg and broken chairs around my torso. My arms were all tangled in them. The wood was splintered everywhere. All the small things from the room were broken and pushed up against me: vases, jewelry, hair brush, shoes, everything. I felt like I'd been run through a washing machine on "heavy." I was covered in bruises. Every single inch of my body was bruised: my legs, my ribs, my feet, my face. The back of my head had a huge gash and a goose-egg that would make a field-surgeon cringe. I think that's why I can't remember what happened. But I know it was bad and I know it was Jesse.

She rubs the back of her head as if expecting to still find the bump there.

When I woke up, I tried to push all the splintered wood and things away from me. Every part of me hurt; I could barely move. Right then, out of nowhere, a little red-tailed hawk came screeching into the screen of the big sliding door in our room. It hit so hard its feathers flew off around it. It picked itself up, flapping its wings, and flew up against the screen again. Screeching even louder. It grabbed the screen in its claws and flapped and flapped, pulling at the screen and screaming. I heard it. It was saying, "Run! Run, Glory!" It was a hawk scream, but on the inside I heard it: "Run! Run Glory run!" And so I forced myself up. I grabbed my backpack and blanket, a handful of clothes, some cans of food and all the money I could find. Then I opened the screen and I ran. I ran as fast as I could. That hawk flew straight away south from the house and I followed it. It disappeared above the forest, but I just kept going in the direction it went and never veered. I walked for two days and then I came to this homestead. Which I knew. Which I'd often stopped at on my way in here and I knew. I was safe and it was that bird that saved me.

Jesus, Glory.

She pauses to look up as the hawk swirls higher. I watch as she contemplates its flight.

Well, what's it saying now?

I don't know. But I'm not ready to leave this place. It's the only thing that's felt like home to me in a long time. And right now, that's what I want. But thank you for the offer. I hate to think I won't see you again. It's strange, but you feel like a friend already and I haven't had many of those. If any.

We both watch the hawk lift higher and eventually fly beyond the clearing, out of sight. The low rays of the waning sun lay flat and bright against the valley floor, lighting the blossoms of the gnarled and ramshackle apple trees like fireflies. Gnats and mayflies lift up from the marshy grasses and fall into an erratic dance with the dust and dandelion seeds that drift gently on the breeze toward the canyon. I look over the little homestead. The few things there are tidy and cared for in their use. A home enough, strong and surrounded in comforting beauty. A feeling stirs in me and it is far closer to envy than pity.

Very well. Have it your way. But I won't sleep at night picturing you out there digging out a springhouse with a bedpan. I'll come by in a couple days and bring a few things from the winery. A shovel, for one. And a sharpening stone maybe.

You don't have to, but I guess you know that. I won't turn it down.

With that and an unceremonious goodbye, I get in the 'Cruiser and turn back onto the dusty evening road toward home. The homestead recedes behind me as I wind away into the forestland. Giant slash piles as tall as buildings loom among the roughly harvested sections. The miles disappear into my wandering thoughts, dappled here and there with images of my new and unusual acquaintance, but mostly, as I draw near town, the blunt and relentless demands of my own life grow upon the horizon. A blaring horn rips me from my meditations and I swerve to miss a sun-bleached blue 1970 Ford F100 whose lane I was claiming more than my share of. I slow down. The truck comes to an unnecessary sideways halt in the middle of the narrow road on a blind corner. In my side mirror I see an old man in greasy jeans and a cut-sleeved shirt that exposes dark and muscle-braided arms jump out of the driver's side. He slams the door and stands with his meaty hands spread open in a questioning, or challenging, posture. His dirty trucker hat is pulled low enough to hide all but a menacing, white and straight-toothed smile.

My stomach turns cold. I step on the gas as the bend, the truck and the man retreat and shrink into the landscape of the mirror. I immediately think of Glory, alone in her homestead. It's not just Jesse that she has to worry about out in this neck of the woods. There's nothing and no reason to be here. So when someone is, it's worth wondering about.

# Little Tin Cup

*June 7*

The children run screaming in circles around the dusty barrels of the old
sherry house. Sweat drips from my forehead, leaving a trail of dark spots
on the pale sheath of dirt and spider webs that have claimed the old
floorboards. I spin an empty barrel on its edge across the room, making a
temperamental scratch along the floor. It's not the first today and it won't
be the last. Dad stacks old cases of wine against the wall, the contents of
which have long lost their labels, their color and their efficacy. Ace tips a
stack over as he lunges for Lyla's hair.

> Hey you two! Get on outside with your roughhousing. Damn it!

Dad mumbles as he bends to retrieve the bottles. I turn to the hesitant
kids with a wink.

> Go on and listen to Papa. There's 120 acres out there for you to
> play on. I don't know why you guys are always underfoot.

They scurry out and up one of the gnarled, bulbous fig trees out front and
watch from a safe distance. Our goal is to clean up this barn of forgotten
alcohol and make it the respectable little sherry house it once was back in
the gold rush days. It's a side project of Dad's that hasn't garnered anyone
else's attention but mine. He already has a few years-worth of sherry aging
but the tiers of barrels are buried deep within this tomb of mislabeled
vintages of wine, old boxes of labels and rusted car parts, all laced
together by the strong and persistent webs of the black widows watching

with idle curiosity from every nook and rafter. Dad guides another barrel into place in the corner.

> You've been bringing the kids to work a lot lately. Can't Leo watch them?

> He has a hard time dealing with kids in the morning. Says he just can't do it.

Dad stops and wipes his brow with the faded blue bandana that is ever present in his back pocket.

> Aw hell. People have to do things. They just have to get up and do it, that's all. *Can't* do it? What's that mean anyway?

> He works on projects 'til late at night. Sometimes until two or three in the morning. But he's always done that. It just never mattered until the kids. You know, 6:00 am happens for them regardless. Anyhow, it's fine. Our counselor told me I had to accept him how he is, not try and change him. So, I'm trying to do that. He doesn't like mornings. I do. So I'll do it. I'm trying to make things work, Dad.

> Yeah, well you're taking care of the kids *and* working, both. That doesn't seem fair.

> Life's not fair. Isn't that what you always told me? Anyhow, I have an in with the boss.

He pretends to miss my joke and we return to work in silence. By noon the old wood floors are mopped and clean. The gallery of rejected wine, the rusted parts to unknown equipment, the decomposed labels and twenty-two or so stout black widows have been replaced with rows of sherry barrels stacked three high. All that remains in the place are things that are needed, and nothing that is not. The kids are calling for lunch from the treetops and I can't argue. Dad comes out and stands under the towering old fig tree peering through the dense leaves at the kids.

Run up and see if your grandmother has some lunch for us, will you, kids?

Aw Papa! Can't we get a ride in the jeep?

You can walk. Go on now. Rustle!

Disappointed, the kids start a half-hearted search for their shoes.

Dad, do you mind if I take these extra lug boxes here?

What for?

Who cares what for? Do you need 'em?

Well, no. But you're sure making off with a lot of stuff lately. For that supposed fisherwoman you met in the woods?

He says with a laugh.

Maybe. And she's not *supposed*, she's actual.

Sure you're not selling this stuff on the street?

Because there's such a hot market for broken old boxes and bailing wire? No. Just trying to help her out is all. Might head out there later, if Leo will watch the kids. She's trying to scoop out a springhouse.

What?

He shakes his head at the thought. Dad can stand the thought of a lot of things, but he can't stand the thought of someone doing a job the wrong way. I see an opportunity here and exploit it.

Yeah, I don't know anything about springhouses and how they work, but it's ok if it's full of mud, right? Just as long as there's water on top? And she shouldn't worry about the cracks too much, right? I mean, can't she just put a bowl or something under it, to catch the water?

No! What? No, she can't do that. She shouldn't even be messing... I mean, damn it, you got to clear it out first. At the very least.

Oh, sure. She's doing that. She's got a nice-sized garden spade.

He throws down his work gloves and stares at me for a moment, wondering who raised me to be so dumb.

Kids! Get back here. Go put your shoes on. We'll get lunch on the way.

They appear as if by magic in the doorway. They didn't get very far.

On the way where, Papa?

Slab Creek. After I look at this springhouse, we'll do some fishing. Sound ok?

The children run for their shoes, completely forgetting how they didn't want to walk anywhere.

Soon enough we're through the frosty stand and bumping our way along the road to the homestead, listening to the fishing rods roll and clank against the varied and numerous tools Dad loaded into the back of the Landcruiser. The children conspire in the backseat, empowered by milkshakes and dizzy with the aroma of hot grease and French fries. One benefit to having a mother in crisis is that she's less willing to argue over healthy food, reasonable bedtimes or the questionable necessity of shoes. The children hang out the windows to be the first to catch sight of the mysterious encampment.

Why would she live out here? Lyla yells through the rushing wind in her face.

Why not? Ace answers. I would!

It occurs to me this might not be the last time in my life I have to fetch supplies to a loved one out in the woods. I'm thinking of all the survival skills I haven't taught the kids yet when Lyla leans into the front seat with a serious look.

Is she a witch?

No, honey. She's not a witch. She's just camping out.

We round the bend and break upon the green meadow that buffers the homestead. The orchard has lost its blossoms and the unmanicured branches are thick in summer leaves. Glory is leaning on the old cattle chute and if she's surprised to see a car full of people, she doesn't show it. We pull to a dusty stop and pile out. The children cling to my legs and peek out at Glory from either side. She pulls herself up and approaches.

So you must be Lyla and you must be Ace, right?

They say nothing.

> Well, that's all right, but if you guys are interested, I have a pet chipmunk over there in the woodpile who I've been training. If he gets really good, I'm going to rent him to a circus.

The kids take a couple of steps out from behind me, craning to see the woodpile.

> Go ahead. There's a can of pine nuts by the fire-pit. He'll take them right out of your hands.

They try to resist but can't and break away at a dead run for the woodpile. I watch them go then turn back to Glory.

> Glory, this is my Dad Frank.

I gesture toward my Dad who's banging around in the back of the Landcruiser unloading all the tools and supplies. I shrug my shoulders and raise my voice.

> Dad! Stop for a minute and meet my friend.

Dad comes around to shake Glory's hand and size her up. Glory is reserved.

> Nice to meet you, sir.

> Call me Frank. So. You know Slab, huh? Not many people do.

Glory gives him a narrow-eyed look.

I know Slab and some others around here.

Sure, like the American? You fish there? It's pretty good.

The American hasn't been worth fishing in years, but I bet you know that already.

Well! That's pretty true. I guess she's all right, Rose. Well, fisherwoman, why don't you show me this springhouse of yours.

Glory and Dad walk off down the meadow to the spring. I look around for the children, but don't see them anywhere. The homestead is silent except for the buzzing of a few bees and the slight rustle of wind. I get up on the cattle chute and stretch to see the whole valley, but they aren't there. I call a few times with no answer. A slight moment of panic seizes me as I think of Jesse and other potential hazards out here, but then I take a deep breath and sit down. I close my eyes and wait. I see the homestead, the meadow, the orchard. Quiet. I open my eyes, stand up and head way down to the north end of the meadow and through the stand of trees. I come to a rock and call for the children; they come scrambling over almost immediately.

Mommy! We were calling for you but you didn't come. We were scared. Ace got stuck, up on that rock! And we were lost!

You weren't too lost, baby.

I don't like being alone out here.

You're not alone. If you ever feel scared anywhere, just look up. See all those birds? If I have to, I'll borrow their eyes and see you. Ok? No matter where you are, I can find you.

They grab my hands and drag on me as we make our way over to the springhouse where Dad is scratching his head and Glory is holding a handful of shovels. The work Glory's been doing has made a huge muddy mess and one of the side walls has moved substantially with the change in water level. Glory looks hopeful.

> Looks good, don't you think, Frank? I mean, I've already increased the flow by digging some of that stuff out over there and—

Dad shakes his head and waves his hand at her.

> No. This is just, aw hell. Kids! Back in the car. Let's go fishing. I'm going to have to think about this for a while.

> What's wrong? I thought it was going well.

> Let's go to the creek, Glory, see if your fishing is as good as your plumbing. We'll tackle this when it cools off a bit.

We squeeze everyone into the car and make our way down the canyon to the bridge crossing Slab Creek. We pile out and I can't help but be pleased to take the children here to the spot where Dad first put a fly-rod in my hand. We walk a short distance upstream and gather together under a big bragging oak tree. The children have only ever fished with bobbers and worms in the warm and mellow ponds around the vineyards. This is something altogether different, but I know they are ready for it. I string up the rods for the kids. None of the grownups bother to put ours together. The most wonderful part about fly-fishing is that it's exactly as much fun to watch as it is to do. Sometimes more.

Glory sits back against the mossy base of the tree and helps Lyla pick out the prettiest fly from her fly box. I tie Ace's fly on and then walk them out and put each one on their own hole. I give them a few very simple instructions. Start with the fly at your feet, look at the spot you want to cast to, then point at it with the tip of your rod. In a while I'll tell them how to cast it back and forth once, but first things first. This is how I was taught and this is how I teach others.

People tend to get obsessed with the proper technique and the timing of the cast and getting it to look as beautiful as they've seen in the pictures, but that really has nothing whatsoever to do with catching fish. Step one? Get the fly to the fish. However that happens isn't important. What's important is that one of the very first things someone experiences is the excitement of seeing a fish jump at the fly they just put on the water. They'll miss it because they haven't been told how to set the hook. The cast could have been simple and unimpressive, but the moment that first fish appears, that's the hook. The tension and apprehension — watching the fly float on the current, not knowing what will happen but feeling like something *should* happen — all this swirling in the mind, when *whap!* A beautiful wild creature comes out of nowhere for the thing you offered it. That moment, that first time, is the most important thing. And it should not be adulterated with the burden of the "right way" or the history or the expectations of whatever people think fly-fishing is about. It's not about anything except that one moment, where you and the fish meet at the end of the line.

Lyla and Ace do a reasonable job of flicking the flies out there. After a couple of tries, they get the line out pretty far across the pools. I watch Lyla's fly hit the water nicely and I know it's coming and sure enough a little trout strikes at her fly. Lyla screams and doesn't pull the rod up or anything and the little trout can't get its mouth all the way over the fly anyhow and so it just keeps biting at it, following it as it goes down the current.

A fish! Screams Lyla. A fiiiiiiish!

Glory and Dad are laughing and clapping by the shore.

Catch it! Yells Ace.

I can't! I don't know how. Mom!

Laughing and proud, I go over and help her bring in her line for a new cast.

> Try it again, honey. Only this time, hold the line under your finger here, against the handle. Then the line will be tight when he bites. When you see him strike, hold the line and pull the tip of the rod up quick, ok? You'll get him.

She casts out again and sure enough she gets another strike right off. Kneeling by her side, I hold the slack of her line in my hand and when he strikes, she pulls the rod up and I pull her line in with my hand quick enough to set the hook. She doesn't notice what I've done because she is jumping and barely breathing, watching a nice-sized Rainbow pirouette across the surface of the water. It dives and jumps, putting on the best show a new fisherman could ever hope for. I help her bring the fish to shore as everyone crowds in to see. I keep it just under the water. It's nice and healthy, bright silver with a rainbow like an oil puddle swirling all around its sides and belly.

It's so beautiful.

I know, honey.

Good one, Lyla! Dad says as he gives her shoulders a good shake. That's a big one! Maybe the biggest one I've seen in a couple of years here. You're a natural!

I pull the fish a little closer to shore.

All right, I'm going to let it go now.

Can't we keep it?

You can't keep it like this, baby. It's a wild trout. It's only beautiful out here, and we're not going to kill the first fish you catch. Take a good long look at it so you never forget how pretty he is.

I gently back the hook out and it's gone. Back down into the green creases of the riverbed. Spurred to addict-like desires for more, the children rush back to their spots and cast with hyper-focused attention for the rest of the afternoon. Dad and Glory alternate helping and by the end of the day, we have two new fishermen and a small passel of trout to take home for dinner. After the lessons in properly gutting the fish, which is equally enthralling, we pack up and head back on the road to the homestead. Driving up through the forest with the late afternoon sun blinking through the trees, I remember that first Slab Creek Rainbow from my childhood. How I managed to cast the line and even set the hook my first time. How it was the biggest fish caught that day. And what a natural fisherman everyone thought I was.

Say, Dad. I was just remembering when you took us here to fish when I was little and I caught that big Rainbow, remember?

Sure do.

And how I hooked it and everything.

I think of how I held my daughter's line, pulling it in so the fish would stay on. I look over at Dad in the passenger seat. He's contentedly watching the landscape roll by.

Yup. You hooked it. You were a real natural.

We crest the ridge and come around to the bend toward the homestead. Dad and Glory are discussing a plan for the spring as we pull up to the cattle chute and get out. The trees sit still as an air of discomfort blows slowly and stirs around our feet. There are deep ruts in the meadow from tires spinning hard and the gate is open and laying half down on the ground.

Stay in the car, kids.

I say in a stern tone. Glory rushes to the little makeshift room and stops, looking all around her. Everything is displaced. The pine-bough bed is flipped over and ripped apart. The cooking set-up and all the utensils lay strewn about the floor amongst her clothes and the few items she had. Loose stones are kicked over and misplaced. The tarp, no longer attached to the wall, is escaping down the meadow billowed by the down-canyon wind. A giant and slow waving stingray scared from its hideout. Dad makes his way to the ruins.

Ransacked! Jesus. Look at this place!

Jesse. Had to have been.

Maybe, I say. I've seen some pretty sketchy people not far from here lately. Wouldn't put it past any of them. Then again, they might work for Jesse too.

Glory runs to the corner stone of the fire-pit and pulls at a loose stone there. It falls away and she gropes inside and comes up with nothing. She sits back hard in the dirt.

It's gone. The money's gone. I'm so fucked now.

Dad walks down to the springhouse and comes back with a few old tools.

They took the good tools too. Damn it. That was my favorite saw.

I'm so sorry, Frank! And you were nice enough to try and help me. Look what my messed-up life gets everyone. Trouble. Loss. Headaches. I'll pay you back for it.

With what? Don't worry about the tools. What are you going to do about this?

She can't stay here, Dad. Her boyfriend is really dangerous. And if this *was* him, he'll be sure and come back.

I can just move camp. It's ok.

No you can't! Your backpack is gone; all your stuff is trashed. All you have left is the fishing pole you had with you. You're just lucky you weren't here or you might be gone too. This is no joke, Glory, you need to get as far from here as you can.

I'm not leaving the mountains.

Then come stay with us.

Dad interjects. Tossing the old tools to the ground and wiping his brow with his old bandana.

I can't. I don't want to burden your family. I can take care of myself, really.

I'm sure you can. You won't be a burden. You can work off the saw and your room and board since Rose has gotten so unreliable lately anyhow. Maybe between the two of you, we can finally get some stuff done. Just for a little while, until you figure out what to do.

Glory looks around at the remains of the homestead in silent acquiescence. We collect her remaining belongings. Her old denim jacket, clothes, fly boxes. Roll the sleeping bag and blanket into a neat bedroll and cinch it tight. She looks around at the remaining gear and then grabs the old tin coffee cup and ties it to the bedroll.

This was here when I got here. But I think it should come with me.

You want to leave the rest of this stuff?

Yeah. I want something of mine to decompose with the rest of this place.

We load into the 'Cruiser and pull onto the old road that will take us home. The ride is warm and silent. The children are both leaning on Glory in the backseat, fast asleep, mouths gaped open. We begin to see houses, ranches, and soon enough the small tight cluster of old buildings that comprise Hangtown. We skirt town and head up into a lumpy series of vine-covered hills. Through the winery gate and up to the house on the hill. The vineyards are studded in buds and the house is bordered by an orderly garden, a giant oak and some mulberry trees. My mother stands waiting on the path in front of the house. The kids wake up when we pull up and jump out of the car.

Grandma! We caught fish for dinner!

She hugs them as they lumber by, dragging the bulky creels and the little cooler with fish to the house.

Glory, this is my Mom Margaret. Mom, this is Glory. The woman I was telling you about.

How are you?

Says Mom. With a kind but steady gaze. Glory seems dumbstruck and sputters a quiet response:

Fine, thank you.

Mom, I was hoping we could host Glory here for a while. There was someone in her camp and—

You don't need to explain. You're more than welcome.

She says this looking at Glory, not me. After a moment, she turns to glance back at the house.

I'll go get the room ready. I bet that old cat has the pillows all messed up.

She heads for the house. Glory leans in a close and says:

      Wow. Your mom's kind of intense. I mean, she seems real nice. But something—

      Well, you don't go talking to Margaret Waters unless you're ready to say exactly what you mean and you got nothing to hide. Because I tell you what, that woman *knows*. She will never call you out, she minds her own business. But she just looks at you and you know that she knows and then either way you gotta face up to it. Believe me, my teenage years were rough. But she's all right. A good one to have on your side actually…

      Well, don't just stand around all night gabbing.

Says Dad as he walks by with the rest of the fishing gear.

      Glory, you know how to cook?

      Sure enough.

      Good. Those trout aren't going to fry themselves. Let's see what you can do with them. Maybe we can put it toward the saw. If they're really good, maybe even half a shovel!

# Not Lost for Lookin'

Alder Creek

*June 20*

It's that dark twilight when the sky is deep blue-black, but you can still see the outline of trees and hills against the sky. In an old-west town with one dirt street. Wooden sidewalks, four or five buildings. From out of town, over the hill, two giant black horses come charging down the main street. Massive, muscular horses. Draft horses. Percherons. They are almost as tall as the buildings themselves. They come thundering into town harnessed to — and dragging — a giant uprooted oak tree. The tree is on fire. The roots extend toward the horses and the flames are crawling up the roots and up the harnesses to the horses. The horses drag it into the middle of town, stop and stand on their haunches, pawing at the sky and screaming…

It's Wednesday, fishing day. I stand, face upturned to the showerhead, and turn the hot water handle up to full. I want to feel the heat of the fire from my dreams. Steam fills the shower and my skin turns red and mottled where the water hits. But I just can't ever seem to make it hot enough in real life to hurt. I jam the handle hard a couple more times but it's full up. *Damn you!* I say to myself. My new mantra.

You talking about me, sweetheart?

Ghost says from the doorway with a sly grin. Arms folded, he leans comfortably there.

You know I am.

I say through the foggy glass.

What's got you so grouchy this morning? Not sleeping well?

You know what's got me. And I think it's time you did something about it.

I'm trying to.

Try harder. Be here. Be with me.

He walks up and leans his forehead against the glass door of the shower. I lean mine against my side and close my eyes. I open them and he's gone. I stand back and stare at the print for a moment, then with more force than is necessary, I wipe it away. I abandon the shower and make my way around the quiet house. The children are gone early with their father. I make a ceremony of bacon and black coffee, trying to shake off the mood.

Where should we fish today?

I ask the empty table. *Alder*, replies my coffee cup. I look down into the cup, where the coffee moves and swirls a bit before coming to rest. Moves again in the other direction. It's that in-between time of the season where the tiny creeks are already crowded with elephant ears, but the big streams are still blowing with run-off. The mid-sized streams are still just a tad bit too high, but the small-to-middle-sized creeks (or creek, I should say since there's only one and that's Alder), will be perfect.

There's a knock at the kitchen door, then it cracks open as Glory sends a little whistle through the house.

Come in! You should try a turkey call next time.

Hey, you never know. I didn't want to disturb anyone, if you know what I mean.

He's gone with the kids. You want some coffee? I was just asking it where to fish.

Hell yes! And where did it say?

Alder.

Ah! Of course. Perfect.

Alder is a moment. You have to catch it just right. Its elevation is right there at the place they don't measure. This stream doesn't even exist if you go at the wrong time, like in September. You'd drive down the dirt road always thinking it should be right around the corner and next thing you know, you end up where you started, wondering how you could have missed it. No, Alder only exists at the right time and no other time.

It's 8:00 am and Alder Creek is just putting on its finishing touches. Pulling itself out of nothing. Water emerging from the dry bed. Pebbles unfolding to fish, unfurling with a flip and flash of tail. Boulders going under with one last breath. Eddy currents bubbling, falling, stair-stepping waterfalls and pools, spreading out to catch the sunlight and wait for their fishermen.

The morning takes care of itself, and we are soon enough on the eastbound highway to the mountains. We wind along the south fork of the American River, a stunning beauty whose most fertile days are gone. There's always a touch of sadness on this drive. This road whose proximity brings hoards of men to her banks, men who on a daily basis rape and rob her of her fish, her gold and her clarity. She's still beautiful though and though she is, I will never fish her.

We bridge the American and head up the road toward Alder Creek. It's a little-known byway that connects one place with another but is not really a place in itself, or so you'd think. Its shoulders are lined with a thick wall of trees that obscure any view of the country beyond. The hawks circling overhead know what lies behind that green veil. They need only turn eastward in their high perches to see the gentle sloping canyon patched with alder groves and bedded in pine needles. An unseen surface, this canyon is carved and creased by Alder's moving waters and watched over in the distance by the stark and glistening granite peaks of the Crystal Range.

The veil drops for just a moment and I nose the Landcruiser through a gap in the wall of trees and onto a little road that winds down to the creek. We cross Alder at the old cow camp. A gem among stones. The line shack, boarded and swept, waits. In the fall the cowboys from the Nielson Ranch will gather the cattle here and gather together themselves on this porch. I don't know if Alder exists for them then or not. It wouldn't be here for us. Perhaps neither would the cow camp if we drove in. But the boys and the cattle and the creek would be somewhere and they would be together and they would not see people passing through at the wrong time.

We drive through the creek bed; water and fish retreat, come back. The creek is shallow here and only ten feet across at its widest. This camp sits near the headwaters and this water is good for drinking and washing your face in and filling the kettle, but it's not for fishing. This is the nursery. When the small fry get tired of dodging hooves and cowboy piss, they head downstream to fuller waters. And so do we.

The road builds itself in front of us and falls away behind while we wind up and away from the canyon floor. Red bud, buck brush, cedar, fir and ponderosa all watch from the downslope. Cabin-sized boulders sit on their haunches above. I tilt my chin to the boulders; they say, *Humph*. I laugh. I look for the way in. There is always only one. Though you might descend to the creek from any point along this ridge and reach the waters below, that don't mean you've entered. There is always, only, one way in and one way out of any fishing stream. So I watch for the way in. Sometimes you can see it, and sometimes it has to be given to you by someone else. The way into Alder was given to me years ago by an old fisherman I know. He'd fished it for 240 years before he told me about it. And I will fish it for at least 190 more before I pass it on.

The entrance to Alder is marked by an outcropping of granite — intimate, huddled forms stacked one against the next lean over the cliff that rolls itself out to the valley below. I park the Landcruiser under a cranky pine and throw the tailgate down. We shuffle around in the creels, get fly boxes sorted, reels attached. Check the little cooler to make sure the beers are fully submerged in the ice. Chores done, we head for the rim. The hike in is quick and easy and deposits us in front of two perfect little holes. The creek is small water, but I have come to expect good fishing, a term which in my book has to do with a whole host of things, none of which include the number of fish caught or their size. Alder is good fishing because the trout, though small, are wild Rainbows, lightning fast and full of spirit. Alder Creek trout are half bird and when you hook one it shoots straight for the sky; fins splayed to wings and tail flapping.

Glory looks up from her fly box.

What are you putting on?

The usual. You?

The usual.

Royal Wulff. It's all I fish. I am a one-fly woman except for the occasional flirtation with an Elk Hair Caddis or late summer grasshopper. Glory fishes a Stimulator now, but she's more outgoing than I am. Through all the fish and all the streams and all the flies, I've come to the understanding that every fisherman has one fly pattern that's his own. And it doesn't really matter if that fly matches a hatch on the stream. Because you catch trout with will, not with flies. And you can't catch a fish with your will unless you have your fly on the line. That fly is sometimes a beacon and sometimes a siren and sometimes a portal, and when you fish, you send your will up the rod and down the line and into the fly, and from there you can reach the fish. You can sing to them from the fly, call them out from under their rock or out from the shadows and bring them to it. Of course, not every fisherman comes to know this. Most fishermen fish the fly that matches the hatch on the stream. This works too, but it's just luck that the fish takes the imitation over the real one. It's not a question of skill. Indeed, a fisherman must lay that fly out perfectly, but from that point on, it's still just a matter of the fish choosing to take one over another. But to throw a fly out there that at best doesn't necessarily look like the hatch and at worst is offensively misplaced in color, size and shape and then to have a fish come gunning for it like it's a hot saloon girl her first day on the job — that takes will. And when pushed against the wall, I'd rather depend on my will than what I've got in my fly box or in my pocket or up my sleeve...

You seem a little tense today. I mean, more than usual anyhow.

Am I so obvious? I really don't want to be like this, Glory. You know, I was actually really fun once. Ask anyone.

Oh I've seen glimpses! So what's the deal?

Our mortgage doubled. I just found out.

How did that happen?

The re-fi we did wasn't fixed. They just turned around and shivved us, essentially.

What are you going to do?

I could get another job, I guess. But I'd have to quit this writing project. And I have the kids to watch; I can't afford childcare.

Why can't Leo work more?

You don't understand him, Glor. He's a master craftsman. He's an artist. He just *can't* bring himself to do things he considers a waste of time. He won't do anything half-assed. The problem is there just isn't a demand for brilliant, expensive work in this town. He blames this town and he blames me for bringing him here. I think as far as he's concerned, I wanted to move home and so I can do what it takes to support our living here.

It's bullshit.

He's not just sitting on his ass, though. In the meantime, he's been making our house incredible. It's going to be worth double. In a way, he's trying to maintain his integrity. I can see that.

So are you, with your writing. But you're going to have to give it up?

Maybe not. But I'm willing to do what I can to keep things together. He's the love of my life. I have to try.

She sighs and reaches over to brush the curls from my shoulder, saying no more. I tie on my fly while she ties on hers. We exchange one long look held up by a weary but trusting grin, and with a nod we go to our holes. First cast. The fly sits on the water not even a shadow of a moment and a flash and a fin and it's gone and there's a fish on. First cast fish. Always, always a good sign. We fish. Sometimes we watch each other, sometimes we skip each other. I'm on a beautiful hole and Glory watches as I miss four bright strikes then catch two fish one after another, then miss another one. I turn to say something to her and as I pull my line off the water to reel up, I realize there's a fish attached to it.

It's going to be one of those days. Catch 'em without even lookin'. Does that count?

What are you talking about? Of course it counts.

Oh yeah? Then we should add up all those strikes too. Five strikes equals one whole fish. Going to be a two hundred fish day.

I teeter on the edge of a big rock. I'm about to go over and I manage an awkward jump that lands me half on Glory, knocking her creel open.

What the hell are you doin' jumping on me?

Sorry, but sometimes you've got to jump to keep from fallin'.

She laughs at that. We hit it just right, in every sense of that fisherman's term. It was the right day to go to Alder — I know that since it's even here to look at. And the weather is perfect and the fish are throwing themselves at the shore and the rocks are all dry, not slippery, and every time we need to cross the stream the rocks line up near each other so we can hop them, and as soon as we're hungry, Alder lays out a beautiful beach near a perfect hole with a flat table rock to eat off of. The trout are all fatter than normal, healthy and strong. The mosquitoes don't bite and the deer flies don't bite and anything else around that might bite, don't. Today we just rest. We just are. Just right.

After lunch, we fish. And it's just fishing today. Some days it's something else, and I've had my share of that so far this season. In fact, I was beginning to wonder what had happened to me as a fisherman over the last few years and why I've been having such trouble. This summer I've had plenty of ghosts, plenty of tangled lines and hard work and heartbreaks and fights. But not much, or not any until today, just plain old fishing. I guess sometimes you have to drive your spirits down pretty low to get to the point where you just don't care anymore what you're doing. Then all of a sudden you're fishing. Because fishing and thinking don't mix. You can leave all that thinking and worrying and planning and plotting and writing and working up on the ridge. Even if all the thoughts, worries, plans, plots, words and work are all about fishing in the first place, they'll keep you from it if you can't see that one fact: that fishing can only exist when you're fishing. That all those things from the world and fishing are mutually exclusive. And that all fishing requires to exist is a fisherman's spirit. And once you see that, Alder Creek is anywhere.

But somewhere I knew that. The first time I saw Alder Creek was in a Safeway parking lot when I was seven. A fisherman walked out of the grocery store in the dead heat of summer carrying a full bag, and the bag ripped and everything spilled out. Bottles broken and apples rolling under trucks and into oil puddles. The fisherman just shook his head. He shook his head and breathed way in and closed his eyes and didn't bend to pick anything up. He just stood there and he was done. He turned off his head. He sold his car. He quit his job. He left his wife. And he stood there doing those things and shaking his head and breathing. And as he did these things, the water flowing from the broken bottles swelled and pooled and went around his feet and up over his boots. The trucks slumped into rocks and the cars into sand and those little rolling apples began to spin and shine and they popped out of their orbits and swam away fish. The Red Delicious turned into a Brookie and the Pippin was a Rainbow and the Pink Lady spun out into the first Piute trout I'd ever seen. And there around this fisherman swelled Alder Creek and it was beautiful and it loved him. He stood there on the shore and took off all his clothes and put them in his ripped grocery bag and set it on the sand and then he waded into the stream. He walked all the way in up to his chest and it was cold and he smiled and took a deep breath and went face in and swam downstream and away. I saw him round the bend. Then he was gone. And as soon as he was gone the water went down the cracks in the asphalt and drained away. The trucks came back and the cars and the sand disappeared and the parking lot was damp but Alder and the fisherman were gone. I saw the broken glass of the bottles and the bag and the apples sitting still except for that one Pink Lady. She was still spinning and I snatched her up quick. She pulsed in my hand and quivered and I folded her in my skirts and I took her. She was the first trout I ever caught.

I was just a kid then, but I understood. It's just that I've spent the years since forgetting what I already knew. And sometimes it's hard to remember. Like when you work to remember, and struggle and fight to move the mountains that are your life and your habits and your thoughts. In all that struggling, you lose track of what you are trying to get at. You forget why you wanted to remember in the first place. And then you ask yourself what you're doing and why you're doing it and why isn't it working anyhow… and the next thing you know, you're in Hangtown. Or you're at home watching TV. Or you're lost. And all you had to do was just get up and go fishing. And then easy as biting into an apple, you remember that the purpose of your life is to live. Plain and simple. Live as in feeling alive, and that's different than what most people do. You can be plenty dead though your heart's still beating. And the world knows its share of ghosts with more spirit than the walking. So I am here at Alder Creek to fish and somewhere along the way, halfway between the Lunch Hole and the last waterfall, I remembered to live. And though that sounds big, it's really quite basic. In fact, it's as basic as my heart beating. As breathing.

I'll be goddamned! Look at that!

Glory's upstream with a dancing big brown trout. It's leaping and diving trying to scare her away, trying to splash her off the line. I get up there as she's letting it off the hook.

Beauty. Didn't even know there were Browns in here. Look at the size of him! Where was he hiding?

Hiding at the bottom, actin' like he was a boulder.

Alder Creek had really given it up to us today. On top of everything — the perfect day and the beauty of the stream and the kinetics and the sounds and all the hospitality — Alder gave us a few nice big fish. I'm a small-stream fisherman; I don't expect much. So when I get a big one, I sure as hell am appreciative.

Perfect day, hey?

Hell yes, it is.

Ready to go? Where's the way out?

We look around. This canyon is filled in with some pretty thick buck brush, and memories of pushing through chest-high thickets, rod held high over head and brambles ripping through clothing have me a little nervous. I scan the east ridge upstream and down. There's a small grove of pines ascending the slope and a little gap, or maybe just the ghost of a gap, in the brush. I stare at that for a moment. It seems right. Nothing but everything tells me that's the way out.

That's it, isn't it?

I'm thinkin' so.

Glory says with a grin. We break down our rods and start up. As we walk, the buck brush politely steps aside and if it brushes us a little too close, it says, *Oops! Sorry!* We make our way quickly up the first rise. I stop for a breath and look back down at the creek and just around the bend going out of sight, I catch a glimpse of a foot splashing, an arm stroking water. *Hey!* I want to yell. *Thanks for the apple! Thanks for Alder! Thanks for everything!* But he's gone. So I turn around and head for the ridge, for the truck, for the beers, for the writing, for the work, for our lives, for us. Because now I remember what the hell I'm doing this all for. So I can feel like I'm alive, heart beating and breathing or not.

# Angry and Confused, It's the Only Way to Go to Town

Or

Everybody Tells Me I Had a Real Good Time

*June 22*

Glory was surprised when the cordless phone whizzed past her head and smashed into the wall behind the couch.

What the fuck?

Leo won't take the kids early. Says I have to come home and put them to bed if I want to come back here to write.

That's fuckin' bullshit.

Fuck it.

Fuck it?

We're going to drop the kids off anyway, then we're going to town. Because if I go home right now, I'm getting a divorce for sure.

You're looking for trouble.

I'm not tryin' to, but if it happens, I'll probably not say no.

Fair enough.

The thing is, you never know how much you can stand 'til you can't stand anymore. It's a simple thing, a small request. A couple hours. But fate rests in small requests sometimes, and no one sees it coming until the electronics are flying across the room.

We gather up the kids — coats, shoes on the wrong feet, it doesn't matter. Time to go. Sometimes it comes up sudden. We wind down the road from my parent's house, all 1.6 miles from my own. The kids are still fussing in the back so I drive on. Make a few more loops around the neighborhood until the kids fall asleep. Even in my fury I make it easier on him. When we roll up to the little bungalow on the corner of Mason and Spring, it looks happy. Deceptively so. It's not the house's fault, that's for sure. It was always a great house. Strongest part of the family at the moment. Glory waits patiently as I grip the wheel and stare hard at the front door.

How do you want to do this? She asks.

You just wait in the car. I'll take the kids in.

I carry one in, then the other. Leo is sitting on the couch waiting for me to take my spot in the ring, but I just walk by and out the door.

I'm goin' out!

I jump in the 'Cruiser and point her toward town.

We goin' to The Tree?

We're doin' more than just goin'.

The Hangman's Tree is one of the last bars on Main Street. For some reason, all the bars in town are closing. It's a sign of something serious because as far as I understood economics, bars are the very last businesses that are supposed to go under. I think even bars in ghost towns do at least a few rounds of business a night. So I don't really know what's wrong with our town. Gil's closed two years ago and Powell Brother's sold their liquor license for the price of a carton of cigarettes. Rumor has it The Hangman's Tree itself is about to get condemned by the county. And if you could see our county, you'd know that things have to be pretty low-down to earn the title "condemned." This whole place deserves to be condemned. *I'm condemned*, I think, and I gun it up Locust Avenue and run the stop sign onto Main.

Why you goin' so fast?

I want to get to The Tree before it's condemned!

You're speedin'.

What are you talking about? It's not speeding when there's no cops around.

Once The Hangman's Tree goes down, the only bar on Main Street will be The Liar's Bench. And that place is no more than it sounds. A murky back-eddy of bad intentions, blackouts and piss-purified carpets. I only go there when I have to. If it's a mission. Then I go about it the way an eldest son goes to the mountain to shoot down a dragon and retrieve the village's magic rock. I go to The Liar's Bench with eyes open and a billy club in my purse. But tonight I don't need to retrieve any magic rocks and while something needs to be taken down, it ain't a little old dragon. It's my life. So we skip The Liar's Bench and pull right up in front of The Hangman's Tree.

This town's true name is Old Hangtown. It earned it as a gold rush town about as wide open as they came. Since it had a slight bit more law than the other towns in the foothills, it became the territorial seat. In other words, it's where they sent people to get hung. They eventually got themselves a judge too, not that they really needed one. But a hangin' judge resided here, and he would nod his head and someone would slap the horse on the ass. I guess this went on regular enough to warrant an official name for the town. But these days, the judge is gone and even the tree itself is gone.

But this little bar is built right on top of the stump of the original hangman's tree. And that's where it gets its name. And its ghosts. And its fuck-it attitude. Out front, instead of a sign, there's a dummy of a cowboy hanging off the roof with a rope around its neck. It's as good a sign as any. Everyone here acts like they got the rope around their necks, looking out over the faces of the people that do or don't love them, resigned to their fate, hoping for a shootout but settling for one last bummed cigarette.

I got the rope around my neck too, so I jump out of the 'Cruiser and head for the door. Maybe someone can cut this thing off or maybe give it one final tug. I don't care which. I'm at the bar ordering straight vodka before Glory even hits the curb. She comes in checking the corners, behind the door.

What're you drinkin', Rose? Beer?

Beer's not drinkin'. I'm getting vodka.

Didn't know you drank that.

What do you want?

Tequila I guess. If we're starting a new routine.

I'm drinking vodka because no one I'm in love with drinks it. And no one that keeps me up nights or weighs on my mind drinks it. I don't know shit about vodka and it don't know shit about me. Not like wine that tells everyone my secrets. Or whisky that asks no questions. No, tonight it's vodka because vodka is clear and it looks like nothing and it tastes like nothing and it hurts just a little bit. And a whole lot of nothing is what I'm looking for tonight.

I didn't know it yet, but tonight would be the night I'd meet Chicago. You're a fool if you think there's just one world we all live in together. Worlds are organized like a glass of milk that a grubby five-year-old just blew into a mass of bubbles with a straw. World against world against world, all smashed together into a very complex, beautiful honeycomb. Sometimes they pop and get absorbed into the bubbles next to them. Sometimes they merge real quietly where no one notices. Mostly we live in our own milk bubble and pretend not to notice those other ones. Until you stand face to face with the fact that you made promises for life that you can't keep to someone who you're not sure is even the person that you promised to in the first place. And then you realize that there was no way on earth that you should have made promises for the future because you can't know what it'll be and you have no control over it anyhow. So it all falls apart. And you're sorry but not really. It's like being sorry that you got swept off your roof by a flood and sorry that you couldn't hold on to the TV antenna tighter. There's no fighting a flood. Fuck sand bags. Swim. So when you start swimming, you run into these other little bubbles where people are swimming. And they can see you and you can see them, but other people don't see either of you even when you're in the middle of a crowded room. So that's how I see Chicago. I'd downed two vodkas and two beer-backs and Glory'd gone off to the jukebox when Chicago slides up into the stool next to me.

Hey baby! What up, girl! Let me roll on up here and talk to you.

Chicago is squirrely and skinny and smiling big. He's holding a world full of energy, high on several things and drunk too but keeping it together as if he was only a tiny bit buzzed and that right there is a quality I go for every time. He talks like he has one of those replacement voice boxes they give throat cancer patients. But it's not a replacement voice box and he doesn't have cancer yet and he's only 27 years old anyhow. He strikes me as a Vietnam vet with lots of replacements and a strong willingness to be happy about life if life would only give him the chance to be. And if life don't, well, I can see he's got a strong tendency to take shit out, just as likely as not. Under the four knuckles of his right hand he has the letters N-A-N-A tattooed crudely with what must have been a knife and pen ink. His hair is pale and sticking out in a fine mess. His eyes are clear grey, narrowed and smart. And smiling. I like him right off.

So who are you, sweet thing? He asks.

I'm one of those bad people.

Me too! Let's be bad together. What's that you're drinkin', water?

Vodka.

Straight? No mixers?

94

Think of it as a tall drink in a short glass.

What's your name, girl?

Rose.

I order another for me, and the bartender just gives one to Chicago. He obviously lets him drink here, and I'd be surprised if he ever asks him for money. The bartender has an eye on us. He looks familiar. On his head a yellow bandana tied deftly under a fine woven seaman's cap. Arms, chest, fingers, neck, entirely covered in tattoos: some crude, some finely wrought, all swirling in and around a pristine white undershirt. He is exactly medium build with dark hair camouflaged against olive skin that refuses to divulge his age. Deep dark blue eyes sit surrounded by features that couldn't be more sexy. He's a beautiful man who could fuck you with his eyes if you were prone to that kind of thing. I'm not, but the two stragglers at the other end of the bar are. Trying hard to catch one little glance. Sadness and longing gleaming through hedgerows of clumpy mascara. Passion buried in the folds of cheap Wal-Mart sweatshirts. But the bartender only gives them enough to keep them ordering drinks. No, they're not what interest him. Behind him are large satiny photographs of land, city places and women. Naked, bent over, eyes heavy with makeup and vaginas exposed, but too alluring and too terrifying to be pornography. He's got one very keen eye on Glory and the other on the trouble spots elsewhere in the bar: the two guys getting a little heated over the football scores, the parolee with the twisted face and the old-timer he knows is going to slump off the stool for good one of these nights. He wipes down the bar in front of Chicago and gives him an amused grin. Chicago grins right back.

Hey Vincent! You gotta meet my new friend here. Her name is—

Oh, everyone knows who she is. Don't they, Miss Rosewater?

It's "Waters," with an "s."

I say, sliding my empty glass into his forearm where he's leaned it on the bar.

Um-hmm. And what brings you into Hangman's?

Lack of better options. If it's any of your business.

Everything that happens in here is my business.

He says and cracks a pleased smile.

Well, Chicago. She's all right. Snappy enough to handle you, anyhow.

He freshens our glasses then moves down to the other end of the bar to tend to the stragglers. I swivel my stool back around.

So, you from here, Chicago?

Yup. Born right here.

He taps the bar twice with his finger.

Yeah, me too.

You was born in The Hangman's Tree? I thought I's the only one! Shit, girl.

I look at him stupidly as he tells me the story. Turns out Chicago's mom went into labor right here in the bar and with the help of a level-headed bartender and a few very drunk but supportive patrons, this little screamin' outlaw was brought into the world right on the spot where many an outlaw went out.

Chicago gives me tonight's tour of The Hangman's Tree from his stool, telling everyone's story in his gravel-road voice.

> That one over there is sleeping with that one's boyfriend. And that one knows about it but won't say shit because she's like that. But she's going to scratch that bitch's eyes out one of these nights. And that one over there, that's my cousin. I kicked his ass last week in the pool hall, but we can't remember why. I'm sure he deserved it and when I remember, I might have to do it again. But we're solid now...

Chicago goes on. I nod my head, hearing all the ins and outs of this little quagmire community of which, I realize, I am about to join. As he gestures from one group to the other I notice his hand again.

> What does "N-A-N-A" stand for?

I ask, picturing it being the last thing one would see before getting a fist in the eye.

> It stands for Nana, obviously. My grandmother. Whenever I win a fight, it's only thanks to her.

He says, contemplating his hand, then drops the conversation for a quiet moment. He seems to go somewhere else, then snaps out of it.

So what's the story with you chicks?

Chicago asks, gesturing to Glory. Something about him compels me to just tell the true story.

> That's Glory. I met her in the middle of the woods out fishing a few weeks back. Been on the loose ever since. I'm working on a fishing book and she's hiding out from a dangerous and unpredictable boyfriend. Been runnin' and fishin' all spring.

I'd leave it at that but the vodka prompts me to keep talking.

> She needs a bodyguard; you want a job?

I say, 95 percent joking. He shakes his head and almost chokes on his drink.

> I don't know about no job, but I'll take a fight or a fish anytime, girl! You can pay me in drinks and kisses.

> We're not giving out kisses. The drinks can be handled.

> All right then. I'll help you girls out and show you a thing or two about fishin' around here too! Damn, you don't even know.

But I do know. I can tell a home-brewed fisherman a mile away. Though I suspect he's prone to throwing lures and power bait around like rice at a wedding. It's no matter. I can tell Chicago's the kind of guy you want on your side of the pond rather than not.

> Hell, I'll start my job right now. See that old dude at the back table? Hasn't taken his eyes off your girl all night. Noticed him right off.

At the deep end of the bar sits a man tilted uncomfortably forward in his booth. The low hanging bulb casts a pool of light over his hands, covered in fingerless woolen gloves and delicately choking a lowball glass with drops wet and gold. I can't see his face. Glory is busy searching the jukebox for something besides Metallica, Lynyrd Skynyrd, Anthrax and Willy. Not that we don't love Metallica, Lynyrd, Anthrax and Willy, it's just that they are so unavoidable. But everything tonight is unavoidable, so she just puts on *Ride The Lightning* with a "To hell with it," and comes back to the bar.

What the hell is that? Metallica?

Yeah. I put some Ozzie on too.

Jesus, it's like I'm having a high-school reunion with myself right now.

She takes a stool away from me and Chicago, then starts chatting up the bartender. Chicago gestures toward him and leans in close to me, whispering:

That's Vincent; he stays pretty straight. He drinks but he don't never get drunk. Takes them photos too. He's damn good.

Vincent's eyes are working on Glory, but she's throwing a bit back to him as well. And it dawns on me that there's a difference between someone looking, and someone looking *at* you. My hairs are up, there's something about him I don't trust. Well, not not-trust exactly. I have a pretty clear vision of something I can't see, but somehow understand. He's capable of things, things far beyond what I'm capable of. And he seems sure about it. He is controlled to the core. *He is an assassin*, I think, *who just isn't for hire.*

I turn my attention back to Chicago, who has moved on to telling me this story about his girlfriend and how crazy she is, and I think, *He's an assassin too! But one who might only kill for love.* Chicago is my kind of assassin. Apparently, his girlfriend just recently broke up with him after he caught her cheating, but now (as in right now), she's trying to get back together with him. Then it dawns on me that this short little girl with long blond hair who keeps storming through the long hall which constitutes The Hangman's Tree is his scorned, cheating love. I've been seeing her all night. The door at the far end that comes in from the back alley flies open and she stomps in, charges through the bar, looks at Chicago, huffs and without breaking stride, continues toward the swinging front door while glaring back over her shoulder. She pushes the door out with one stiff arm and storms out. Ten minutes later, it happens again, just like that.

That's your girlfriend? She sure seems mad. I say.

Fuck her! She's not my girl no more. But do you mind still sitting here talking to me? It's really pissing her off. She wants to get back with me, but I don't want nothing to do with that bitch.

Hell yeah, I'm not goin' anywhere. Fuck her anyway! I can't believe she cheated on you.

I'm getting more and more irritated thinking about it. This little muffin of a girl treating Chicago so terrible, cheating on him and now torturing him. I can see he'll go back to her the second I stand up from the stool or the drinks run out or the bar closes, whichever comes first. And after everything I'd figured he'd done for her. *He's an assassin for love!* I wanted to yell at her. *Do you know what kind of heart that takes?* I was really feeling it now. Their story unfolding in my mind. He'd obviously have put his blade away for her, if only she could have loved him. Now he'll have to use it. Cut her heart out or his. It's just not right.

It's just not right!

Chicago whispers into his glass. Staring hard into the grain of the bar.

I know, man. Fuck her. Let's keep drinkin'.

I say as I scoot my stool closer to his.

Here she comes again.

Do you want me to kick her ass for you?

Naw, naw. It's cool. But I'm surprised you'd do that, nice girl like you.

Well, something about this seat makes me an asshole, dude. I don't know. Maybe it's just this place has me on edge.

Yeah, fuck this place. Half of 'em don't care for you and the other half don't like you, but they're always nice to you.

Uh oh, incoming…

Again she comes in the back and heads out the front door, but this time she turns and looks at Chicago with a whole new brand of serious and says real low:

I ain't comin' back.

Then she turns and walks out the door. Chicago hops up so swift, I don't know he's left the stool until I see him catch the door just before it swings shut and he disappears after her into the night.

Aw hell.

I sigh and swing back around to the bar, wondering what I'm going to do now. Glory is engaged down at the end of the bar with a medley of suspects. The two guys watching football are leaping out of their seats, cursing and spitting at the TV screen. Vincent watches them calmly from behind the bar. The man in the booth is gone. His glass sits empty and enshrined in a hot puddle of electric light. I order more vodka and sit with it, or three, for a while.

At this point, someone pulls the handle that lets time out the chute, like rice out from the bottom of a silo. One minute I'm looking around the bar after Chicago and the next thing — *whoosh!* — time slides away and takes everything down with it. There in the rustling sound and the sliding away are the people: yelling, laughing, bar girls getting their T-shirts cut and tied, drinks clinking and splashing over their rims... place becomes space. The yelling football men are gone, popped out the end of the chute already. Vincent is still there slowly working a towel around the edge of a glass, the solid and quiet axis around which we swirl. *Blackened is the end!* Metallica throbs from the jukebox, hurtling. *Blackened! Blackened!*

But Vincent isn't having any of it. He pulls the plug on the jukebox before we find out just how black the end is going to get, and he switches on the lights.

We're closed! Everybody get the fuck out.

All right, we better get the fuck out then.

I mutter as I look around for Glory. She's right there.

Time to go, Rose. Let's get out of here.

Right. Let's go before I sober up enough to remember any of this.

We head for the door, but Vincent steps in front of it and puts his arm across the door jam.

You gals aren't driving, are you? There's cops all over out there, and your car's the only one on the street.

Uh, well, I guess not. Fuck it, we'll walk home.

Walk home? Wait a few minutes while I close, and I'll walk you both home.

Perfect!

Glory!

I grab Glory by the elbow and drag her out of earshot.

Are you fucking crazy? He can't walk us home!

Why not? It makes sense. It's not safe out there.

No, it's not safe in here. The only thing we have to worry about walking home this time of night is skunks. This guy I don't trust.

Man, it's fine. You're crazy. Let's just wait for him.

I throw my purse on the bar and hope she's not as drunk as me. Vincent cleans up and puts the stools up on the bar and everything gets shut down and we step out into the cool night. We turn east and start hoofin' it up Main Street. It's 3:20 am.

The streetlights are bright but the night is silent. I'm struck by the oddness that an empty street can make even bright lights seem lonely. We walk toward home to the sound of our own footfalls echoing down the empty set of Old Hangtown. The cameraman and the boom operator and the wranglers and the caterers are gone from this gig. Gone back to 1952, drinking bourbon and sucking on ice cubes outside the trailer most likely. We keep walking. Glory and Vincent are chatting, and I'm working on forgetting all the things I don't know anyhow. We pass the Landcruiser. It's the only thing on the street save for the moths and a handful of strays. I pick up the pace, wanting to get up the road and let these cats get to their hunting. We cross the threshold of a deep alley and I glance in, hoping to spot a mouse or a ghost, and I'm hit with the sight of a young cop leaning against a patrol car parked half in and half out of the alley shadow.

Whoa. Look, Glor! There's a cop in the alley.

Damn! He's a cute one.

Yeah, makes me want to do something illegal.

I say as I cross my wrists in front of me.

Don't you have any respect for the law? Vincent asks sarcastically.

The law's an affront to my heritage!

Glory and Vincent laugh and shake their heads. I laugh and shake my head too, but then I don't. I stop walking. Glory and Vincent continue a few feet before Glory turns back to me, on her face a question and then a knowing and then a hard look. She furrows her brow and gives her head a three-quarter tilt, shaking it slowly back and forth. She's about to say, *Don't...* when I turn back to the alleyway.

Hey motherfucker! Are you seriously hiding back here in the shadows? What are you doin' here? Waiting for drunk drivers?

He gets up from leaning against his patrol car.

Or walkers.

He says, taking a step toward us.

Hey, don't you worry. We'll walk while we can still walk. After that, we'll start hollerin'. And anyhow, we're just tryin' not to drive drunk. Isn't that what you guys want? I should be insulted by that shady threat, but you *are* sitting here in the shadows waiting to spook people, so I guess that says a lot about you.

I'm laughing. I think the cop is laughing too. His face looks like he's trying to hide a smile, but maybe he's just trying to figure out what he's dealing with. It all seems ridiculous to me. Tiny town with nothing going on except moths buzzing lights and the stars shining, and here's this cop staking out the place. What did he think he was waiting for? People don't bring real crime down the center of Main Street. If you want to find bad shit, you have to go looking for it. No, he's just loafing and I know it. Looking for some dumb-ass like me to get in a car and drive into his shady little trap. Glory gives me the hard look again, then she turns a soft look to the cop.

> Don't mind her, officer. She has a hard time keepin' her mouth shut. Especially since she started talkin'. We're just on our way home. Come on, Rose; let's get going.

> You girls on your way home to Mason Street?

> What? You know where I live? How do you know that? You ran my fuckin' plates, didn't you? That's bullshit, Mister Po-Po! Just because my car is on the street late at night, you assume it's trouble? Can't park in front of The Hangman's Tree without getting run through the computer?

In my mind, I'm watching this scene in the editing room back at the trailer with the actor in the cop uniform and the starlets drinking scotch. The room is filled with cigar smoke and we're all laughing. *Oh here comes my favorite part*, someone says from a shadowed corner. *Where they all get arrested and that thing happens with the billy club. Oh yeah, this is the good part right here...*

> Did your computer tell you I was a law-abiding citizen?

Glory grabs my arm and tries to pull me away.

> Rose, stop. Come on. Let's go.

> Did it tell you I was irritable?

> Rose! *Come on.*

Glory is tugging at my elbow while I give the cop my best tough look: the one where I squinch my left eye shut more than the right one and furrow my brow and purse my lips… and I was even getting ready to put my hands on my hips when Vincent steps in front of me and puts his forehead right to mine.

Careful you don't get what you're asking for, Wild Rose.

He holds my gaze for a long moment, then steps off the curb and disappears around the corner. *Told you he was trouble*, I tell Glory with my eyes. Things are shaking out now. *You're fucking trouble*, she eyes me back. We'll have that conversation later but for now there's just some things I won't abide by. Unfortunately, those things include authority figures in dark alleys. The cop is looking at me with pure confusion at this point. He's scoped me for signs of drugs and signs of insanity and signs of everything else from the rookie checklist, but the rookie checklist never said a thing about a the signs of a broken-hearted woman out to make the world feel what she's feeling.

Well, there's one way you can make it up to me and it's not by standing there looking cute.

I say to the cop as his jaw drops just a little bit. He's wondering if he's supposed to shoot me or something.

Are you looking for trouble, lady?

Hell no! When I look for trouble, it's not with the law, buddy. But you can sure give us a ride home since you already went through the pains to find my address.

Rose! What are you doing? I'm going to shoot you myself! Whispers Glory.

What the hell for?

Jesus. Because you know I can't see a stranger kill you, dumb-ass.

It's cool, Glory; chill out. He knows where I live and I'm sure it's no problem to take a taxpayer home.

You're not a taxpayer.

That's not the fuckin' point! He should give us a ride! I'm pissed.

The cop takes his hand off his holster and walks to his backseat door and opens it.

All right, girls. I'll give you a ride. Get in.

I jump in the back seat, throw my purse against the hard plastic seats. Give a little rattle to the cage to see how tight it is. Glory is standing outside the door looking more pissed and more desperate than I've ever seen a woman. She gets in. I give a little tap to the cage behind the cop.

Wow, thanks for the ride, man. It's been a really tough night, you know? I got kind of pissed at my husband. I'm pretty sure it's over. Then there was the bar and all, but this here is real nice of you.

No problem.

He pulls the squad car out of the alley and turns up Main. I settle into the seat and press my forehead against the cool glass. Make my breath known upon the window and through it, I catch sight of a figure standing dead center as we cross the next alley. The man from the booth. On his head a dark porkpie hat and his face still a shadow. As we go past, he begins to raise his hand toward our car. What gesture there, only the strays will see. I shudder. We drive down the dark end of Main, turn left over the little hill and roll down Mason to the front yard of my house. The cop stops the car.

Here we are. Is that your husband?

I look through the cage and see Leo sitting on the front porch glaring through his cigarette smoke.

That'd be him.

Are you cool?

Yeah, man. I'm fine. Thanks for the ride. Really. Can you take my friend to the Waters' place?

He turns to look more closely at Glory.

She a Waters?

I look at her for a moment and grab her knee.

Yeah. She is. And sorry about the "motherfucker" and all that.

It's all right.

I give Glory a quiet hug, then pile out of the patrol car. Straightening up, I walk up the steps past Leo. He breathes out a wave of smoke with the word "nice" wrapped up disdainfully in it.

I'm going to bed.

I inform him as I head into the house and straight back to the bedroom.
As drunk as I am, I move silently since I know the children are sleeping. I
walk through and push the door closed behind me. I wait for the sound of
it closing, but there is none. I turn around and Leo is standing in the
doorway.

What happens next is a blur. A blur punctured every ten minutes or so
with glinting images and words ripping through the room like shrapnel.
Like bullets. Me huddled on the edge of the bed, arms locked, staring at
my feet around which there are wet smears from tears. He's blocking the
door and screaming. I see his face contorted but I don't hear what he's
saying. I don't need to hear the words. He says I am a terrible mother. I
am a terrible wife. I do unforgivable things. I am responsible for
everything. I am making him furious. It's me. It's my fault. And I have
gone too far. Who I am, is too far. Too much to put up with. And it's me
and who I am and what I do that will destroy him. Fuck up the kids. I'm
selfish. I'm driving him to this place. He's not screaming at me, he says.
It's not him. It's me.

It goes on. He leaves. He comes back in to start anew. Over and over. It
goes on. All I can do is hold on to the edge of the bed and hope the
children don't wake up. *Just please don't wake up the kids* is the only thing I
say the entire time. I don't fight with him. I don't try to defend myself. It's
pointless to do so. It's a one-way flood. When the dam breaks, you just
hold on to something you trust will stay rooted. Hold on and stare at your
feet until the river is right again. It's not how I want to be. I'm ashamed
that I don't fight, but I just don't want the kids to wake up. I used to fight.

110

Fight like hell. No one could punish me like that, not without a battle. But the kids. The kids change everything. I have to keep my wits about me even in the middle of the night, broken-hearted and three sheets to the wind.

He goes out. This time, he doesn't come back. I slip down into the bed and sleep. Dark and sad, that sleep, until the door creaks open again and this time it's a child's voice that stirs me. Dull sun like flour spilled on the floor, lifting and falling through the air. I watch it float and it brightens. The color comes in gently. The flour is gone and Lyla steps silently through the golden pools and green reflections of leaves drifting through the window. I am amazed that the world remains always beautiful. Regardless.

What's for breakfast, Mommy?

Anything you want, baby. Anything you want.

The children eat breakfast then drift out to the yard, innocent of anything more dramatic than the latest petrified beetle on the doorstep. Glory emerges from the sunny street and gently takes a seat in the corner rocker. We settle into the morning kitchen with hot coffee in old diner mugs. I watch Glory stir honey into her coffee. She doesn't look the worse for wear.

How'd you get here so early?

Had to ask your dad for the spare key and a ride to Main Street to get the 'Cruiser. He was on his way to some farmer's breakfast. He didn't ask me to explain.

Well, it's sure not the first time he's had to do that, unfortunately. Jesus, Glory. What happened? Where did it all go?

Don't worry, Rose. It's going to be all right. Your life is going through a huge change right now and it's hard to get a good perspective on it.

What?

It's just your instinct to cling to the things you've become used to, regardless of whether you really want them or not. You're missing them already and that's normal.

No dude. Where are my house keys? Where's my wallet? Fuck...

You lost them? Shit, I'll give you one guess where they're at.

I'm not going back there. No way.

Oh you have to. It's "the morning after." Buck up, baby, your journey to become a complete motherfucking asshole is almost complete.

She says with a grin.

Can't I just call a locksmith?

I ask with that familiar sinking feeling. It's one thing to freak out and take the town down, but it's another thing altogether to have to go back and sift through the ruins searching for your lost chingaderas. Keys to a doomed house. Cards to shared bank accounts. I don't want them, but I'm going to need them, so I clean up the half-eaten oatmeal bowls and call up Mom. Margaret Waters, the one thing you can always count on.

She'll take the kids for the morning and thank god. The little winery, their house, that land… the only constant in my life at the moment.

Come on, kids! Get in the car; we're goin' to Grandma's!

They run to the car. Visions of cartoons and ice cream sandwiches pile into the back seat with them. Me and Glory exchange a deep look. Back to town. I feel sick when I think about going back there in the bright light of day with all I've done and all that's been done splayed upon the ground bleeding out and drying in the sun. You can never escape anything, really. No more running, I guess. If I have a responsibility to look at the vows I'm questioning and the lives I'm threatening to break apart and stand behind my intent, then I guess I have to be able to walk back into The Hangman's Tree, look the 9:00 am crowd in the face and humbly ask them if they've seen my keys, my wallet or any other casualties of my civil war. We load up the car and pull out. I have no idea where Leo is. We take the familiar turns up Cable Road to my parent's house, two tires barely over the line. This road will never be straightened out. We pull up to the gate, drop down the little road that dips into the gully surrounded by mounded vineyards and swing left to the top of the hill. Sunny house, green grass, old Mulberry tree with its old swing stands quietly remembering me, but waiting for my daughter to take her place at the end of that sturdy rope. Waters learn how to hang on young. Mom walks up and collects the kids. Looks at me. *Don't ask*, I say with my eyes and she doesn't. She already knows. We leave them to their playing and head back toward town.

Glory. About last night, I'm sorry. I know you don't want to be exposed to the cops. I wasn't thinking.

Honey, I can handle it. I've been where you are and I'm here to stand with you. If you need to drink a gallon of whisky and shoot guns at the moon, then I'm here to drink a gallon of whisky with you and reload the bullets. I never had a friend like that when Jesse was gettin' bad. It's why I had to run to the mountains. It's the only protection I knew. It's the only friend I thought I had until I met you. And now that I have this friendship, I'm not leaving these hills ever and I'm not leaving you. All right?

All right.

Was it bad last night? Did he hurt you?

Yeah, it was bad. No, he didn't hurt me. He's not violent like that. He just says terrible things sometimes.

Words can be worse than a punch, Rose. Has it always been like this?

No. And believe me, I've sorted and sifted through my memory to see if there were clues I could have seen, but there weren't. At least none that a young, love-struck girl could have seen. We met at a crowded party and when we saw each other that first time, Glory, the whole room stood still. The two of us had to lean way out a window just to get some privacy. We looked east from the valley and talked about where each of us would most want to live. It was our first conversation, but we knew we were talking about our future together. It was just like that. Like it was all written already.

What happened?

I said the mountains. He said the ocean.

Uh oh.

Yeah. And I made us come here. In the end, I think he's just out of place. That phrase is used so often, it's cliché. But I'm beginning to realize that being in your proper place should be the most important concern in your life. Because if it's wrong, you're not going to be right. And if you're not right, you're not yourself. And the longer you go not being yourself, the farther you get from ever being able to find your way back. Then you're lost.

But you're not lost, Rose.

No, I'm not. I am this land's person. I belong here. But Leo? He doesn't. Back at the ocean, he was right. He was perfect and poetic. And he loved me more than anything.

Glory graces me with a long, deep look as I pull to the curb across the street from The Tree.

Here we are. Would you look at that scene?

Apparently, the stage crew had come back and told the extras where to sit. Chicago is reposed on the bench outside of the bar, arms folded over his chest, butt on the edge of the seat, legs outstretched and crossed at the ankles. Head tilted back against the brick wall. Sleeping or feigning sleep behind his sunglasses. Vincent stands to the left of the bench a bit and leans a casual shoulder against the wall, smoking a cigarette. Everyone's set and waiting for the cue as we roll to a stop across the street. Vincent pops off the wall and tilts his chin at us. Chicago doesn't stir until Vincent whacks his shoulder as he strides by. He steps off the curb toward us and threatens to flick his cigarette at the oncoming traffic. They stop. Chicago stirs, sees the Landcruiser and hops up with a grin. He trots up to the driver's side window. Vincent comes round the side, leans against Glory's window and nods a sly smile to her, flashing those eyes. Chicago slaps the hood of the 'Cruiser.

What is up, girls!

Hey there, Chicago, Vincent. Uh, we were just coming back to look for my wallet and keys. You haven't seen them in there, have you?

Maybe we have. Maybe we haven't.

Yeah, sometimes, we can be real forgetful.

Vincent says as he leans further in through the window, his eyes on Glory. I catch her eye and wonder about a graceful departure. Chicago cuts off the escape with his Labrador-ish enthusiasm.

You girls comin' in?

Oh no, can't. Got to work, get the kids, you know.

Yeah, and I think we had enough last night anyhow.

Glory tries to come to our rescue, but Chicago shakes his head at me.

What're you talking about? You-all left *early*!

Early? What are *you* talkin' about, man? You were out of there so fast, you didn't even finish your free drink! I was looking for you.

You were? Damn, girl! I knew you was and I sure as hell tried to come back. Didn't they tell you what happened?

No.

Shit, girl. This town... I was out there in the parking lot getting a blow job from that girl in the chinchilla—

You mean your girlfriend?

She ain't my girl no more. I already told you that part.

But you're having sex with her still. Seems pretty boyfriendy to me.

Honey, I'm just makin' sure I'm over her. It's just like when a dog takes to killin' chickens. You got to hang a whole bunch a chicken heads around his neck till he gets so sick of them he won't never look at one again.

I just stare at him blankly as Vincent chuckles.

But anyway. Continues Chicago. I was out there in the car and she was suckin' my dick when all of a sudden, there's some asshole knocking on my window and it's a cop! I was like, "Damn, man! Can't you see I'm getting my dick sucked here?" And then I just went back to my business, but he knocked on the window again. I told him to go to hell and he told me to get out of the car and then he arrested me. So that's why I couldn't get back here and hang out with y'all. I sure am sorry.

Jesus.

Yeah well. So! Are you comin' in?

No. We really can't.

You want to go to the river?

Yeah, you should come for a swim.

Vincent repeats the offer, directing it at Glory. We shake our heads no. Chicago slaps the car again.

Whatever! Go on then. Take care of those little ones. We'll be seeing you around for sure. Right, Vincent?

Maybe. Vincent says, standing back from the car. If someone else doesn't see them first.

What are you talkin' about, V?

Oh, nothing big, Chicago. Just last night when I left these girls to their little cat-and-mouse game with that cop, I hung around long enough to see that it didn't go south. After the squad car pulled up the street, that old dude from the corner table came out of the alley, got in an old blue Ford pickup and followed them up the street.

Hey! I was watchin' that guy last night too! Until I kind of forgot to keep an eye on him. He sure has a thing for ol' Glory here.

Chicago raises an eyebrow at Glory, and I look at her for a reaction, but she seems unperturbed.

Who is that guy, Glory? Is he one of Jesse's?

Hell if I know. I still can't remember shit from before the homestead. Yeah, maybe the truck rings a bell. I don't know. Jesse didn't run with any old guys, though; that I'm pretty sure of. It's probably nothing to worry about. Just some geezer trying to get his rocks off.

Chicago laughs, kicking the front tire.

Well, maybe you girls better keep us around just in case. I'm a real good fighter, 'specially against old men and teenage cops! And besides, you promised to take us fishin'.

"Us?" I ask?

Yeah, me and Vincent. We cleared our whole schedule for you ladies for the rest of the summer. So where we going next week?

I didn't know you fished. I say, looking at Vincent.

I don't.

Vincent takes a final pull off his cigarette and, with a very satisfied look
on his face, blows the smoke out gracefully while giving us a comfortably
beautiful smile. He reaches around to his back pocket and pulls out my
wallet and tosses it in Glory's lap. Then he reaches in his other pocket and
produces my keys. With a jingle, he hands them over. Me and Glory just
laugh in surrender and agree to all go fishing together. We exchange
numbers and say more goodbyes and wave and pull sunglasses down and
pull away from the curb. In the rearview mirror, both are standing in the
middle of the street holding up traffic. Vincent with weight on one hip,
crushing his cigarette, Chicago with thumbs hooked through belt-loops,
bent at the waist, spitting on the ground. Both of them watch the
Landcruiser pull away down Main Street. We reach the bell-tower and
only then do they slowly make their way back to their stations at the
entrance to The Hangman's Tree. Glory is quietly studying them in her
mirror, thinking intently about something. I shake my head.

What the hell was that? I ask.

Army. Serious Army.

Those guys are not in the military, dude. Jail, for sure. Some other
organized shenanigans, maybe.

Army.

What are you talking about "Army?" What Army?

*Ours.*

# Caples Creek

*July 12*

Caples Creek. I've been in and out of this creek since I was a kid. I was too young to fly-fish the first time I ever saw it. We used to backpack into Caples Canyon with a few other families from town. My first memories of it are calves and hiking boots, slouching wool socks of some grown-ups' legs hiking up the trail in front of me. Stepping over rocks, a dirt path. Smell of pines laced with Mountain Misery and a chorus of clanking sierra cups. Camp is pitched in a meadow of grass, miner's lettuce and cow patties. A meandering stream. Submerged boulders. Cold water. I remember a slight yet constant anxiety that the cows in the distance were going to tromp into camp and get crazy. Topple the cook stoves and drag tents hooked on horns wildly through the meadows. I watched them with a wary eye until Uncle Ralph distracted us with a demonstration of cow-patty burning. That was very exciting shit, as he liked to say.

Evening was hot food on cold tin plates, drizzle of rain and everyone huddled under blue tarps around a smoky fire, passing the flask of sherry around and listening to Uncle Ralph tell, once again, the story of how he chased a bear out of camp one time. Ralph was camping somewhere, maybe here. Maybe near Yosemite. Maybe in his backyard. And he's cooking a gourmet dinner out of dried morels and 40-year-old balsamic that he'd packed ten miles into the woods. He was cooking up some grub for the camp — morels in sherry sauce or something — and the pasta was almost done, boiling gently in the aluminum camp pot, imparting tiny toxic particles, and he's telling everyone how delicious this dinner's going to be, and he leaves the cook-stove for a minute to do who-knows-what and when he comes back there is a great big black bear sniffing around his dinner.

The bear starts getting into the sauce and lapping it up and knocking the pasta pot off and just generally causing mayhem. Uncle Ralph in his fury yells at the bear: "Hey bear! Get the hell out of my morels!" and grabs a wine bottle and charges the bear. The bear, for some reason, sees this as a threat and takes off running. He runs around and around the ring of light from the campfire with Uncle Ralph at his heels yelling at him about the morel sauce. Everyone around the fire is watching in disbelief. Then at some point, when the shock of the situation wears off, Dad yells: "Hey Ralph! What are you going to do when you catch him?" And Uncle Ralph just stops, as if he crotched into a fire hydrant he didn't see on the sidewalk in front of him. And he drops the bottle and the bear runs off a little, stops at the edge of light and looks back over his shoulder disdainfully, mushroom sauce dripping off his chin, then shrugs and saunters off into the night.

This is the story I hear my first night camping on Caples Creek, and it will be the story I hear every night I camp there for the rest of my life. It steps into my thoughts when I'm gutting fish for dinner creekside, floats into my dreams half-twisted in a hot sleeping bag, makes me chuckle over camp coffee, tin cups full of grounds as Caples' morning mist rises off the deep pool outside the tent. When I'm sixteen, when I'm twenty-four, when I'm one hundred and seven, I laugh. Because Uncle Ralph was funny as hell and Caples was a hell of a place and still is.

Shit!

Glory yells, spilling coffee from her tin mug as the Landcruiser hits another bump in Upper Broadway's unkempt and forgotten asphalt.

Can't you keep it straight?

Hey I'm trying! They don't put much effort into this end of town, you know. Guess they figure everyone out here either can't afford gas or has had their license revoked.

Where the hell is this supposed "garage" anyhow?

I don't know. Every place out here looks like it could be a garage.

Upper Broadway is a long, straight, end-of-the road zone lined by run-down motels, scrap yards, auto repair, liquor stores and old line houses. We are looking for Chicago's place so we can pick up him and Vincent and head out to Caples before the morning gets too far along. After a couple of weeks of distracting them from the fishing idea with mellow, if not amusing, get-togethers around town, we have finally relented. Now we are packed and ready to see exactly what these men are made of.

Hold up, Rose. Stop here at the post office; I need to check on something.

Check on what?

As I pull up, Glory takes another sip from her coffee and sets her jaw as she stares intently at the post office building.

Look, I've been avoiding it, but I think there might be something in there for me. Before we had the house, when Jesse had to skip town, or go lay low somewhere, or if I did, he'd send me letters through general delivery. And if I knew what town he was in, I'd do the same. After the beating, I didn't care if he had anything to say, but part of me wants to know what his game is. Or if he's trying to find me.

He almost killed you! You can't possibly be considering communicating with him.

Of course not! But if he's focused on finding me, I want to know. Or if he's not and there's no letters, then maybe I can start to sleep a little easier. I have to know either way.

She steps out of the car and heads through the front doors. After a few very slow minutes go by, she comes out, walking as if walking were an afterthought. An envelope and half-open letter dangling by her side. She climbs into the passenger seat and, sinking down, says nothing. I pick the letter off her lap. Unfold it to expose a brief note written in dark and purposeful script:

*Babe,*

*I know you're back in town. I've seen you. If I wanted to find you, you know I could. But I'm not going to. I can't even believe you're here at all after what happened. You should be gone, but you aren't and I hope that's because there is still a part of you that wants to see me. I'll be waiting. You know where.*

*I love you more than anything. I know that now more than ever. — Jess*

I fold the letter and as I open the envelope, a photo slips out. It's a picture of Glory, sitting on the steps of an old porch under the arm of a giant of a man. He is broad and strong. Even when seated on the tall deck with his feet on the ground, his legs are bent. His hair is blond and bristled. His jaw is set and his chin, defined by a deep cleft, has a slight five-o'clock

124

shadow. They look happy. I stuff the photo and letter into the envelope, feeling slightly sick and more than slightly afraid. And just under that? A little touched, perhaps, by the eloquent letter coming from someone who I had neatly categorized as a brute and a monster. I stuff this feeling away quickly before letting it get a foothold. I turn to see Glory, still slumped down, still staring straight ahead.

What are you going to do?

She takes another sip of coffee.

Absolutely nothing.

She says without emotion. I start the 'Cruiser and we pull away in silence. We proceed up the street and turn onto a dirt driveway that has a short wooden sign in the ground with the word "Nowhere" and an arrow carved into it. We bump up to small old adobe bungalow snuggled up to a big open-front garage with faded trucks, tractor parts, rusty trailers and every part and parcel of any vehicle from 1962 to 1987 littered and laying around the perimeter. We pull up and I jump out. Glory takes her time getting out, slowly rearranging the things around her that don't need re-arranging. Chicago is at the workbench in the garage, hunched over an oil pan scrubbing some old piece of metal frantically with steel wool and turpentine. I approach and give him a little pat on the butt as I peer over his shoulder.

What are you doing, Chicago?

Just cleaning up this old belt buckle I found out in Dry Creek last week.

What were you doing way out in Dry Creek?

Findin' shit. Like I said.

Vincent walks into the garage from out of nowhere and sets his heavy camera bag and gear against a pile of fenders stacked against the wall.

Chicago has a real knack for finding things. I've seen him drive out to the middle of a field, get out of the car, walk fifty feet and bend down and pick up an arrowhead. I've made a decent buck or two betting on him over the years.

Hey! I didn't know you was makin' money off me, V! Where's my cut?

Let's just say I've been putting it toward your fifteen-year-old bar tab. You ready to go yet, cupcake? These girls are starting to look impatient.

Hell. Yeah, let me just wash up and grab my fishing hat.

Chicago disappears into the back of the garage and comes back a moment later with a faded-to-pink foam-fronted trucker hat with a picture of a leaping big mouth bass. In old print it says: "Gone Fishin'." Across this Chicago's scribbled in black sharpie pen: "Fuck You." Glory strolls in the garage doorway.

That's a real nice hat you got there.

She quips as she stops next to Vincent and slips an arm around his waist, leaning in for a morning hug.

Thanks, honey! You gals ready to learn a thing or two? Let's hit the road.

We throw all the gear and a cooler full of beer into the back of Chicago's jacked-up International and head east into the mountains, bound for Caples Creek. The windows are all down in an effort to retain the morning's coolness. At this point summer has no doubt about itself, cooking the days with dry and relentless determination. Nightfall brings little relief and most people sleep bared and naked under windows propped open with box fans. We have chosen Caples Creek. Maybe as a punishment. Maybe as a test. The hike in and out of this river is long, steep and exposed. A granite expanse that lays prone to the sky with few trees to give reprieve until you reach the river's edge.

If the men are worried about this hike, they aren't showing it. Chicago has his arm out the window whistling Dixie and Vincent sits in the passenger seat systematically organizing his camera and lenses into his black backpack. Chicago doesn't ask for directions and hits every unmarked forest service road and logging offshoot necessary to get to the seldom-used trailhead on the north rim of the canyon. He comes in hot down the last quarter mile and pulls to sideways stop, kicking rocks against a closed and locked forest service gate posted with a sign that reads: "No Motor Vehicles." I lean out the window in disbelief.

What the hell? This never used to be here.

Goddamnedmotherfuckingforestservice. Mumbles Glory.

This ain't no 'Motor Vehicle.' It's the Scout!

Says Chicago as he yanks on the e-brake. He looks over at Vincent. Vincent studies the gate, then puts down his camera gear, gets out and walks to the back of the truck. He opens a big metal toolbox welded to the back and pulls out a battery-charged saws-all. He walks calmly to the gate, revs it up and proceeds to cut the gate into four pieces. Chicago gets out and they haul the sections out of the road, then they hop back in and without comment, Chicago throws it in gear and continues. *We're the new Forest Service*, I say to myself. We pull to a halt at an old logging pad where an overgrown wall of buck brush and a bunch of misplaced ducks hide the entrance to the trailhead. The nice thing about the few locals who come here is they have enough respect for the rest of us to at least attempt to throw outsiders off the trail.

We pile out and stretch our legs. I pull my dirty salt-stained Smith and Wesson hat down tight, close my eyes, and wonder if he'll be here today. People piss, grab rods and gear and head for the drop-off. The drop-off to Caples is one of the most beautiful sights in all this range. We break through the tree-lined rim and stand, toes over, a fall of tumbling granite and tangled berry brush. It falls away, exposing a nestled valley of pines and shy meadows. The head of the canyon is an enchanting maze of stacked granite, walls, cliffs and wide open bowls of grey rock — as well as a few gnarled and deformed pines that strike their life from cracks you'd be hard pressed to wedge a penny into. They live on nothing. They live nonetheless. Through all of this runs Caples Creek, a green river of plunge pools and pocket water, long flat runs and lost spaces. Big, healthy rainbow trout swirl in the rockbound pockets, and monstrous brown trout, like submarines, line up under the shady overhangs of brush in the forested flat water. I prefer the fast water and deep pocket pools where you can throw a giant Royal Wulff or Humpy into the foaming water and catch a leaping Rainbow. But if you're more patient, which I'm not, the largest fish are the big Browns that you have to stalk with care and quiet. A black ant cast on the flat water here is a deadly proposition.

This river will tell you about a fisherman. It's a good place to find your water. At some point a fisherman comes across the water that matches his heart. Comes to the water that runs seamless with the blood through his veins. It resonates. The pace of the water is the speed that you naturally fall to, and the sound or the silence is a language understood. Some people are lake fishermen for a reason: it speaks to a still heart and patience. Steady, subtle, observant natures can coax fish from slow-moving flat waters, a surface with little information but underneath, complex and changing. I'm none of these. On Caples I found my water and it was jumping through the exposed granite expanse, swirling, falling, running, chatting all the while. Water with no gradual transitions, it runs fast and shallow, punctuated abruptly by deep beautiful pools. This is where I fish best. Where I *am* best.

We step off the edge, gain momentum and walk with hard footfalls down this steep and sandy trail. It's a couple miles to the river and if coming down the canyon wall is a hot and joyless task, hiking out is tenfold so. There is not a stitch of shade for the descent and the occasional towering granite boulder makes for uncomfortable passing. Mountain lions love this country as much as we do, and though they don't have a taste for humans, we don't like to push it. You never know what lean times will make a critter do. We level out onto the valley floor as the trail winds through tall pines and aspens and detours into Government Meadow. Through the round-up site, a hundred yards more and we're on the stream in front of my childhood family campsite.

We take seats on rocks and stumps and begin assembling our gear. Chicago pulls a two-piece old bamboo fly-rod out of his pack and puts it together. It's dark and patinaed, with bright silk wraps and a dark and scrolled inscription near the stained cork handle. I give it a closer look. It's a thing of beauty.

Where did you find a rod like that?

My grandma gave me this the day my momma dropped me off at her place to stay for the summer. That summer lasted about nine years. I was seven. Nana said my great grandpa made it when he was working back in Michigan. He was a boat-builder, but he used to make rods for folks from time to time.

Did you know him?

Hell no. He died and then the family came back out here. Wish I did, though. He was the last man to stick around the family more than a year or two. Never knew my grandpa or my father neither. Aw, don't look sad, girl! My grandma was the best damn woman in California. It don't bother me none.

She must have been to keep you! And to give you that nice rod.

She gave me this and let me come out here and camp alone for weeks at a time if I wanted when I was just a kid. Shit, people would get arrested for that now. But she just let me be and do what I wanted. She's Miwok, was raised like that herself. I sure can't complain.

She sounds wonderful. Do you see her much?

Naw. She quit a few years ago.

Quit what?

Quit livin', what do you think? Just said she was goin' and she loved me and then she died.

I look at Chicago as he happily strings his old rod, and I wonder about this woman taking death by the hand, or kicking it in the balls, however you might like to look at it. I have an impulse to wrestle or tease him. Or just grab him up and hold him like a little brother. Instead I stay put on my stump and think of my own raising-up and my mother, tough and good in her own way.

> Hey, Chicago, since you're so good at finding things, will you do me a favor? My Mom wants me to collect heart-shaped stones from all the rivers my Dad fishes. She's making a big pile of them and, I don't know, making some shrine or something. Anyhow, she's trying to heal his heart. I thought maybe you could help me find some.

> Oh hell yes I can!

He says, kicking some gravel on the sandbar at his feet. He sticks his fingers in a small pile, flicking the rocks around and comes up with a very lopsided heart-like rock. He examines it, then tosses it into the river.

> Naw, that one's likely to give him a heart attack on the spot. But I'll keep looking, Rosie-pants. Don't you worry about your daddy!

We turn our attention to stringing up and tying on flies. Choosing the right fly depends. Depends on things you know but can't explain. I study the fly box. That I'll be using a Royal Wulff today is a given, but which Wulff is another question. I stare at the rows of flies, old and new, crammed in one after another until the right fly shows itself. I take out the fly, hold it up for Glory to see. Hold it up to the stream for the fish to see, a little fair warning.

It's a large — or *was* a large, I should say — Royal Wulff that's now so tattered and beaten that the once fluffy white wings are but a few delicate strands and the peacock has unraveled into one long wisp followed by a cropped bristle brush where the tail used to be. The body is held together with a wrap of red silk that had obviously come off at some point and was tied back on in a crude knot. It's perfect. This is my oldest mojo-fly — made with my own mojo, that is. I have some very old, worn and used flies of my Dad's and my Papa's, but this Wulff has only been used by me. It's ten years old at least. As old as these jeans, this wedding ring. It's no small task to fish with, and keep, the same fly for ten years. In it is every fish, submerged log, tangle of weeds and overhanging branch that ever tried to take it and failed. This fly has seen edges, dark places, depths. Has traveled with me, walked and changed with me. The first cast with it is the turnkey that opens the doorway to the world of fish. Glory takes the first hole. Chicago takes the second. Things fall natural and easy today. I turn to head upstream and Vincent is perched on a rock by the side of the trail, focusing his lens.

Oh no you don't. I don't want to be in front of your camera, mister. I've seen your work.

Now what makes you think I even want to take a picture of you?

He says with a serious stare.

I just thought…

I'll let you know if I want to take a picture of you.

He holds my eye, then a smile unrolls across his face like a magic carpet. He's ruthless and beautiful. And honest. *And if that's a tough thing to face*, I think, *that's my problem. Not his.* I head upstream alone.

Around the bend is the first run of forest flat water. Deep green channels pressed in by shady pines on a mattress of pine needles. The realm of the big Browns. Not my water. I'll throw the Wulff out there a few times but I'm not going to bother with changing the fly just to lure one of these submarines out. I know a black ant or a wet fly would turn a bronze side, but I'm not interested in pursuit. I don't like having to convince a fish that it wants what I have. I prefer the Rainbows up in the plunge pools that throw themselves on my fly like a pileup on a quarterback.

Across the river from me is a deep running channel that has undercut the bank. The water there drinks the sunlight and swallows it black. It's the places you can't see where you know that things are. I cast my line aloft, strip out until the Wulff makes its turn directly above this chasm. The line moves right today. Things feel good. The fly traces a figure eight through the air, above the water, over and over. Because it's the right time I break the eight and lay the fly down at the top of the channel. It sits for a moment on the still water at the edge of the current, then gently dips into the line of moving water. This old fly knows what to do. It imperceptibly makes its way across the channel and heads for the undercut. The current here picks up and sweeps the fly out of sight for a moment underneath a fan of overhanging pine needles, back under the ledge. The light directly underneath the spot where the fly went changes suddenly. Where it was black it flashes to a bright green. Fish and shadows are the same until they move. I know it's striking, so I pull the tip of the Sage up quick and strip an arms length of line in and *whop*! Resistance. The rod doubles over. Two hard tugs from the other end then *snap!* The line retracts from the water, floats back in a trailing wave and falls in a pile at the base of the big ponderosa behind me.

I stare dumbfounded at the channel for a moment then turn around to see a ghost untangling the line from around his boots. He looks at me, questioning. Raises an eyebrow. I should be happy to see him, but I'm in shock. He has no idea what I just lost. But I do. I can't even cuss. It's too much for cussin' and it's too much for explaining. A fly that I have been creating, been saving, that tattered and perfect Wulff was taken in a sliver of a moment by something that I had underestimated. And that was my mistake. I got surprised and reacted too quick. Pulled the line too tight, too fast and broke it. I lost the fly and the fish.

I let out a long breath. It flows into a sigh as I look back at the spot in the channel. Black again. Right back to the same place as if it wasn't bothered in the least. Under the water, an ancient brown trout frowns with twenty-four hooks in its jaw. Some so old and rusted that they are just an orange stain and some are mangled lures and several are black ants. And one of them is a Royal Wulff, trailing a silk thread and the remains of a wing. The remains of memory lodged deep into the bone of this Brown, it and they facing the current, suspended fatefully and unmoving by the slow wag and pulse of his green fins and fan of tail.

I shake my head, feeling a little sick.

Damn!

I'm reeling up my line when it snags.

134

You're standing on my line, darlin'.

We laugh at the joke. The line jumps through the dry leaves, returns. I see how this fishing is going to go, so I decide to hike far and fast ahead to the lunch spot to buy ourselves some time alone. Through the pines I catch a profile of the red granite cliff that overlooks the little beach where we always stop. At the base of this cliff runs a deep narrow channel cut through solid granite that is a guaranteed catch. *I'll save it for Glory*, I think. I've fished it plenty since Dad almost always saves it for me.

I head for the cliff, picking my way through the brushing arms of cedars and piñion. The trail here is more rumor than anything else. I push through a thicket and am deposited onto a delicate little beach surrounded by infant trees and bordered by a small beautiful plunge pool. Looks inviting and this hot day begs for a swim. But before I do any swimming I decide to see if any of those agreeable Rainbows are in there. I pull out my old tin fly box and poke at the flies in there. I eye the old Wulff of my Dad's, but I'm not sure I can suffer another loss like that again today. Stimulator? Too forward. Humpy? No. *Damn you, Brown Trout!* I shake a fist at the river. Poke around the flies some more as if I might find something new there. *Well, there is this new Wulff. It's the right size anyhow.* I take out a brand new fly. It's clean, pristine. Every hair in place, perfectly white fluffy wings. Why not? My mojo-fly was new once. And I guess sometimes you just have to start at the beginning. I show it to the ghost. He gives it a speculative glance.

All right, fly, let's see how you do.

I tie on the brand new Wulff and step out onto a sunlit boulder in the stream. So familiar. I never plan it. I never look at a stream and say, *Oh there's the rock I'm supposed to stand on to fish this hole.* You don't think about those things. But as soon as I hop out and both feet come to balance on it, I have a sublime moment of recognition. Of comfort. *This rock. This place.* I come to it every time. Absolutely every time. Not because I remember but because it is the right place to be to fish this hole, and every fisherman knows this. So I hop out to this rock that I have stood balanced on so many times before and strip out some line. Breathe in and cast out. Lay the fly in the bubbles fanning out from the tiny waterfall between the two boulders at the head of the pool. The Wulff dances at the edge of the riffle then slides into the current and now's the moment, and I know it is, and I'm expecting it and I'm ready and *whomp!* Bright silver steam train hits my fly and takes it under, but not for long because I set the hook and then *look out!* Fish comes shooting straight out of the water and does a dance three feet above the surface. A big bright Rainbow trout and it can fly. And it is strong because it dives back down, bends the rod in half and heads for the big rock at the bottom. I play it away from the rock, but this Rainbow is also smart so it heads for the waterfall. But I am smart too, so I let it go over into the long flat-water pool below and now it's simply a matter of patience. The Rainbow gets tired. I guide it to me, run my fingers down the line and under water until I feel the fly. I grab the hook and pause for a moment to look. I keep the fish under water, where it's most beautiful. It's big. Very big and very healthy and very wild. I give the hook a little turn and it comes out. The fish swims there for a moment looking at me. It doesn't seem to be overly mad about it.

Sorry about that, fish. But you learned something there, didn't you? Learning's not always easy. I know. You can ask your big brown buddy down there all about it. Go on now. Next time, maybe you'll keep that fly, eh?

136

I give the fish a little pat under the tail and it swims off. I reel up my line and turn around to see the ghost laughing at me.

> What's so fuckin' funny over there? Never seen a woman talk to a fish before? I'll tell you what's not funny: this heat! Let's go swimmin'.

He grins, nods his head and starts undoing buttons. I start in on my own buttons, looking him in the eye. He pauses while I drop my shirt from my shoulders. Jeans, bra. Clank of brass belt buckle and zippers. Boots on the pile. I leave the hat on though. I'm not getting into this frozen water coming straight out the depths of Caples Lake alone. I walk shining to the edge of the stream and survey the situation. Look over for some help; ghost just shrugs.

> I can't keep you warm in there, honey. He says.

> You can't keep me warm anywhere.

He threatens to push me in.

> Just try it.

I open my arms in a challenging invitation. We smile at each other. The sun is shining. We turn to the pool where I caught the Rainbow and wade in. I gasp with the cold. We look at each other with wide eyes. Caples Creek is cold enough to take a ghost's breath and that's saying something. We step close until we are belly to belly, then we drop beneath the water. We stay under for a second, pulsing, surprising the fish for as long as we can stand it, then pop up cussin'. I pull myself out and spill onto a big flat granite slab in the middle of the pool and lay supine to the sun. Take the soaking hat off and lay it on the rock next to me. Palms down to the heat of the stone. Ghost lies down beside me, turns and lays a hand gently upon my cold chest. I speak without opening my eyes.

Do you remember what it's like to touch me?

Of course I do.

You can have that again. It's up to you. It doesn't have to be like this.

I know, Rose. Today, right now, I feel like I can make it happen.

I take it in. Take it all in. What a perfect day. This is what I want. And I know. *This is how it's going to be.* I fall asleep to that thought and into a dream. The dream is of the sun on my eyelids. The dream is orange. And warm.

And something comes into the orangeness. It's a twig snapping, and then it's my eyes snapping open to the white sun, and I slap myself in the face trying to push it back out of my eyes.

What the fuck? Oof!

Hey, there you are, Rose! Naked already? The fishing that bad?

It's Glory, congealing into shape out of the sun. I sit up.

As a matter of fact, no. It was so good I thought I'd better give them a rest.

Oh I see.

How bout you? Catch any?

Pretty good. Not bad. Browns.

Yeah, I had a little run-in with a Brown down there. You didn't happen to see a submarine with my mojo-fly in it, did you? Because if you did, I expect you punched him in the nose and got it back for me.

What? Not your mojo-fly!

Yeah, well. Hell. Anyway. Want to come swimmin'?

Ok. Yeah I guess so.

She undresses on the shore.

Is it cold? She asks.

I'm sorry, did you just ask me if it was cold?

Right. What the hell. Here I come.

Watch the rock there, it's loose.

Shit! Where'd you go in? Here?

Yeah, there. Anywhere in there.

It's kinda shallow.

I guess.

It's fuckin' cold, Rose.

Umhmm.

I'm not sure if I want to go in.

Glory stops for a long moment and locks her gaze onto the wet hat dripping on the rock over the pool.

No. I definitely don't want to go in.

Why don't you? It's not even as cold as Slab.

She steps back out of the water and stumbling back over a rock, turns and grabs a tree branch to stop herself from falling. She lets go and kneels down in the sand, doubles over and throws up, retching. When she sits up, her face is as pale as quartz and beaded with sweat. I hop from my rock to the shore and grab her around the shoulders.

Glory! What's wrong?

She leans into me and starts crying. I hold onto her.

What the fuck, Glory? What is it? Tell me!

She shakes her head, grabs my arm tight, trembling.

I don't know. I just… I saw that hat all wet. And the water. I just got sick. I was terrified.

I help her to the lunch spot and bring her her clothes. She settles down under a tree, looks far off and says nothing, so I give her a little room. I go to my clothes and pull jeans over wet skin, get my blouse buttoned up just as Chicago and Vincent come around the bend.

Aw hell! We're too late! I told you we shoulda hurried, V!

Chicago laughs. I gesture toward Glory, and they both fall silent. Chicago
steps closer to me and lowers his voice.

What's wrong with our girl?

Vincent puts his pack down, walks over, leans down and gently lifts her
chin, tilting her face to his. He studies her face. She looks right at him a
long while without saying a word. She grabs his hand and pulls him down
to sit beside her.

> I don't know. I must still be kind of fucked up from that
> knockout I took. That or getting that letter from Jesse has me
> freaked out.

> Jesse contacted you? Why didn't you tell us?

> I was going to. I just got it this morning. He says he's waiting for
> me.

Vincent takes that in and focuses a silent glare into the distance for a long
moment. A thought crosses his face that he dismisses with an abrupt
snort.

> It's all right. There's not a goddamn thing that's going to happen
> to you while we're around. You understand?

She nods and with a faint smile, relaxes against him. Chicago looks from
Glory to me then back to Glory. He grins and his eyes narrow.

> I know you've had a hard run, but ain't no one going to hurt you,
> girl. And if they do? Well, as you lay there dying, you can have a

smile on your pretty face, because you'll know that within twenty-four hours, that bastard will die in way more pain than you.

Well... thanks? Don't worry about it, guys. I'll figure it out. Let's eat some lunch, hey? I want to hear how all your fishing was.

She gets up and starts unpacking the food. Chicago digs hands-deep into the bulky pockets of his army pants and pulls out two huge fistfuls of heart shaped rocks and drops them in a pile by the old campfire ring. He reaches into a back pocket and pulls out a handful more. He grins and goes about his business. We follow suit and all settle in to a big spread of the usual. Chicago pulls a can of tuna and a fork out of his pack. We all pause and look at him. Glory almost chokes on her mouthful, laughing.

Really?

He shrugs and peels back the lid. *Everyone's got his traditions,* I think. We find places to lean back and relax in the warm summer afternoon. I pull out a Swisher for me and offer one to Glory and Chicago. Vincent has a cigarette hanging off his lip as he deftly switches lenses on his camera. Chicago leans back against a young juniper, lights his cigar and puffs a few warbled smoke rings into the air in front of him. Vincent directs the lens to where Chicago is sitting and adjusts the focus. Chicago just pulls the brim of his Fuck You fishing hat down tighter, takes another puff and smirks.

You're comfortable with him taking your picture? I ask. I thought you said you shouldn't get in front of that camera unless you're prepared to have your very soul exposed.

That's what I said, all right. Vincent's taken a hundred pictures of me. You think I give a shit? I don't give a shit. There's nothing

142

about myself I didn't know by the time I was ten. Girl, it ain't that hard. There ain't nothing I can do about myself and I sure don't give a good goddamn what other people think. So put my picture up. It ain't news to me. And if it bothers you, well, that's your problem.

Vincent takes two deliberate shots. Then puts the camera away. I instantly regret my bluntness.

I don't mean to come off like that, Vincent. I think your images are beautiful. They're perfect actually. They scare the hell out of me, though. Where did you learn to do that?

Chicago laughs, smoke swirling from his mouth like volcano waking.

Oh you hear that, Vincent? The little lady wants to know where you learned to take them pretty pictures. Why don't you enlighten her.

He sits up from his tree, props his chin on his hand and gives an exaggerated inquisitive look to Vincent. Vincent looks at Glory, then to me, then down to his pack. He begins to lace up the cinches. When he speaks, his voice is flat, like it's someone else's story he's just repeating.

My dad was a two-bit pornographer in Reno. He used to work out of the motels down on 4th Street because he didn't have a legitimate studio. He used hookers from that neighborhood because the pros on the strip had standards too high to go with him. They weren't all prostitutes either. He got others sometimes.

Vincent sets his pack aside. Then he looks at us. His gaze is straight and sustained.

I watched my father go from B-movie porno straight down to something you couldn't even rate. He was trying so hard to capture something about these women, and he was never able to do it. It eluded him and frustrated him, and he thought that if he could just expose them more, make it more raw, more dirty and rough, then somehow they would finally show themselves to him. They never did. He could have shoved that lens all the way up their pussies and never seen anything deep about them. But he couldn't see that and so he just pushed the scenarios further and further. By the time I left, he had done things that you'd never want to know about. I was fourteen. One day I just went into his motel room, took his camera and walked to the highway. I stuck out my thumb and took the first ride that was offered.

Jesus. I don't know what to say.

You don't need to say anything, Rose.

Vincent tilts his head back and slips into an easy smile.

Part of me thinks you relish the discomfort of others.

I say, shaking off the mood.

No. I don't relish it. But I do find it interesting.

He stands and throws the pack on his back. Chicago slaps his knee.

Story time is over, kids! Let's hit the trail. This all just makes me want a drink. First one out gets the extra beer!

He jumps up and throws his gear together. We all rush to break down and pack up our rods as we push to get in line on the trail. The enthusiasm wears off as soon as we climb out of the forested valley and up into the vast sun-bleached granite slope that is our fate for the next couple of hours.

Welcome to God's graveyard! Yells Chicago from the front.
Wonder how many devils he's got buried here?

Glory scoffs at that and yells loudly to make sure he hears her from the
back of the line.

Better move quick before he sees you, Chicago. He'll realize he
missed one!

# The Right Jack

*August 7*

The benevolent apple orchard that guards my parents' house greets me and the children with knobby and outstretched arms. The orchard is old and the varieties are unknown. Long forgotten and out of favor. These trees were planted in the first years of the gold rush by homesteaders who quickly realized that produce and alcohol were more dependable than the flash of gold in the pan. I stop to admire the old sherry house, its stone walls still strong and its tin roof ablaze in a red and orange patina of rust. The morning is sunlight and green leaves and thousands of little green apples. My children are little green apples as they chase each other up the rows and toward the family house on the hill. A walk this morning was necessary. I left the foreclosure notice on the table in the beautiful breakfast nook that Leo'd built by hand. These days, he doesn't wake up before he hears me leave. It's just easier I guess and I guess I'm glad for it.

We make our way up the dirt road to the house. The children quicken their pace when they see their grandfather working in the garden ahead.

Papa!

My father is wrestling with some deer fencing. Glory stands there beside him, hands on her hips and shaking her head. They are both smeared with red dirt and sweat.

Frank, I'm telling you there's no point in putting this fence up this late in the summer. Shoulda done it in the spring when they were eating all the blossoms and baby peppers. I warned you about it then!

No, no. I saw a big buck come in this morning, and I know there's already three or four other deer in here. They're going to destroy this garden! Have I ever told you how many grapes they ate in the Zinfandel block last year?

Five tons of grapes.

Five tons of grapes!

That's impossible.

No it's not. They get in here in the spring and they eat all the buds. They go right down the row and just clean 'em off! Do you know how many grapes a bud turns into?

A lot.

A lot! If you multiply the number of buds they eat by the average amount of fruit they yield, it comes out to tons. Tons of grapes! Here, hold this post while I get the sledgehammer.

Glory looks at me and winks.

Why don't we work on fencing the vineyards then and just leave this to that old buck? This garden could use a little thinning out. You have fifty tomato plants in here.

He's a farmer, I say to Glory. He can't plant anything smaller than an acre. Even if he doesn't have an acre to plant in. And shouldn't you be taking it easy, Dad?

Dad just mumbles and rolls a heaping wheelbarrow full of tomatoes out of the way. Glory puts the post down and walks over, wiping her face with a dirty bandana.

You guys are over here early. What's up?

Came to see Mom. Shit's coming to a head, I think. Got the final foreclosure notice today. I don't know what we're going to do.

Well, Margaret's got company. It's cribbage day.

Aw hell! He here?

Yeah, he's here. Weirdest friendship ever.

Makes perfect sense to me. He says she's the only honest woman he's ever met.

I make my way to the house as Glory goes back and wearily hoists the post back upright. On the patio, I find Mom at the picnic table playing cribbage with Vincent. They both glance at me and say nothing. The children sit next to Vincent with black ink markers, tracing outlines and images on their forearms. They check Vincent's arms to see if they've copied his tattoos correctly. Lyla adds a few cats and hearts. Next to the cribbage board, I notice a nice piece of rose quartz, in the perfect shape of a heart. I nod toward the beautiful stone.

Did you find that, Mom?

A gift from your friend Chicago. Vincent brought it. I'd like to meet him some day.

He's real shy.

I turn to the kids beginning to roughhouse at the table.

> You kids go play in the hose. I need to talk to Nanny alone.

They run off to the mud hole behind the chicken coop, tugging boots off on the way. I watch Vincent peg six off three-of-a-kind. Margaret has a wide lead.

> You're here early. That guy still not getting out of bed?

Vincent asks, knowing the answer.

> The final notice came in. We have thirty days to move. Leo wants to live separately for a little while. See if that's any better. Or any worse. I haven't told the kids yet.

Mom speaks without looking up from her cards.

> Well, you need to tell the kids. The sooner the better.

> I will. I've already explained how their daddy and I are thinking of spending more time apart.

> The kids don't need to be there while you guys break down that house. Why don't I take them for a couple of weeks to Aunt Ruth's.

> Jesus. Thanks, Mom. Yeah, I think that would be the best way to do it.

> And you and the kids can move into the old stone cottage in the orchard. We can fix it up. At least for now.

Vincent looks up from his hand to share a knowing look. Mom's taking care of me like she always does and like no one else can. This is the third time I've seen Vincent over here and I wonder if she's taking care of him too in some way, subtle as that can be. Maybe that's the point. Maybe for some people, detachment is a comfort. Not me. I prefer the emotional trenches. Which reminds me of someone.

Hey, Vincent, have you heard from Chicago? He was going to look at my radiator, but he's not answering his phone.

He's out of reception.

Where's he out of reception?

He'd probably prefer it if I didn't tell you. At least not until he gets back.

Great. A mystery! I just hope that rig doesn't overheat in the meantime.

I leave them to their game and go take a seat in the Mulberry swing to watch the kids play. Glory comes up from the garden and sits down beside me. She crosses her dirty boots and leans back heavily in the seat.

So where the hell is Chicago? Vincent won't tell me. Do you think he's back with that crazy girlfriend?

Maybe he got arrested again. Indecent exposure or assault on an officer. I don't know; he was grilling me yesterday about Jesse's outdoor grow, though.

Like what?

Like how big it is and how we run it.

Oh god, you don't think he'd go mess with Jesse, do you? Did you tell him where it is exactly?

Not exactly. He was asking more about how we sourced water and stuff.

Right. So he can figure out exactly where you would need to be in Rock Creek canyon to do it.

Or maybe so he can start one himself?

No way. He wouldn't want that much steady work. I bet he's gone out there.

You think he could find it on that little bit of information?

He could find a BB in a beanbag.

Fuck. Well, let's just hope he's in the drunk tank then.

We swing quietly for a minute, listening to the faint screeches of the children playing with the hose in the distance. Glory has her head drooped over the back of the bench seat, staring up and through the tangled branches.

I remembered something last night.

I look at her and wait. She takes her time.

I was helping your mom make dinner. She took a big bag of flour down from the shelf and thumped it onto the counter and *wham*! Right in that moment, it just opened up in my mind. It was just there, all of a sudden. There was a kid. Young, like twenty or barely more. He got hurt. Or maybe killed. Something like that. Something bad happened to him, and I think it was Jesse that did it. I have a picture of this kid being alive, working on a line of pipe or something. Then I have an image of him being dumped on the floor of the equipment shed. I remember the sound of him hitting the floor. It was dull. And heavy. I think I was going to tell. For sure it was why I was going to leave.

Holy shit, Glory! What are you going to do?

What can I do? I don't even know for sure if it's real.

But if it is real, then Jesse has a real good reason to find you. His letters could be bullshit. Maybe you should go to the cops.

Maybe I was involved. Maybe going to the cops is going to get *me* in a lot of trouble. I don't want to do that until I know exactly what happened. I think I just need to wait.

Glory, I'm so sorry.

Don't be. Even if I can't remember it, it's my own doing and my own destiny. I'll deal with it.

She turns to look at me. Maybe she doesn't like what she sees.

How are you? Things still coming down over there?

It's all coming down, all right. Leo is moving out. I'm moving here. We're going to separate for now. We haven't decided about divorce.

What are you waiting for? It seems inevitable.

I'm waiting to see if he comes around. It's hard to believe he can really walk away from it.

Do you really want him to stay?

I don't know. It's all just gotten so hard. It didn't used to be like this. Love doesn't just disappear. Does it?

Glory gets up, pulls the dusty gloves from her back pocket and slowly slides them on. She doesn't look at me, instead directing her gaze down to the garden where Dad is wrestling with a new roll of fence.

I don't know where love comes from, Rose, and I sure as shit don't know where it gets to sometimes.

She watches as Dad attempts to stand the roll on end. It's not going well.

I better get back down there before he kills himself.

With that, she jogs down to the garden and grabs the other end of the fence roll before it topples over. I sigh and look around at my old stomping grounds. Across the road, my childhood tree house still sits perched in a low fig tree. The kids use it occasionally, but apparently they don't have the driving need for solitude and secrecy I used to have. Still have, maybe. I get up and saunter over to the faded old ladder and, hand over hand, make my way up. A tattered old quilt hangs by a few nails over the little entrance. I push it aside and hoist myself in, slide my back against the wall and cross my legs beneath me. I lean my head back and, comforted, close my eyes.

A dull gnawing sound and squeak of metal wake me. Ghost sits, cross-legged and back to me, at the opposite wall. He's carving into the wood with a pocketknife. He turns and smiles over his shoulder, leans to the side so I can examine his work. It says "Billy" with a heart under it.

Lookin' pretty good, isn't it? Thought I'd freshen this up for you since I was here. It's so sweet. Your Billy...

You should be jealous; he was my first love.

Oh I'm not jealous. He was a lucky kid. You must have broke his heart, though.

No, he never even knew. I was too afraid to tell him.

Well, that's a shame. Looks like you've learned a thing or two since fourth grade.

He says, folding the blade and tucking it in his front shirt pocket.

Lot a good it's done me. I don't think I can tell you one more time I need you. It's getting embarrassing.

I laugh and scoot over closer to him. He doesn't laugh with me. He looks away, raises his hand and slowly traces over the old carved heart.

Rose, I have to go for a while. That's really what I came here to tell you.

A lump immediately begins to swell in my throat as I wrap my mind around his words. I choke on a response, unable to get anything out. I shake my head in frustration to loosen my tongue.

What do you mean, 'go?' I thought you wanted to be with me?

I do! It's just... well, it takes a lot to come to you like this. You have no idea. It's not easy. If I'm going to commit to it, I need to be sure. And in order to be sure, I need to be away from you.

That doesn't make sense.

Yes it does, Rose. You're a pretty powerful influence. I can't think straight when I'm near you. I just don't want to have any regrets. Do you understand?

I lean toward him, reach into his pocket and take out the pocketknife. I flip the blade up with a delicate snap.

You know what I regret, honey? Not telling Billy Hendrick I loved him when I had the chance. I see him around town sometimes now. He's old. And sad. And not doing what he wants with his life. He used to breakdance. That's why I loved him.

I flip the knife from my fingers to my palm, make a fist and, with a thud, lodge it firmly into the wood beside the heart.

He doesn't breakdance anymore. I should have loved him when it was the right time to love him. So take your time, but don't forget: time can be a tricky thing.

I look back to face the ghost, but the tree house is empty.

Fuck!

I yell and slam my fist into the old plywood floor.

You hear me, ghost!

I yell again and look around. He's gone. Nothing left but me, an old quilt and the obsolete markings of youth. I pick at the peeling paint of the floorboards. Look at the knife and decide to leave it there. Lyla will probably need it someday.

Momma just hopes it'll be sharp enough.

I mutter to myself as I sweep the quilt aside and climb down and away to the sound of the hose beating water against the hot afternoon pavement that sizzles with the footfalls and laughter of children.

# Pour 'em Deep, Keep 'em Coming
# and Forget to Put 'em on the Bill

*August 16*

Ever been stabbed in the belly in a bar fight by a broken-bottle-wielding ghost? Me neither. But that's just because ghosts don't get drunk. Or if they do, they don't effect your life the way a real drunk does. They just stumble through you, not into you. If they slur and spit and make offensive remarks, it's only in the shadow of a whisper, easy to tune out. If they barf, it doesn't stink and it doesn't get on your shoes. Ghosts can't pay bills and ghosts can't sleep in and ghosts can't waste your time. You can't get fucked by a ghost. But you can't get much else from a ghost either. Especially when they ignore you for days at a time. I watch the corners now relentlessly. At dusk and at dawn, his favorite times, but nothing.

> Hey Vincent, why do you think Rose has that ugly expression on her face?

Chicago asks from the back seat, snapping me out of my thoughts. He makes an exaggerated study of me in the rear-view mirror.

> You'd think she was drivin' to traffic court.

> Don't mind Rose's face. She's just not getting any attention from her man.

Vincent says, not knowing the half of it.

Aw hell! You need some attention, Rose? Well, you should of said so. Here, let me hold your hand and tell you how pretty you are.

Chicago reaches around from behind my seat, groping clumsily for my hand on the gearshift. He yanks my arms, popping the 'Cruiser out of gear.

Settle down, Chicago! You're going to make me crash.

Just let me hold it for a second. C'mon, Rosie, I haven't touched a female in a month. How bout you, Glory? Want to snuggle a little 'til we get there?

He pats the seat beside him. Glory gives him a dubious look.

Hell no. I have no idea where you've been. Anyway, neither one of us is lonely, for your information. Rose just had to say goodbye to her kids for the rest of the month. She's sad, so get your head out of the gutter.

I wouldn't have any idea where else to put it! You two just don't know what you're missing.

I pull the car over with an abrupt jerk of the wheel and come to a sliding stop on the shoulder and turn around to face Chicago lounging in the back.

Did you go out to Rock Creek last week? I demand.

Vincent shakes his head with *a tisk-tisk*.

Uh-oh.

Maybe I did. Who wants to know?

We do. You can't just go fucking around in Glory's business. You could get hurt, or worse yet, get her hurt!

Ain't nobody hurtin' nobody. Now settle the fuck down. I just went out there to take a little peek and see what he was up to. Just keepin' an eye is all. It's what you hired me to do.

We didn't hire you!

Just because I ain't been paid doesn't mean I ain't been hired.

This is a dangerous situation. We didn't expect you to actually get involved in it. Why would you take a risk like that?

Well, I'd like to say I'm a romantic fucker and I'm trying to impress you girls. But really it's because I don't like it when dicks get too big in this town, know what I mean? There's a certain balance to the shit that goes down in Hangtown, and this guy in particular is fucking with it.

Seriously, he could have seen you.

Aw, that's funny, Rose.

It's not funny at all.

Nobody's going to see Chicago if he doesn't want to be seen.

Vincent says casually.

Ain't never gunna happen. Hell, I've been sneakin' up on you girls all summer and you have no idea.

Seriously?

You'll never know. Either way. And neither will Jesse. Anyhow, he wasn't there.

This gets Glory's attention.

How do you know?

Because no one was there. The whole place was packed up and cleaned out. Looks like your boy has moved on. Thank you very much and you're welcome for that information.

He must think she's talking to the cops.

Who cares what he thinks? He's long gone now.

He's not gone.

Glory says this matter-of-factly, but I don't buy it.

How do you know? How *can* you know?

She reaches around to her back pocket and pulls out an envelope folded in quarters.

There was another letter at the post office yesterday.

Chicago snatches it out of her hands and hurriedly unfolds it, clears his throat and straightens up to read aloud:

"I can't stop thinking about you. Last night I woke up and thought you were beside me. I saw your breasts, the red curling hair of your cunt, your legs dropped open, and when I reached to put my hand inside you, you disappeared—"

Give me that!

Vincent snaps as he grabs the letter out of Chicago's hand.

Spare her, would you? She doesn't need you reading that out loud.

Oh, I don't mind.

Glory says. She looks back out the window as she recites from memory:

"You disappeared. And then I remembered you were gone and I cursed myself again, for the thousandth time. I would give anything to touch you again. Please come back. Jesse."

Vincent folds the letter up, reaches back and takes the envelope from Chicago, puts it back inside. He hands it to Glory and looks at her steady. She folds it up and puts it back in her pocket.

Don't worry, Vincent. I still can't shake the image of that dead kid on the floor. That's what I see when I read this.

I put the 'Cruiser in gear and pull back onto the winding two-lane highway. I turn up the music, but not everyone gets the hint.

Where are we going fishing anyhow? Yells Chicago from the back. This ain't the way to Silver Creek.

We're going to Jackson.

Jackson? What the hell? There's no fishing in Jackson.

Nope. But at this point, fishing is not what we need today.

Jackson is a little tiny gold rush town to the south of our little tiny gold rush town. It's got old western fronts, crumbling stone buildings, junk shops and old diners. Just like our town. The only real difference is that there's no freeway running through Jackson, so there's no importing of culture and no exporting of bad habits, and those last ones tend to multiply when there's nothing to do. The idea of ambushing Jackson puts everyone at ease. We settle in. Rolling down windows, rolling through mounded hills with dry grass toasting in the sun. Massive oak trees announce themselves and we can breathe. Hills roll into washes roll into ghost towns roll into Jackson.

Your best bet for a good drink in a tiny gold rush town is to seek out the oldest hotel on Main Street. There's usually only one, typically a tall three-story brick job with leaded glass windows, red velvet wallpaper and gilded chandeliers. When you're a stranger in a gold rush town, it's wise to pay your respects right off to the oldest place on the street. So after parking head-on into the curb across the street, we head into The Jackson Hotel and order up beers for us and a whisky for the dead miner in the corner. Looks like he could use one. He nods and lifts his glass in welcome. We tip our bottles in return and we all drink. This is a fine town, just fine. We spend a pleasant pace watching the gilded mirror behind the bar. Watching our every self. Watching every miner, every cowboy, every saloon girl, every businessman who ever got drunk, fell in love, fell out of love or killed himself or someone else in that place.

Man, I'm hungry.

Yeah, me too. Hey miner! Where can we get a good burger in this town?

He gestures across the street to the corner bar with a dim old sign reading "The Fargo Club." I can see where this day is heading: straight to Hell. Glory and Chicago race each other across the street. Chicago pushes Glory into the door jam as she tries to get in ahead of him. She sticks out her foot and trips him as he passes her and he goes stumbling into the darkness. She follows. Me and Vincent make our way across the street with a little more dignity, even if we both know it won't last. He pauses at the bench outside to light a cigarette and I pause with him. The street hosts old dented and rusted pickup trucks ferried by dented and rusty old men. They form a slow and questionable parade that seems to have no climax. Vincent flicks his cigarette butt into the street and we turn into the swinging doors of the bar. Our eyes adjust and shapes emerge: red leather stools, pool table, miles of bottles, antlers, overalls, straw hats and a brood of ninety-year-old forty-year-olds. It's 1:30 in the afternoon.

Glory and Chicago are hunched over the bar engaged in an argument in front of a barkeep who looks slightly confused. They have two whiskies and two beer-backs in front of them and two shot glasses already empty and stacked to the side. Glory is yelling and Chicago is yelling, and it seems to be about who can out-drink the other. Chicago seems to be yelling only because Glory is yelling. His face is calm, confident.

> Sorry, girl, but I'm the better drinker — and a better fighter to boot. I'm half Miwok, and half-Indian beats full-blooded-anything anytime.

Glory throws back her whisky with a snort.

> No Indian can out-drink the Irish. Or out-fight us.

Oh, you are crazy, girl! My Nana would have had you hog-tied before you even cracked a beer. And she'd a done it after two pints of Old Crow.

I thought your old gramma was from Michigan. There's no Miwok in Michigan; they'd freeze.

She was only there for her man. We're from here. Right here, and don't you forget it!

I don't believe you. Look at you: you're a scrawny white dude with freckles. You're no Indian.

Chicago downs his whisky and orders another round.

My blood's on the inside, Miss Ginger-head. How do you think I never git lost? And how do you think I find all them things I find? My ancestors show me. That's how. They stand right up and point at the ground. I walk over and there stuff is. There's no Irish who can do that. When your ancestors die they're just gone. Leave you all alone.

He leans back on his elbow and nods at her with a self-satisfied grin.

Glory's face turns redder than normal.

Well, that's because the Irish don't need their old dead nannies holding their hands. The Irish are not afraid of anything.

Miwok ain't afraid of nothin' either!

Chicago shouts, disturbing the bartender. Glory grabs her beer and waves it in Chicago's face.

Bet you're afraid to play pool with me. Now that you've had your drinks, you know I'm gunna school you.

166

There is no way in hell you could ever beat me at pool, missy.

Want to bet?

Hell yeah, what do you want to bet?

Your pants.

Oh, you got it. I sure hope you're wearing pretty panties today, girl. Whoop!

Chicago grabs an armful of half-empty glasses and stumbles over to the pool table. Glory follows. Vincent walks up to the bar and nods at the bartender. Tossing two crisp hundred-dollar bills on the counter, he makes a swirling gesture over the mess Chicago and Glory left.

Better get burgers for all these fools and whatever else they ask you for.

The bartender scoops up the bills without expression and goes into the back. We lean against the bar to survey the room just as a woman walks past. She struts away from us down the bar, and Vincent and I both watch her. She's wearing tight high-waisted jeans, the seam of which disappears between two firm and perfectly formed cheeks. She's compact and tight, and right off I think of all those skinny little rocker chicks from high school who always had that same figure — long hair, electric blue eyeliner and a thirty-year-old boyfriend by the time they were fifteen. She rounds the end of the bar and helps herself to a fresh draft. She looks up at us and I flinch. I'm expecting to see the young rocker girl of my memory, and instead I'm looking into a face drawn and haggard. Deep lines. Cigarette hue. Tan upon tan upon tan. The hint of a black eye or fifty. She could have been ninety. She could have been sixteen. She could have been brought into town with a wagon-load of moonshine and opiates a hundred and fifty years ago, but was probably just dropped in town last month by a primered Chevelle with two missing hubcaps and a warrant out for its impound.

She comes over and puts two stacks of quarters on the bar in front of me, leans in close and rests her chin in her hand. She gives me a look, closing her lids halfway down and drawing a creased and leathered smile.

You want to play?

Play what?

I ask her back, leaning in on my own hand. We're nose to nose. She doesn't flinch.

Anything you want, babydoll.

I glance at her stack of quarters.

I don't do anything for less than ten dollars.

I say with a wink. She straightens up and with a huff scoops her quarters off the bar and walks over to the pool table, lining her coins up on the felt for the next game. I exchange a smile with Vincent.

Well, you're a tease. Playing hard-to-get are you?

Oh, that's no game, love. There's a difference between playing hard-to-get and being hard to get.

We clink glasses and finish our shots. The bartender comes out with our food.

I see you met Roxanne.

He says, sliding baskets across the bar and gesturing toward the pool table where Roxanne is leaning over in front of Chicago helping him place his cue ball in the right place. He's staggering and leaning over trying to steal a look at her ass. I've seen this behavior before.

Look at that! Do you think he's going to go there?

No.

The bartender interrupts, overhearing.

She likes the ladies. She's just toying with your friend so she can talk to the redhead.

He adds, then walks away down the bar, leaving me and Vincent alone.

Too bad. I say. He seems awful interested in her good side. I could never.

Why not?

What do you mean why not? She's not, well, I wouldn't be attracted to her, I guess.

There's plenty to be attracted to there. What kind of lover are you?

Well, yeah ok, she does have a great body. I guess I can focus on that.

No. You don't focus on that. You want to be a lover? You want to fuck someone for real? You look right at the ugliest part about them and make it sexy. Let their scars and their anger and their bruises and all that shit give you a hard-on. How do you think Beauty felt every time she was thrown across the bed by the Beast? She liked it. She wanted him to be as ugly as he could be.

Is that how you love someone for real then, too? Look right at the worst part and love it?

I have no idea.

But you just said—

I said *fuck*. I don't know the first thing about *love*.

We settle in with our food. As I watch the balls gracefully banking around the table, I wonder about the ugly parts in me. The games roll by, and Roxanne seems less and less interested in the game and more and more interested in Glory. Chicago calls his shots, but the women don't hear him, laughing and chatting over the side bar. Vincent and I watch him run five stripes down then miss his shot on the eight ball. He sits back on his stool to give them their turn, but they don't notice a thing. He stands back up with a huff and, swaying and glaring for a moment, he goes back to the table and starts shooting their balls. He drops their last three, then hammers the eight ball into the corner pocket loud enough to get the bartender's attention. But not Roxanne's. He slams his cue down on the table with an "Aw Hell!", turns and storms past us through bar. He strides to the door, tugging his hat brim down to his nose with one hand and slamming the door open with the other. He disappears into the bright flare of sunlight.

Well. Would you look at that.

I say and we laugh as we watch the door swing in and out a few times before it comes to rest, sealing us back into our tomb of comfortable darkness. We're about to go back to the serious job of drinking when the door creaks open again. At first we think it's Chicago returning, but the backlit shape of a large man slowly and deliberately steps into the room, stops and looks from one end of the room to the other. After a long moment, he moves into the bar light.

Mother fuck!

Vincent says, sitting up straighter. I sit up straighter too.

What's the problem?

It's that old dude from Hangtown. The one I saw watchin' you two the night we all met.

The man takes a stool at the very far corner of the long bar, takes his porkpie hat off and lays it on the stool beside him. The bartender meets him there, snaps the towel from his shoulder, wipes down his spot with one hand and tosses a coaster in front of him with the other. He orders a whisky and while the bartender pours it, the man leans in and talks a long while. The bartender looks down the bar toward us, then toward the pool room. He nods his head yes. He shakes his head no. He says a few more things, then leaves the man with his drink. Vincent stares hard at the man, but he doesn't even notice we're here. He watches the pool table intently. Every time Glory moves, his eyes move with her.

He's up to something.

Vincent says, without taking his eyes off the man.

Yeah, up to being a creep. But he's harmless. There's tons of shady old characters around here. It's just a coincidence we ran into him again.

There are no coincidences when it comes to evil men, Rose. No accidents. They do what they want.

Well at least he's making an effort to be with the object of his desire. It's more than can be said for the men in my life.

What's wrong, Rose? No one parading for you? No dramatic stunts in front of your window? You want to be pursued constantly, don't you?

Occasionally would suffice.

The old man in the corner turns in his stool and stops, staring into the room where Glory is laughing and leaning over the green table through veils of amber light. He looks at her as if he's trying to make something out on a distant horizon. He steps away from the bar and heads toward Glory. Vincent jumps to his feet and in one step is planted in front of the man, chest to chest. His voice is flat and low.

Where do you think you're going?

The man shakes his head like he's in a fog or not quite aware of the situation, straining his neck to keep Glory in view over Vincent's shoulder.

Who is that? What's that girl's name?

The man asks. Not taking his eyes off her. Vincent leans to the side to block his view.

Betsy Ross. Who wants to know?

Is her name Glory?

He asks and puts a hand on Vincent's shoulder to push past him. Vincent grabs his hand, bending his thumb back against his wrist. The old man buckles under the pain and backs up, snapping out of his haze. Vincent lets go and the man stands back up straight. Focusing his gaze on Vincent, his eyes become sharp as a slow smile crawls across his lips. He is not afraid. Far from it, in fact. He turns his back on Vincent and strides casually back to his stool, where he grabs his coat and hat and walks to the door. He pauses for a moment to look back at us, then a last long look at Glory. Then he is gone. I wait for Vincent to take his seat next to me at the bar.

What the fuck was that?

I'm not sure.

Vincent leans over the bar and calls into the back room.

Bartender!

The bartender comes out and Vincent starts in on him.

Who was that old man in the corner and what did he want?

He's been a regular around here for ages. Quiet. Don't know much about him. He sure was interested in your friend over there, though. Grilled me hard about her. I didn't tell him anything because I don't know anything.

What's his name?

Parker.

Parker what?

Just Parker. Don't know his last name.

Glory, oblivious to anything outside the pool room, knocks the cues from the wall rack onto the floor with a clattering crash. She and Roxanne laugh and make a painful attempt at putting them back in straight. They fail. Glory pokes around the room to gather up her stranded things while Roxanne struts toward us. She pauses in front of me.

I'll be seeing you later.

She says with a wink then continues out the door. I watch her go, then raise my hands in surrender to Vincent.

Jesus. Can this shit get any weirder?

Sure it can, Rose. Here comes the champion.

Vincent stands up to help Glory manage a straight line.

174

Onward!

Yells Glory, pointing toward the wall clock. Vincent corrects her arm to point to the door.

Eggggzactly! She drawls. Follow her!

We push out onto the bright street and stand, hands in front of our eyes for a moment until our eyes adjust. On the bench in front of the club is Chicago, sprawled long, one boot up on the arm, one down on the ground, and arm draped heavy across his face. Glory stands over him, casting a shadow across his seemingly lifeless body.

Shhhhh-cago! Get th' fuck up! What're you doin' down there?

I'm not down. I'm just savin' up.

Good! Cause yer gunna need it. You're gunna sleep with Roxanne.

Chicago springs up like a cat, suddenly alert.

What? When?

Right now. Get up!

What the fuck are you sayin', girl?

Roxanne said she'd sleep with you, if I slept with her after. So c'mon. I'm doin' you a favor.

Well hell, all right! Damn! Where to?

She's across the street at the Jackson Hotel.

Glory gestures to the old brick building across the street. Chicago pats his shirt pockets. He gets up checking around his feet.

Hold on.

Then he walks down to the corner of the building, looks around, bends down and picks something up. He walks back and, fishing a lighter out of his pocket, lights a brand new cigarette. Glory shakes her head in amazement.

How'd you find that?

I told you, girl. I find things. When I need 'em, I find 'em. And when you need 'em, well, I can find them too.

He grabs her elbow and they walk across the street and into the hotel. Vincent, for the first time ever, looks completely dumbfounded. I can think of nothing to say in this situation, so I gesture toward the coffee shop. We get a couple of cups and head to the Landcruiser to sober up before heading home. Vincent gets into the driver's seat and I don't fight him. We quietly watch the steam from the coffee float up and commiserate on the windshield. Vincent shakes his head. Then he chuckles a little, to himself. I shake my head. I look at him and catch his eye as we burst out laughing.

Holy shit.

Yeah, holy shit is right. I really ought to be writing this down. It is technically a fishing journal day after all, and I sure can't make this shit up.

Just then the back door flies open and Glory rushes into the backseat, slamming the door behind her.

Go! Go! Go!

She yells, flailing her hand forward. Then looking frantically out the back window. I follow her gaze. There is nothing, nobody behind us.

What? What's going on? Where the hell is Chicago?

She reaches into her purse, grabs on to a dark wad and flings it up onto the dashboard. Vincent grabs it and unfolds it. It's Chicago's pants.

Go!

She demands, slapping Vincent's seat. Vincent throws it in reverse, then heads out for the two-lane highway that will take us home. We drive a short way, Glory watching intently out the back for followers. I reach back and yank on her shirt to get her attention.

Jesus, Glory. What did you do?

She looks back at me with a smile.

He bet his pants he could beat me, and I saw him cheatin'. Now we'll see who wins the Irish-Indian war of Jackson County!

She cackles. Then, just as fast, she sprawls across the back seat and promptly passes out. I look to Vincent; he's smirking. I'm at a loss.

What about Chicago? We aren't going to leave him there, are we?

Cheatin's cheatin. He made his bed. Now he's going to have to lie, or whatever he's doin', in it.

# The Big Dipper

*August 23*

Indigo soaks across the evening sky as the light from the old army jeep pans over the thick head-pruned vines. Maimed and tangled old heroes, they line up in orderly rows along the bumpy vineyard road. We take the drainage ditches at high speed because the old hill road is too steep not to. With every bump, the few logs for the fire lift and thud on the metal floor in the back. The Top of the Hill. It is a place.

Winding up narrow rows through the oldest part of the vineyard, we climb away from the small and modest winery barn, made even smaller from this perch on the hill. Cresting the final slope, I pull to a stop at a perfectly round irrigation pond surrounded by peach trees and pines. All around and descending in every direction are the vineyards, pooling around the winery below.

Glory and I hoist the logs out of the back and carry them to the edge of the pond and set them down at the old fire pit surrounded in stumps. Glory walks off into the dark vineyard to gather up kindling. I watch the stumps and wait patiently for a ghost to appear. Nothing. Crickets chirp and exaggerate his absence. I fling a few rocks into the darkness in the hopes I might hit one by luck. No luck.

Glory returns and sets sticks, dried vines and logs to fire. There is a peach tree with handled cups hanging here and there on the branches. Glory selects two as I pull an old stained cork out of a scuffed and unmarked bottle of wine. With cups full and red, we settle back against the stumps and listen to the sound of the sparks snap as they ignite upon the night air.

You are so lucky, Rose. Look at the stars! Look at the view. This is such a beautiful spot.

I know it. And I never forget it. I've never looked around here and not seen it for exactly how amazing it is. Every damn time.

That's good because most people don't have this. Some people may be rich as fuck, but they don't have this. It's going to be hard to leave here.

Oh come on. What are you talking like that for? You aren't leaving.

Sometime.

Yeah, well sometime is some other time. So just stop thinking about it.

I have to think about it.

Why?

I got another letter from Jesse.

You need to stop reading those.

This one's different. He told me to come back.

He wants you back, that's not news.

No, first he said he knew I wouldn't come back, then he asked me if I would. This time he told me I had to.

Well, you don't have to. You don't have to do anything he says anymore.

I don't know.

She says, poking at the fire unnecessarily. I set my cup down on a flat rock.

What do you mean, "you don't know?" You can't possibly be considering going back to him. Just because he said so? What's wrong with you?

You don't understand. No one tells you what to do, Rose. No one ever has, that's obvious. Hell, Leo's trying to control you just a little bit and you're furious over it. Jesse has always been there for me. For every detail. He makes me feel secure somehow. I'm sure that's hard for you to understand.

Help me understand, because you're right. I don't.

He just took care of things. He used to choose my fortune cookies for me. You know, like after dinner at the Chinese restaurant. They'd give us a few and he'd look at them and select one for me. Whatever the fortune said, it would make him happy. Because in a way he was responsible for giving me something nice. And promising.

You were a prisoner, Glory.

Maybe I wanted to be.

But you're free now.

I am. But maybe I don't know how to be.

She says, looking straight at me. And I know it's true. I struggle to think of something to say but before I can, the faint drone of an engine sounds up from the gully followed by two columns of bouncing light projected into the canopy above our heads. Dad, out for a night drive in the old CJ5. You'd think it was a family pastime and it might be. We wait as the jeep clears the horizon and pulls up alongside ours and parks. Dad hops out and comes walking through the darkness to our campfire. Glory cleans off the top of a big stump with her hand and pats it.

> Hey there, Frank! Have a glass of wine?

> Don't mind if I do!

He plucks a cup off the tree as he walks by.

> Saw your headlights from the house. Thought I'd see what you two were up to.

> Just talkin' and watching the stars. Same old.

I say and pour him a cupful.

> Anything important?

> No.

Glory answers, shooting me a warning look. Dad settles in.

> Well, I've got something of interest then. Just talked to Henry up at the Mitchell farm. That nice little cottage they have in the cherry orchard just opened up. Rent's cheap — free if you want to care-take for old Mrs. Mitchell. Pretty easy. Cooking meals some nights and keeping the place up. Anyway, I thought of you,

Glory. Took the liberty of saying you might stop by next week and check it out. But between you and me it's as good as yours. Henry said he'd arrange it. I told him you were perfect for it.

Glory looks at Dad, stunned for a moment and unable to regain her composure. She looks to me for help, but I give her none. *She can have her freedom if she wants it*, I think. So I pick up my cup, sit back and sip my wine instead.

Frank, I don't know what to say. I hadn't thought much beyond the immediate summer. I certainly never expected to have any opportunities.

Why not? You're a lovely and capable woman. You can do whatever you want. So, I should tell them to expect you then?

She looks at him a long while before answering.

Ok. Yes. Tell them to expect me. I'll get up there as soon as I can. Soon as I get myself together, I mean.

She smiles. Bewildered. Relaxing against the stump and nodding to the fire as if it had said something she agreed with. Dad finishes his wine then shakes the last drops into the fire with a sizzle.

Good then! I'll leave you young ones to the night. Your mother is supposed to be calling me from Aunt Ruth's, I better get back. Don't want to disappoint her!

He walks off to the Jeep. He hops in, turns the engine and pulls around and disappears over the next hill toward the house. We see the light from the headlights bounce jerkily around the distant vineyards long after the sound from the engine has faded.

We settle back into the shadows cast about by the fire, drink wine and watch as the stars emerge in ever-receding pinpricks of light. The Top of the Hill is a place. If you look toward this hill at night from any vantage point on the property you will see that the Big Dipper sits directly above it, hovering and poised to ladle into the irrigation pond, the vineyards or into the hill itself. It is a very beautiful sign, one that hangs right up there for everyone to see. It says, *This is the land of plenty*. And we know that it is.

# Dead Man's Lake

Or

You Take a Chance, Living
Mokelumne River
*August 28*

A ghost was born today, in Mokelumne Canyon.

Mokelumne. It always takes something from you. This is how it's always been. My best hat rots at the bottom of the reservoir. Ripped off my head by the afternoon wind that tears up that canyon, running hard from the sun as it sets. The first time I fished there, it took my favorite tin fly box. It had been my Papa's, and I lost the box when I hooked the biggest trout I'd ever seen and it threw me off balance from the rock I was perched on over the churning waters. There was a moment, a timeless space where I was neither falling nor standing firm, and I knew that I was going down. But I had a choice. *You can fall*, I told myself, *or you can jump*. And so I jumped in after that fish. Because sometimes you have to jump to keep from fallin'. I just stripped the line in hard with my left hand, held my rod over my head and jumped in. My creel spilled its guts, and me and that fish went downstream together, tethered, drowning and fighting with my lunch and my leaders and my fly boxes trailing us. I went under. It was too deep for footing and you can't swim with a fly-rod in your hand, but I'd sooner die then give that river my Sage. That thing is an instrument, a divining rod that shows me the right water and all its secrets. And if the bottom of that cold river was where I needed to go that day, then so be it.

But I got footing. And I worked my way to some shelving rock and I pulled myself out. It was too late for my fly box and my sandwich, the latter of which gave out a little pathetic yelp as it disappeared over the waterfall downstream. The fly box, however, went with more dignity. It floated for a while, crested the waves, then sunk as the water penetrated the air holes in the tin. It went under in a deep pool trailing a perfect bridal veil of bubbles. My Papa's flies. The tattered Coachmen and the McGintys that my aunt tied. That perfect Parmachene Belle with the silver thread that no one ever used because it was just too beautiful. Disappearing. Disappeared. I didn't even think about diving in after them. I couldn't get those flies back any more than I could get my Papa back by swimming to the bottom of that hole. No, they were gone. Mokelumne took 'em.

But in return, it gave me something. I pulled myself onto the rock, the river pouring off me, and my line went tight and the rod bent nearly in half. The fish was still on! I made sure my footing was good this time and I brought that fish in. I reached in to unhook it and cradled it for a moment under the water. It was nearly as long as my arm. It was reflecting the sun and all colors and none, a true Rainbow trout. *Shit! Where's my Dad?* I looked around desperately. *Where the hell is he? Someone's got to see this thing. No one's going to believe me, not ever.* I yelled for him. Nothing. You can't yell for your Dad or for help or for anything in Mokelumne Canyon because of that eternal wind and the raging water. Voices don't exist. *So it's just us, fish. Well fine. I see you. I know you exist and you know I do. I'm sorry if I scared the shit out of you jumping into your hole like that.* One last long look and I let that fish go. It swam down into the depths. Disappearing. Disappeared.

Why the fuck is everyone so quiet?

Vincent asks from between drags on the cigarette he holds draped over the Landcruiser's steering wheel.

I feel like there's a plot I'm not in on. You guys planning to kill me or what?

I look around the car, Glory is absently twirling the leather pouch around her neck while Chicago lays half across the back seat, knee propped up against the window, hat pulled over his eyes.

Fuck, yeah we are, Vincent. He says. Just as soon as we get you far enough up Mokelumne Canyon so no one can hear you screamin'.

You're too hung over to kill anybody.

I say, reaching back to pat his leg. Vincent doesn't look convinced. But then again, Vincent is the only one who's never been here.

It's Mokelumne, Vincent. That's why we're quiet. You'll see.

We'll see if I'll see. I'm not a superstitious fool like the rest of you all. I'm sure it will be fine.

Oh, it'll be fine.

Chicago says tipping his hat up so he can see Vincent in the rear-view.

It's almost always great, in fact. It's just things happen is all.

What kind of things?

Just things. There's always somethin'. Right, Rose? Can't get out of there without Mokelumne giving you one little kiss.

Yeah. I suppose that's true. For most of us. But not my Dad. Every time he goes there, it's just as fine a day as you can have.

Glory laughs at that.

Wherever Frank goes, it's just a fine a day as you can have. That man is blessed.

We make slow time down the winding two-lane highway due to Chicago's boat we're trailering behind us. Today the plan is to get deep into Mokelumne Canyon where the fishing is epic and the granite forms a cathedral-like empire around this powerful river. Vincent asked each of us to name the river we revere the most and each of us answered the same. Mokelumne. Astounding since very few people know of, or go to, this wild canyon. We expect nothing short of wild solitude as the backdrop to this trip. Vincent turns off the main highway and begins the eternal decent into a deep and winding canyon. After an hour of switchbacks, we finally hit the valley floor, follow the river a ways, then climb again, up the height of the massive dam. We crest a hill and drop into the dirt parking lot near the boat launch. It's full.

What the hell?

There's never anyone here, ever. But today the place is crowded with vehicles. Official vehicles. At first I think it's the power company looking over the dam, but then we get close and read the sides. Search and Rescue. Trucks everywhere. Medical vehicle. Refrigerated van. A truck is pulled up to the boat launch and a man sits perched on the hood with binoculars to his eyes, fixed on the water. Looking up-canyon.

Maybe they're doing drills?

There's bodies in the river today.

I don't think so.

Chicago hops out and I follow him up to the man on the truck. He's a seasoned-looking man in official uniform, side arm and huge walkie-talkie at his hip. Chicago approaches him confidently.

What's going on?

He looks us over.

You going up the reservoir today?

We're plannin' on it. What happened?

There was a drowning. We got teams up there looking for the body.

Me and Chicago look at each other. The question floats between us. We walk back down to the parking lot where Vincent and Glory are waiting at the Landcruiser. Chicago walks ahead to tell them what's going on. The lot is full of Search and Rescue vehicles, but I stop short. Parked on the edge of the lot is a small, unmarked pickup truck. The only non-official car here besides ours.

A dead man's truck.

*There's a man underwater in Mokelumne and this is his truck*. I can't stop staring at it. Things and objects become strange when they're owned by the newly dead. Because they aren't owned. Not anymore. That truck is nobody's. It is not even a truck. It's a marker.

We come together at the Landcruiser. Lean on the hood. Kick some dirt. Look up-canyon. Look up. The sky ain't nothing but blue right now. We kick a few more pebbles, then look each other in the eyes. We all nod. We're goin'.

Chicago and I hold a longer gaze. We know. It's not just that there's a dead guy in there. It's that we know Mokelumne's heart. Mokelumne takes, always. And the question is just: has it had enough yet? It's either the very best time or the very worst time to go up that river. And I guess we're just willing to find out. We have our own agreements with this canyon. We know about the spirits that linger in the oak groves along the northern shore. The spirits there are old, and they follow old rules. This canyon has been inhabited for thousands of years. The Miwok Indians traversed this river from the headwaters to the foothills trading salt from the big salt-spring upstream. And after them, trailblazers and gold miners. But not many found any reason to stay. The trail is ancient and visible even over the half-mile wide solid granite rock that guards the entrance to Blue Hole. A clear trail across solid rock. Living souls wore a path into the face of a granite mountain and ghosts maintain it.

We pull up and unload the small and dented aluminum boat. We have to carry it down the fifty-yard dilapidated ramp to the water. They cut off the trailered boat launch years ago, so now the only people who boat up the reservoir are people willing to lift their boats and motors over a five-foot locked gate and walk it down to the water. We canoe this from time to time, but you can only paddle across at dusk or dawn, when the canyon sleeps. Any other time, at best you don't get anywhere and at worst you're tipped and sinking. The winds in the afternoon scream the lake into a frenzy of white caps. The Search and Rescue squad eyes us as we struggle with the motor, setting it down every four feet with a huff.

We all gather at the boat. Load up our fishing rods, water, lunch, Vincent's cameras. The squad is watching us. I can tell they're deciding things. Wondering if they're going to have to make a second mission up this canyon today. Our old boots and military issue packs give them confidence, but the boat doesn't have registration or life vests so they're weighing our odds. Chicago faces the group of men.

You got a problem with us goin' up there?

The captain, his face weathered and his disposition even more so, looks at him steady for a pregnant moment.

It's your ass.

He says without the slightest look of concern.

It always is.

Replies Chicago. With that we pull away from shore, pick up speed and put some distance between us this dubious start to our day. We cross the reservoir slowly but without incident and approach the inlet at the far shore. We maneuver through the maze-like channels as far as we can go, then we pull up to a sandy shore. It takes all of us to haul the boat up and pile out. We grab our gear and step toward the trail. Vincent stops us.

Not so fast girls. I'm taking your pictures today.

What? No.

I say, clumsily. Glory just shrugs and acquiesces.

What the hell.

Chicago slaps his leg.

Aw right! You gunna get them skinny-dippin'? Cause I'll hang around for that. I don't care how good the fishing is.

Fuck off, Chicago! I snap. Why don't you hit the trail or I'll see that you're skinny-dippin' with your clothes on.

I look back to Vincent.

All right I'll do it. But no nudie shots and no lesbian-mermaid shit. Ok?

A perfectly satisfied smile is his only reply as he shoulders his heavy pack and heads toward the first series of deep blue channels that empty into the lake. Chicago strides without comment up the steep granite slope to a different trail. One that will take him deep into the canyon ahead of us.

We fish a while. Vincent takes a few pictures. It's hot as hell and the river here is surrounded by solid rock with few trees and scarce shade. This canyon, its walls and peaks, are pure granite. Not broken and cobbled either, solid. Have you ever stood in front of a rock the size of a mountain? We're surrounded by sheer faces, lover's leaps, a thousand opportunities to jump. The fish aren't biting.

Fuck it. Let's swim.

We're at a big deep pool headed by a waterfall and surrounded in jumping rocks. We take off hats, boots, jeans. Set them in piles near our creels, look at the water, pick our marks and jump. We swim. I float on the current, tiny bubbles talking through water. Just my face and my toes out and drifting. I listen to the river from the underside and wonder how you hear a fish coming… or a dead man. Eyes to the sky with clouds turning or I'm turning. A hawk flies over heading south. I hear the water and the bubbles and the sand crawling along the riverbed, and I hear the hawk's wings beating. But the hawk is gliding. *Weird*. Wings beat and beat. The hawk flies out of sight and is replaced by a helicopter heading the other way. Blades beating, moving the water around me. The helicopter moves slowly over, drying my face and toes with its wind. It hovers, moves on upstream. I'm not the body he's looking for.

I right myself in the water, listen from the dry side of the world. Vincent sits up on his rock. Glory looks up, shields her eyes from the sun. The chopper is already a quarter mile gone, it's hovering somewhere near Blue Hole. Smart pilot. Blue Hole is a likely place for a body. Most things that fall into the water eventually end up there. It beckons for swimming, but the waterfall is violent and the bottom unseeable. I never swam it. I stick with holes deep enough to jump into but not so deep that anything is unknown. We watch the chopper navigate the bends of the river. Search and Rescue workers file along the trail heading upstream. More rafts with outboard motors are coming up the reservoir. Every one of us is still searching.

I wonder where he is.

There's a man in the river today, and we're swimming with him. I run my hand through the water in front of me. This water has already passed him by. It knows where he is. I let it drip from my hand. Watch the last drops cling to my skin, holding on, reflecting the sun and the world. Sky. Hawks. Why does the last drop always hold on so tight? *Did you cling so tight?* I want to ask. *Did you have something to hold on to? Was the world reflected in your eye before you went under? What was there? Clouds? Land? Did you actually see air in that moment?*

Where is he, water?

The water doesn't answer. The drop lets go. Falls into the river. Takes the world with it.

I guess I should have known something like this was coming. There has been synchronicity all summer as far as knowing things. Or maybe, there is always knowing, we just don't always believe it. But this dead guy, this is no surprise. Yesterday at the Liar's Bench, old Patrick was pouring our drinks and talking about the draining of Caples Lake. They're draining that lake to fix the dam and things are getting exposed. Old ground. Old fish. Old bones. There's a whole town under there, Patrick says. People just walked away from it when the dam was built. Unhitched their horses, collected their children and their winter stores and backed up. Held their children in their laps and watched the water spill into windows and down chimneys.

All month Fish and Game has been working to save the trout from Caples Lake and transport them to other waters. Most fish survive this shock, all except the very young and the very old. They found a forty-two-inch Rainbow trout in there this week, Patrick told us. They estimated that she was around thirty-five years old. *We could have had the same birthday,* I think. I would have liked to have seen that fish. Most likely she had spent the last twenty years way at the bottom of the lake. Maybe she lived in the old post office building, chasing small fry through the windows. She's probably the oldest trout that any of these guys have ever seen. They pulled her up from the lake floor in a net and by the time she came to the surface she was dead.

But I think about that fish. And I know there is no way that she survived for 35 years in an underwater wild-west ghost town only to be killed by a little decompression. No. That bitch ended up in a net somehow. And when she realized her mistake, saw the boardwalks, old shoes, gold coins and the ruins-entire of her town dropping away from her into darkness, she fought. Not to get out of the net, because that was hopeless. She fought to die. Die herself, by her own will, and so undo the taking away of her world.

She could not live in different waters, not because she wasn't strong enough, but because these waters were her. And when they pulled her up from that deep lake, they undid that world. That rotting town, its half-buildings and toppled gravestones and buried secrets disappeared. With every league closer to the surface she rose, that place receded. Sank into the muck and was swallowed. And all these people standing around the shores watching the water drain out and the nets of fish come up and waiting expectantly for the day the town is revealed are going to stand in wonder. They want to see. They hope for bones or exposed gold or pretty bottles. They barely flinch when Fish and Game holds the giant body of that Rainbow trout aloft. There are a few around here that look at that carcass and wince. Have you ever seen the heart of a fisherman break? In the crowd there are one or two. A brow furrowed. An imperceptible shake of the head in utter revolt, and a spirit turning itself inside out and out and out again. A muttering: *What a shame.*

Someone in the crowd says, "That ain't a big fish; you should have seen the sturgeon my uncle caught last year…" Those people look away, move on, watch the shoreline again for trinkets. But the few fishermen stay. They stand. They witness. It's a funeral and you don't chatter and you don't turn your head. They see the entire history of this landscape, its waters, its fishing, fading away in those drying scales. As all trout fisherman here know, the rainbow on the sides of these fish begins to disappear the second they come out of the water and death dispels it almost instantly. So these few watch her scales graying out and darkening. The Rainbow, all forty-two inches of it, forgetting. An entire world lost. The fishermen clutch at their shirtfronts. The last rooftop sinks under the sand and mud and a spectator on the shore turns quickly, looking at the ground at his feet, grabbing at his pocket.

What's wrong?

Someone asks.

I don't know. Felt like I just lost something.

Bodies of water and bodies in water. It's just how it is. Sometimes they fall in. Sometimes they mean to and sometimes it's a mistake. Sometimes they're put there. Like New Melones Reservoir. Caples Lake made Patrick think of bodies, and he poured more Maker's and said they ought to search by the dam at New Melones.

Chock full of bodies.

He says with confidence. It's the dumping ground of choice for the gangs and mob working out of Stockton. A short enough drive up from the valley and a place where people tend to keep their eyes on the road at night.

Yeah, he says. They ought to drain that res. if they really want to see somethin'.

Who really wants to see something? Maybe we do. Or we think we do, until we see it, that is.

It reminds me of a story my friend Mary told me when we were in Tahoe. Lake Tahoe is the deepest and coldest body of water in the Sierras and it has mysteries. Some parts of it they have yet to find the bottom of. And there is a certain depth where the temperature and consistency is such that things stop sinking and are suspended. The temperature is so cold at this place that things are preserved. Mary's brother had his own boat with high tech diving equipment, and the local Sheriff's department used to call on him to dive down to this layer and retrieve things that were lost.

Back in the 80s, there was some guy, an inventor, who wanted to break a speed record by boat on the surface of the lake. He designed a rocket-powered boat to shoot him across the surface with a giant parachute that would unfold to slow him down before crashing through the boat houses in the marina. The local authorities thought this would be a fine idea and the media from the region where all a-buzz with the prospect of an exciting day's news. The whole town turned out to line the shores and watch history be made. The man started up his rocket, roared across the lake, got halfway across and then his entire contraption exploded into a shooting ball of flame. People on the shore felt the heat. Flames licked at the surface of the water and disappeared, bits of parachute-turned-smoldering-ash alighted at the reporters' feet.

The authorities called Mary's brother to come and find the man. Mary said he took his boat and his gear and a small team and went to the spot where the rocket-ship-boat had exploded. They dove. They went down to the level where things are suspended and saved. They found parts of the wreckage. They found bits of burned clothes. Then they began to find pieces of him. An arm. A foot. Another arm. And when they almost had enough to make a man, they found him. Intact.

There's mob in Tahoe because there are casinos in Tahoe, and there's people who lose and there's people who take what's owed. It's no surprise. And it's no surprise that there's dead gangsters stuck to the draining grate in the spillway at New Melones either. People do. People die. People make choices. But Mokelumne is not the settling ground for petty disputes and greed. Mokelumne settles debts of the heart and grievances of the soul. It's no one's business. It's between a body and Mokelumne. And every body that goes there has to reckon with that.

198

And I reckon with that as I sit here in this pool with the river in my skin, meat, bones. I feel sad all of a sudden. I hear my pulse and my pulse is answered by the chop-chopping of the helicopter coming back up the reservoir. It's coming back and flying with purpose. Straight back to Blue Hole, and we see it descend below the trees.

Shit.

What is it doing?

Landing.

All beating hearts in the canyon skip three beats. It takes the time of three heartbeats to unzip a five-foot zipper. I sit on my submerged rock, half in and half out of the water. Watch the surface, through the surface, watch the surface again. Watch the tree line over Blue Hole. Watch the ridgeline. Watch Vincent. He's watching up-canyon. Glory's eyes are closed, but she's watching too. The chopper revs up and the blades blur and it alights from the rock shelf that drops the waterfall into Blue Hole. We see it break the tree line, straight up into the air, turn and fly due west, right over our heads. We look up and strapped to the running board on the pilot's side is an orange bundle. It's the size of a man.

Is that him?

I think that's him.

Shit.

I watch the pilot and his cargo clear the river and head toward the open water. Five buzzards rise in a flurry from the old oak at the river's inlet and circle the chopper, through its blades. They're ghosts. They're ushering. We have held company with birds all summer. Ravens, hawks, buzzards, this chopper. They usher. They ferry. They have talons for holding onto and for letting go. The helicopter takes this man out of this canyon but it doesn't, not really. It's only taking flesh. It will ferry the body across the water and deposit it with the people who loved him. They need that body, his family, so that they don't have to know what the wives, brothers, mothers of the bodies of New Melones and Lake Tahoe and Caples know: that you can wonder forever. That you can hold out hope beyond all reason in the absence of proof. That the sight of a cold and bloated body in a cloak of trailing algae can be the end of suffering. That a mother can long to see the dead face of her son to dispel the misery of seeing nothing.

I watch the chopper recede into the distant ridgeline. Quietly we all are watching. Respectful of this flight. But the man, he's not going home. He's in this canyon and I can feel him. He is watching a giant bird wrap its talons gently around an orange body bag, the beating of its wings disturbing the water above his head. He watches it lift off of the water, drops falling away. He wonders at the sense of loneliness. We watch the chopper until it disappears. Then we all get in. Swim. It's just life. It's just death. You take a chance, livin'.

Let's get to work!

Vincent says, getting out and heading for his camera bag.

Guess you ain't going to waste too much time cryin' over lost souls.

Glory says with a sigh as she reluctantly makes her way to shore. We struggle wet legs into tight jeans, fish a few holes. Nothing biting still so we head upstream. Weird, since this river has always been unbelievably good fishing, even in the dead heat of summer.

You all want to see Blue Hole? I ask. Seems like we can't come all the way up this canyon and not look at it.

That's what I'm here for.

Says Vincent. We walk the ancient path worn into the rock face for a quarter mile, then drop off the edge to the old salt spring hidden in a crack in the massive rock mountain. Glory kneels down at the edge of a bright white salt pool and scrapes a handful of salt into her leather pouch. Big, beautiful perfect crystals with tiny specks of granite and Mokelumne dirt mixed in.

We head upstream again. By this time the chopper has circled back to the lake's shore and is picking up a couple of Search and Rescue workers. The day's not done. Now they need to ferry all the live bodies out. The sun's just turned up the heat, and as we make our way across the exposed rock, wind licks our backs, pushing us and trying to take our hats. The trail drops into a confused manzanita grove, and we follow an invisible trail that turns at sharp angles and around, spits us out on a tumbled rockslide. We pick our way across this and round the ledge that drops off into the rippling waters of Blue Hole. Vincent whistles when he sees it.

Yeah. It's really somethin' isn't it?

It's really something. We gather under the reaching branches of the old oak grove at the west edge of the vast pool. Stand quietly for a moment, watching. Vincent wants to take some swimming pictures here, but something's not quite right yet. Me and Glory look at each other, knowing we can't just jump in Blue Hole like this. She shakes her head.

This hole ain't right.

I doubt he actually drowned here.

I reply, with more conviction than I actually feel.

Probably not, but he was headed this way, that's for sure.

Maybe he didn't drown here, but this is where they brought his body for flight. And I have to wonder about that man. Did he give his life or did Mokelumne take it? All bodies of water are the meeting of three worlds: the world of air, its reflection, and the depths below. The surface of the water is the boundary between them. This line is evident in the long evening light where ground meets water and the world of air is reflected on the surface of the water. An illusion, but not a very good one. An altered rendition of the trees, rocks and hills that misrepresents one world while hiding another. But there is a clear line between the reality that we perceive and the reflection of it. And when things come to a settling on this line, it's not a give and it's not a take. It just is. He broke through that surface alive and was pulled back through it dead. And this place, Blue Hole, on the surface, is a point of departure while its blue depths are a place of gathering. Everything, eventually, ends up here. Unknown things are gathered at the bottom of this hole. And sometimes the things that end up here leave, and sometimes they don't.

202

There's something we have to do. The question of whether that man gave his life or whether the whole thing was a surprise to him lost its importance with the last bubble of air out of his nostril. The important question now is: has Mokelumne had enough? Chicago has been upstream for hours and god knows what he's seen, could easily have been the body itself. A guy died here today, the spirits are stretching their arms and cricking their necks, a new-born ghost probably don't even know he's been killed, and Mokelumne is taking roll call. You need your eyes open in this canyon today. Search and Rescue was sent in here to clear out a body, but someone needs to evacuate some restless spirits.

We take Glory's salt pouch and scale the rock face around the south side of Blue Hole to where the waterfall careens into the pool. It's steep and slick and fast enough that you don't want to fall into that frothing current. We walk as close to the waterfall as we dare, water lapping at the toes of our boots, and Glory loosens the leather string and holds it aloft. She's silent for quite a while, looking at the water rushing by as if it's telling her something. She nods in agreement.

     Everybody goes when it's their time.

She says to the water.

     Yup. Amen.

     Jesus fucking Christ.

Vincent mutters, shaking his head and turning his attention to setting up his gear.

Glory casts some salt into the waterfall, which carries it down into Blue Hole and away. We stand for a moment then unbutton shirts, pull off boots and pants and throw bras across the rocks and stand at the fall's edge over the darkening pool, and with a laugh and a whoop, jump in. Down. Break the surface and dive down with the submerged granite cliff a foot from my belly and the bubbles from the falls caught in my wake and head for the deep blue. What a color. What an amazing color, swimming down to nowhere. I turn around, pull for the surface, break through for a gasp of air.

This pool is *dee-eep*!

Hey! Swim over here. I want to take some nudes!

What? Goddamn, Vincent…

Glory looks at me, laughing.

You knew this was coming, Rose.

Yeah, but let me pretend I didn't. Hold on! We're just finishing up with a funeral! Then we'll do your damn pictures. Shit Sandwich.

I hate it when you say that.

Shit Sandwich.

Fuck you and swim.

I swim. I'm going to make this last because I'm not quite ready to sit down and have Vincent take pictures, however artfully done, of me in the flesh. So I focus on this swim and this pool. Glory is wringing her socks out on the ledge so I take a deep breath and dive straight down into the darkest part of the pool. Breast stroke and kick down past the reaches of light. This is the place where everything ends up, so I figure I might as well look for my grandpa's fly box or my hat. I swim down past rock ledges and on them are wallets and delicate chains of gold tangled in fishing line and dark braids. Baskets, backpacks and memories litter the sandy floor. A drop-off and there in the dark edge is a familiar shape. Color of straw and that familiar bend… my hat! I swim toward it with effort. I can't hold my breath much longer, but I've missed this hat more than I could ever say. A strong stroke and I reach for it, grasp the crown but it's firm. I let go, repelled. A head turns, my hat on it. A man climbs out from the depth, makes his way to a boulder resting on the pool floor. Sits against it and rubs his chin. Pulls the hat, my hat, down tighter. He looks around, slowly registers me floating there.

Hello.

He says, a statement verging on a question.

Have you seen my shoes? He asks. I've been looking, all day it seems, for my shoes. I just can't seem to find them anywhere.

What?

My shoes. I need my shoes.

I look at him. He's shaking his head and looking around, bewildered. Wearing my hat and searching.

Have you seen my shoes?

No. No, I'm sorry. I haven't seen your shoes. I'm so very sorry.

Oh...

He sits there, looking around himself at the pebbles and fish. Pulling again at his chin as though he'd had a beard there, recently shaved. The habit of grasping for something you had become accustomed to but is no longer there and all that remains are the motions. The reflex of familiar embrace with no weight to justify it. I feel the pressure of the river on my chest. I need air. I try to look the man in the eye, to communicate something, some understanding, but he's scratching and searching the millions of grains of sand leapfrogging themselves across the river's floor and I can't linger because it hurts.

So I turn and kick and tilt my face to the sunlight beaming through the water. I swim like hell for the surface. I swim and swim, but I was further down than I thought. Fingers break the surface first, then me, and I'm gulping air and flailing and breathing and no one even turns. Glory is still wringing socks and Vincent still setting up his shot. I gulp air again. Stroke the water. Breathe out. In. Close my eyes. It's fine. Mokelumne is fine. The spirits are fine. It's not that things are right, things just *are*. The world and its reflection meet on a boundary that has been broken, but can stand to be broken. I sink into the water until the surface is between my lips. I smile. I say nothing. I am in the world breathing reflected breathing on Mokelumne, and underwater? Another me, holding my breath.

We swim a bit more. Casually. In the space of a breath, everything came to rest. It's just another beautiful Sierra granite pool for now. Spirits lift their chins with an imperceptible nod and slip back into the cracks in the granite walls. The wind sits down. Hawks cry from the grand oak, throw sticks out of their nests.

Get over here!

All right, Vincent, where do you want us?

Right there in that sunny patch, facing the pool.

Vincent is up under the oak trees about thirty feet away. Me and Glory are standing out in the open at the water's edge. This isn't so bad. Our backs are to him and the shot's from some distance, so this really wasn't anything to be so worried about. I'm beginning to relax, and I can see Glory never even had a qualm to begin with. We smile at each other, laugh, watch the dragonflies intercept insects in flight. We're laughing and warming in the sun when we hear Vincent say something low.

What Vincent?

Search and Rescue.

Speak up man, what?

Search. And. Rescue.

He points to the trail above Blue Hole. We turn and look up the face of the waterfall and there, on the trail that skirts the rock above the pool, is an entire team of Search and Rescue workers. Probably eight or nine men. We look at them. They're stopped mid-step, looking right at us. Not glancing sidelong. Not looking discreetly as they walk. No, they're all stopped in a line, looking right at us.

Oh shit!

What do we do?

If we sit down and try to cover up, we'll be right out there in front of them, but if we turn around to head for the trees, they're going to be staring at our bare asses. This is a dilemma. Instinct kicks in and flight beats fight, so we turn around and head for the oak grove where Vincent is standing, laughing his ass off.

Fuck you, Vincent!

It's like he planned it! He probably had Chicago tip them off.

Fuck you! Stop laughing, goddamn it. I can't walk in this shit!

The bank is a mess of driftwood, rocks and debris. So instead of fleeing the scene before those guys figure out it's not their imagination, we're having to awkwardly pick our way up the slope to Vincent who is now rolling on the ground, holding his sides and laughing noiselessly.

Motherfucker!

Fuck! Where's my shirt? Where's my shirt! Give me that!

That's mine! Ah hell... shit sandwich.

Glory and I drape ourselves in a tangle of clothing. I sit down behind a small shrub with a leg of jeans over one shoulder, a cotton blouse wrapped around my ass and pair of panties clutched over my chest and look back up at the trail. The Rescue team is still standing there, none of them saying a word. No laughing, no taunts, just looking. Then, one by one, they turn and start a slow pace on down the trail.

All right, show's over. They're gone. Get back out there so we can finish up.

We get up with caution, pull leaves and stickers off with some discomfort and make our way back to the sunny patch.

Ok. Good. Now I want you to embrace.

What! No way.

Glory turns toward me, arms open.

Ok.

What? We said we weren't going to let him talk us into any lesbian-in-the-woods pictures.

You said that. But you know me, I won't do anything… unless someone asks me.

You're retarded.

I'm more of an idiot savant.

Vincent throws some clothes at us.

Here, put these blouses on and you stand there, and you stand behind her and put your head on her shoulder. Yeah, like that.

Jesus.

This is going to look like a cougar-lesbian senior portrait.

All right, you two, we're done; stop your bitching.

Vincent starts packing up his camera while Glory shuffles around for her gear. From the rock overlooking Blue Hole, we hear a shout. Chicago is back and waving at us. He grabs his crotch, then gestures to the beach upstream. Lunchtime. Glory and Vincent stand by the trail waiting for me to lace up my boots. I'm suddenly feeling uncomfortable in front of them.

You guys go on and feed that banshee. I'll be right up.

They shrug and move on. From the top of the waterfall, Glory looks back concerned. I wave her on. I cinch my laces down as tight as I can, hoping to distract from the sick feeling in my stomach that I'd just done something wrong.

What were you thinking?

A voice says from behind me. Ghost, arms folded, looking irritated.

You posing nude for men now?

I concentrate on my laces, hoping that if I ignore him, he'll disappear. He doesn't.

It's getting a little frustrating that you're always around when I don't need you and never around when I do. I say.

Looks like you're getting on just fine without me. You've got a nice little gang here. Real close-knit. I just can't figure out which one you're in love with.

What the hell do you care? You have no right to be jealous. You have more than an invitation to take pictures or go fishing. You have an invitation to this life. You have a seat at the table. But if you get up, then someone else might sit down. They're more dependable than anything else in my life right now. I need them... but I need you more. You need to get here.

It's just not that simple!

Sometimes it is. A man does what he wants.

If a man knows what he wants.

As he says this, he takes a step backwards, hovering just over the edge of the river. Reminding me that he can't be killed. Can't be pushed. Can't be kissed.

I just want to know if it's real.

He says as he looks away downstream.

Is it real? I reply. Of course it is. Of course it isn't. It's neither, it's both. It's a stupid question.

I pick up some rocks, zing them at him with perfect aim. One through the heart and one through the head. No use. The only way to kill a ghost is to stop believing in it.

Your time is running out.

I say, standing up. I pick up my gear and for the first time, walk away from this ghost. From the waterfall, I look back. The trail is empty.

I pull my hat down low and stride off. I can walk without touching the ground when I need to, a gift I inherited from my Dad. It comes in handy for crossing streams and fishing, but it also helps when you need to get some distance. I fight every urge to go back and find him. The tears rolling down my cheeks are immediately whipped away by the eternal Mokelumne wind. It's good for some things, that wind. I'm in stride with it now and in stride with the dead of this canyon.

Across the massive rock face, I begin to run. Old echoes arise and collide. Boots strike fast and heavy on this ancient trail. Moccasins and hooves sound at my flanks. All running to and running from. Arrows begin to wing past on my left and on my right. I pull an arrow from my quiver, aim straight ahead, pull the string, let it go. A young girl running at my side pulls a dagger from her skirt-waist, behind her ear with it for a flash, then she throws it. With tears. With fury. With love. An army of the dead. On the flanks of love are sorrow and joy. And in the face of it? Fear. Fear is what makes ghosts out of men. I run. Shoot arrow after arrow and grab for more. There's none left. The rock face swings up to my right and falls away to the river at my left. The trail banks blind around the face and I, at full speed, run straight off the edge into oblivion.

A primal yell breaks unbidden from my heart and I fall, kicking, screaming, through the air. Sound of helicopter wings beat to the time of my arms swinging at the warm and rushing wind. I hit the sand in a dull thump. Out of breath. Out of hope. Out of time. Hooves fade in the distance. Warriors step off the trail two by two and head to the cliffs. My feet are on the ground. My ground. I'm tired. I'm not crying. I'm alone.

I look around and realize I'm at the campsite where I used to camp with my family. A gust of wind clips the top of the massive old oak that is the centerpiece of this clearing. I see leaves rain down from the branches, and then I see they're not. They're blackbirds. A dozen or more and they resist the ground and tangle away above the river, heading for the far shore. This is my family's spot. Smoke drifts over from my Aunt's campfire where she's frying venison steaks and trout. A zipper from the tent disturbs the quiet. Voices in the distance dispel the smoke and smell of meat. Glory and the boys are upstream lounging on a long sandy beach on a deep green pool. I make my way to them. Not because I need them. But because I love them. And they are real.

Finally! We thought you might-a got snake-bit or somethin' down there.

Says Chicago as he hands me a hunk of salami. Vincent sits patiently peeling an apple and grinning.

Any snake that bites her is going to be sorry. She's got more venom than any creature I know.

Glory kicks Vincent's boot for that as she walks up and puts her arm around me. She bumps her head against mine, tousles my hair and kisses my cheek. She turns abruptly face the guys.

Let's go motherfuckers! It's a long way to the boat.

Chicago jumps up and gestures to the north.

Let's cross the river here. There's a quicker trail back on the other side.

Quicker because it's steep as shit.

I say, collecting myself.

You a pussy now, Rose?

Laughing, we traverse the strewn boulders across the river and head up a steep and poison oak-infested trail that disappears up a crack in the cliff face. We scoot our way up this face and ascend to a high plateau of granite and dry grass. This meanders high above the riverbed for a mile before dropping down onto a jagged granite outcropping situated high above Blue Hole. We climb down to this perch and there in the center are the remains of an old fire-ring and a half circle of boulders filled in with dense manzanita. Vincent pauses to look at the spot.

Stop! Let's catch our breath. And I want to get a shot from here. Damn, that's a long way down.

He whistles as he drops his pack and digs for his camera. I sit down in the shade of a tangled manzanita and close my eyes. Chicago goes scurrying up into the boulder-strewn backdrop.

This here's a real interesting place.

He says, picking around through the rocks.

Um hmm.

Is all I can manage as the weight of the day threatens to catch up with me. Chicago whispers something from the rocks.

Oh, you don't say?

I didn't say anything.

Well, I'll be damned!

Yells Chicago. I open my eyes to see him twisted up under the ledge of an overhanging rock, working something out of a dark hole. He forces it out and stumbles back, holding aloft an ornate shoebox-sized, pressed tin box. He smiles at me, then something catches his eye beyond me. He drops the box, stretching his arm out.

Glory! He yells.

I turn around to see Glory teetering on the edge of the jagged cliff. She slowly scoots her feet toward the edge, leaning out over Blue Hole below. I try to stand up to stop her, but I can't move fast enough to get there in time. She's beginning to fall forward when Vincent comes from nowhere and grabs her waist, yanking her back into the rocks. He falls against a rock wall, Glory pinned in his arms.

What the fuck are you doing? Glory! Answer me! What the hell are you thinking?

He yells at her, but she doesn't move. She doesn't say anything. I scramble up to her. Her face is blank. She's staring at nothing and not answering. Chicago walks up and slaps her in the face. Then grabs her by the chin hard and looks her in the eye.

Glory! Glory. Come back here, girl!

He's shaking her face in front of his. Her eyes slowly begin to register him there and she goes white. A look of total fear runs across her face as she breaks free of Vincent's grasp and jumps up toward the cliff again. Vincent grabs her arm.

Oh no you don't!

Is he gone? Do you see him?

Glory asks, pleading. She scrambles to the edge on all fours, dragging Vincent behind her, looking desperately into the waters below. Chicago and Vincent wrestle her to the ground and hold her until she settles down. We sit like this for a long time as Glory stares at the ground between us. As she slowly comes to her senses, the rest of us look at each other in total bewilderment. The only sound, our deep breaths. After a few minutes, she sits up and hangs her head into her hands. Her long red hair mingling with the dust at her feet. She moves to get up. Vincent and Chicago both jump up to stop her, but she holds up her arm to stop them.

I'm not going to jump, goddamn it. Just let me sit up. Fuck me.

She breathes out low, shaking her head. I watch her for a moment.

What the hell is happening, Glory? You have to tell us.

She leans back against a rock, hands clumsily brushing the hair away from her face. She looks at me, then nods.

I remember.

We know. This is what we've been waiting for. No one says anything. She gestures to the edge of the cliff.

> He made him jump. That boy. The one I told you about. His name is Jason. He's a kid who works for Jesse. He's a smart one, that's why they hired him. He's impulsive, though. He... he cares for me. Jesse knew about it but tolerated it. When things were getting bad, Jason said we needed to get out. Get away from Jesse before it was too late. There was all kinds of hell closing in.

She looks back toward the ledge. Covers her face with her hands and breathes in. Then out, and looks at each of us.

> There were some bad people Jesse was crossin' and he was getting unpredictable. Jason had this idea that we, that I might be with him. I wouldn't. But I let him believe I would. He had a plan for us, and I didn't see any other way to get out. He was going to steal Jesse's payment to one of his suppliers. Instead of delivering it, he was going to bring it to the old abandoned cabin way upstream near the Wolfe Creek crossing. I was supposed to join him, before Jesse figured it out. The plan was to meet here, on this spot, and he'd show me the way in to the cabin. It was going to work.

Glory grinds her heel into the soft dirt as she speaks. A dusty trench forms around her weathered boot.

> I left home and told Jesse I was going to town. I didn't pack anything. I don't know how he knew. But when I got here, Jesse was already here. He had Jason sitting under that tree right there with a gun on him. He was so angry. Kept accusing me of being with him. He tried to make Jason admit that he was in love with me. Tried to get me to admit the same, but I refused. Because I didn't. I told Jesse that I still loved him, it's just that I was afraid of him. He just smiled and took me under his arm. Then he put the gun to my head and told Jason to jump. He said, "Jump or I'll shoot her pretty little face off." He wanted an answer. Jason just

looked me right in the eye. Then he walked to the edge and he jumped.

Glory stops talking and looks far up-canyon. Chicago puts his hand on her shoulder.

What happened then, Glory?

Glory shakes her head and looks back down at her boots.

I'm really not sure. He must have took me home and dealt with me there. That must have been how I ended up with that beating. But I sure deserved it. I used that kid and it got him killed.

I thought you remembered him dead on the floor of the tool shed?

I do. But maybe he was just beat up. It's all a fucking mess in my mind. My head fucking hurts. I need to get out of here, you guys. I don't even know what to do.

You got it, honey. We're taking you home. Right now.

Home.

Glory repeats the word with a shake of her head and a huff.

Where exactly is that?

She gets up and wanders back to the trail. We fall in line behind her. Chicago scoops up the tin box he found. He can't help but test the lid, but it's locked tight. He slips it into his pack, pulls his hat down low and catches up.

The end of day is on us; sun nestled between the canyon walls downstream. We arrive at the shore of the lake, take our rods apart, clip flies off, deposit them back in the box or on the hat. Vincent bends low while loading the boat, and his cigarette case falls into the water and disappears before he can catch it. We all watch it sink into the darkness. Mokelumne takes. Sometimes you know and sometimes it takes a long time to realize. I get into the bow, use my rod case to push off from shore. We drift away quietly for a while, everyone watching the widening gap between us and the day. Chicago pulls the engine and we nose west, sun dipping into and shattering upon the waves. We ride back with the sound of the engine, the wind and the waves hitting the stern. Weary looks. Sun on tired faces.

A traveling seed floats by, carried a couple feet above the surface, puffed out white and buoyant. Glory points at it.

Make a wish!

But she's not smiling. She made one. Can't tell if Vincent did. Chicago can't hear over the engine, but smiles anyway. I look at the poof of seed carried on the wind and I am empty. I can't conjure a single thought. Time goes by, doesn't, and another seed approaches. Glory smacks my arm and nods toward the seed.

Make a wish, Rose!

She's laughing now. I shake my head.

It's not that easy.

The seed approaches slow, flies by and disappears. Nothing. *It's just not that simple*, I tell myself.

Shore approaches and we straighten up. Survey the gear and each other. Cut the engine and gently bump up into the rocks. I jump to shore and hold the boat steady on the waves.

Hey Chicago! Give me your fly from today.

All right. What for?

A little good luck for the next fishermen.

Chicago hands me a tattered Coachman with orange thread hanging off and I unhook the big Royal Wulff from my hat. Scrounge around for an old piece of cardboard and hook the two flies into it. Grab a pen from the boat and scratch a hasty note and wedge it under the post at the end of the launch: "Here are our mojo-flies from today 8-28. Good luck and enjoy the fishing." I stand back with a satisfied smile. I think, *Whoever comes here next will have great fishing with those. They don't need to be worrying about spirits or rambling ghosts, not that they would. Those flies can do it for them, though, just in case.*

Glory walks up, reads the note and looks at the flies for a long moment. Then she lifts the leather pouch of salt from her neck, drapes it over the post and wraps the leather strings three times around, cinching it tight. She turns without comment and walks off the ramp.

We hike our stuff up to the parking lot, which is now deserted. Even the dead guy's truck is gone. We pop open the tailgate and drag out the cooler. We pull out beers and pop the caps on the Landcruiser door jam, sit on the tailgate and around. Deep sighs and settle in. We each drink two beers before we say anything. In the excitement I'd forgot that Chicago had trekked far upstream, further than I usually get to go.

How was the fishing up there anyhow, Chicago?

Great, great. Weird.

Why weird?

Well, the fishing was fine most of the day. Then I took a nap on an island in between two forks of the river so I could listen to the water. When I woke up, I fished the hole just upstream from where I was sleepin'. I was casting into this foaming back-eddy and catching fish after fish. But they didn't have no color. They were just these colorless fish. But I kept on casting at them anyway. Then I noticed something purple bumping around in the back-eddy, and so I went up close to see what it was and it was a sleeping mat. Someone's sleeping mat just swirling round and round this hole. Then I thought it was getting close to time to head back so I went downstream. I saw a good spot to fish so I headed for it, but when I got to the beach, I saw all this stuff. A backpack. It was orange. And empty. And next to it was some clothes folded up and a pair of shoes. Like someone just decided to go for a swim or something. A pair of underwear. They were grey. And the shirts were Hawaiian print. It was all just sittin' there.

Jesus Christ, Chicago.

We are quiet for a while, then the conversation moves on. Life moves on. We drink and laugh until all the beers are gone, then we get ready to go. Vincent jumps into the driver's seat. The very last bit of sun disappears as the engine turns. Headlights on the cliff face, trees, grass, road, and we pull away. Fuss with seats, mirrors, music. Roll windows down and settle in. I look at Glory, no need to talk. It all just goes without saying, so we drive. Roll down the windows and let the night spill in. Darkening, everything.

We move through the forest that bottoms the canyon, follow the river glistening. The road departs and we climb. This is the way out. Sometimes, it's the way in. We are heading for the world we left, but we all know it won't be there when we get back. We gave it away. We gave it to Mokelumne. Some made a wish. Some didn't. It doesn't matter. The music plinks out from the CD player wired loosely to the dashboard. The stars take their places. We climb and climb and you can't but wonder at the depth of this canyon. High up the mountain and we drive through a recent burn, trees in their scorched outlines remember. They are ghosts. I look out the window and back down the chasm to the place we left. The mist has rolled in and filled the canyon. Trees burned black and trees turned white march unmoving toward the granite jaws of Mokelumne. Clouds fall from the night sky. Everything, all ghosts. And I'm leaving them there. In that canyon.

Sometimes Mokelumne takes things from you. But sometimes you let them go. Sometimes you give it up. Like that guy. He folded his shirts and he placed them by his shoes and he gave it up. As I did. I folded my hope and laid it down by my faith and let a ghost slip into the churning waters. I didn't jump in after. You can't save a ghost from drowning, but you can sure drown trying.

*He can swim*, I tell myself. *If he wants to.*

# Spells

*August 29*

Leo eases himself forward to the edge of the couch and drops his head into his hands, black hair falling around his fingers. The room is bare but for a few boxes, odd mail strewn about and a ghost pacing uncomfortably across the floor. I sit against the wall, knees up. The now ragged Smith and Wesson hat rests between my feet. I stare at it as if I could move it by doing so. At my side, my left hand works nervously as I spin the wedding ring round and round with my thumb. A habit I've had since the day Leo put it on my finger. People have commented on it, this habit of mine, but I always just assumed it was normal and nice. A constant awareness of something I love. What's wrong with that?

Marriage. Weddings. A ring ceremony. I didn't really think much about "ceremony" at the time. I'm not religious. I'm not superstitious. I don't *believe* in anything. But sitting here with my husband, my ghost and my ring — spinning it for the 486-thousandth time around my finger — that ceremony is all I can think of. And how, really, it cast a magic spell. One we submitted to. It dawns on me then, about weddings. Couples are blinded by the gown, the plans, the cake, the guests and their seemingly bottomless love for each other. In the meantime, they stand before a spiritual guide who, empowered by the focus and attention of a few hundred witnesses, casts a spell over the couple. *That's really what a spell is, isn't it?* I think. *Words. Just words, spoken in ceremony by any powerful spiritual person to people eager and willing to believe.*

The words paint a picture. They fix an idea in your mind. You repeat them and seal it all with a little, tiny, precious shackle. This little shackle is not a "symbol" of your love or anything like that. It's magic. And it locks the spell in place. Makes sure the idea and those words woven together in a lovely and comfortable veil fall permanently over your eyes. I spin the ring again. Leo is still talking.

It's him or me, Rose. Though I already know your answer.

He gestures to the ghost who's pacing between two points like he don't like either end.

In fact, you already made your choice so long ago. It's him you've been in love with the whole time. I never even really had a chance.

Leo runs his hand through his hair again. Ghost runs his hand through his hair again too. Black locks swirling around their fingers. An old habit. The light through the window glints off their rings as they drop their hands back to their sides. I don't try and deny it.

Ghost hurries over and kneels by my side.

I do love you, Rose! I've decided. I want to be here; I want to stay. We can all stay, can't we?

He looks over to Leo in desperation.

No.

Leo says this harshly, shaking his head and speaking directly to the ghost.

224

I don't want you anymore either. Especially you, in fact. This whole thing is more your fault than Rose's. She didn't know what she was doing back then. She had no idea of the spell she was capable of putting a man under. And you... you fell for it. Took me with you. And by the time she decided to turn her light off and let my eyes adjust, well hell, I didn't know where I was or how I'd got here.

The ghost turns to me, eyes pleading. He reaches toward me.

Rose, just say the words. I'll stay, I promise.

I look at him, the texture of the old plaster walls and grain of the hand-hewn wood floor beginning to show through him. He flickers. I strain to keep him solid. I spin the ring again with my thumb and blink my eyes.

He can't do anything for you, Rose.

Leo interrupts as he rises from the couch. He walks over and runs the back of his hand down my cheek.

You need a man who's from your own world, honey. That way it doesn't matter if he goes blind or under your spell because at least when he wakes up, he'll still love where he is. That's the only way things can work with you. It's not even a matter of love. I loved you. I still love you. Love doesn't change anything.

With that, he straightens up. Goes back to the couch and picks up his coat and a few pieces of mail. He looks back at me once over his shoulder as he opens the door. Then he steps through and as the door shuts, I watch through the little glass panes as he walks to the car. He slips into the driver's seat, pulls his long legs in and gently shuts the door as the engine turns. The car sits for a moment, then pulls away and disappears down the street.

I turn to the ghost at my side.

Just say the words Rose, please.

I shake my head "no." I say nothing. I spin the ring again a few times. With each turn he fades lighter. The sunlight brightens and burns through him. Three more turns and he's gone. I pick the Smith and Wesson hat up from the floor and put it on. Pull it tight over my eyes and sink further down the wall. Nothing left but the sound of my own breathing and the delicate sound of his ring as it plinks down and rolls across the floor.

# It's Not Unknowable

*August 30*

I circle the gutted cars, hubcaps and old tires that lay thrown like dice around the little garage below me. I'm tailed by two angry and squawking blue jays that dive toward me, nipping at my feathers. I scream back at them, dipping in irregular patterns, beating at them with my wings and baring my talons. They keep at me, trying to knock me from the sky.

Chicago steps out of the garage below. He lifts a shotgun to his shoulder and squeezing the trigger, blows the first blue jay away and out of sight. He pumps the gun and tracking the second, fires again, leaving a cloud of blue feathers that follow me down as I alight at the window. He walks over to the sill and holds the old and patinaed Winchester up for me to admire.

> Look at this, little hawk. It was my great-grandpa's. Winchester model 97. It's got this tricky little hammer, if you hold your finger on the trigger, it goes off every time you pump it. Comes in real handy for varmints of all types. So you don't have to worry none and neither do I.

He places the shotgun respectfully on the windowsill and goes back to what he was doing at the workbench. He unravels an old brown bag, reaches in and pulls out a beautiful pressed tin box. He sets it on the table and studies the old metal lock. It is not in bad shape. It's not full of rust and it's not worn shut. It just needs a key is all. Chicago doesn't have the key. He could break it open by force. He picks up a bolt-cutter and considers it. But that would be disrespectful. He puts the bolt-cutter

227

down. He sits for a moment, thinking, then goes to the back of the garage and shuffles around in the old greasy dresser where he keeps peculiar odds and ends. All the while chuckling to himself.

> Special tools for special purposes, right, little hawk? All things come into play at some point. That's what Nana used to say.

He digs around, pushing random things out of the way, and fishes out a lock-picking kit. A nice old kit for nice old locks. Chicago hurries back to the box. He glances at me and points to the box.

> This could be the best thing I've ever found. The ancestors hinted at it when they pointed it out, back up there in Mokelumne.

He waves his arms in the air around his head.

> Be patient now! Don't crowd me.

He fans out the picks and singles out the one. Puts it through the keyhole and makes three exploratory pokes, then finds purchase. The lock drops open. Everyone leans in. Chicago opens the lid and peers into its darkness. The light from the open garage door seeps in. He coughs at the dust that stirs from the interior.

He reaches in and pulls out the first thing. He holds it for a good long while. Then he slowly removes more things from the box and places them one after another across the workbench. He peers back into the box, then picks it up and turns it upside down. The lid drops wide as a small and slow-moving hurricane of little paper scraps swirl and lift and fall to the floor.

228

# I Saw the Shadow of a Bird, But No Bird

## Desolation Wilderness

### *August 31*

The phone rings from the glove box. Glory raises an eyebrow.

Not supposed to get reception out here. Who is it?

I peek at the number.

Chicago. He has his own signal, I swear.

I hurry to answer before we get out of range.

Better speak quick, brother; we're almost to Wright's and I might lose you... What? Slow down, I don't understand... The fuck? Ok, just calm down. No, we can't. Heading for Rockbound Pass. We'll see you tomorrow, ok? Hello?

What the fuck?

I'm not sure. He was a mess. Said he needed to see us. Show us something. I don't know.

Well, he'll just have to wait. I'm not turning around when we're this close to The Range.

We pull the Landcruiser into the little parking lot at the east end of Wright's Lake, which sits high in the Sierras, pooled at the nape of the Crystal Range. Desolation Wilderness. I was born to the Sierras, and as much as I know by heart, I have never set foot in the stark and broken granite expanse that crowns this range. A silvery barrier of glittering stone, gnarled pines, snow-fed water and little else. I always believed that the reason for the berth I gave this place was because it's a crowded wilderness. When I go fishing or camping, I don't want to see people — and Desolation Wilderness is a big attraction for backpackers and other outdoor warriors who drive from all over tarnation to flock to the rock-bound Pandora's box of high alpine lakes and peaks.

And maybe I've been jealous. Maybe I've looked at that beautiful gateway that has been a backdrop to my life and felt betrayed that she lets nylon-wearing weekenders trample all through her. *They don't know where they are. They don't know her, and they can't see her.* Because even though I have never walked in, I know Desolation. And we're here now because something has changed. We're alone somehow even though there are other cars parked as we pull up to the trailhead.

We let the tailgate down and pull out our clanking gear. We slide the rods out of their aluminum cases and tug on our dusty boots, raining dirt and burrs onto the road. Old vests, torn shirts, old hats from old loves. Dirt that won't wash out. We look like we're from another time and we are. It's the end of this summer and we are worn but strong. We hit the trail.

Chuck down at the fly shop had talked about the little creek running into Wrights Lake early in the season and said it was good. That was springtime, though. Somewhere in my mind I know better than to fish these tiny high creeks in the fall and somewhere in there I know better than to ever fish in a place you heard about in a fly shop. But it doesn't matter today because something has changed and I need to be here and we need to walk into Desolation and so we do.

230

We follow a path of soft dirt threaded through pungent cedars. The forest is shady and we walk just within the edge of it. To our right is the sunshine and the reflection of sunshine upon a maze of slow-moving channel water entwined on itself and bordered by marsh and tufted grasses.

Looks fishy.

Yup. Looks that way.

We pull out our lines and cast our flies out on the silent water. Nothing turns. For hard looking, I can't spot a single fish under the water. We keep at it though because it looks so perfect. A rocky crag high up on Rockbound Pass groans and leans forward to watch us cast. Boulders tumble down and echo in the distance. Glory stands at the edge of an outward bend in the channel, knee deep in gold and auburn grasses that wave opposite, but in time with, her line. I watch her cast in this place, the deep water and swaying algae, far golden meadow, gathering pines and Desolation, as always, standing witness. And it's so beautiful that all I can feel is sadness. Because somehow, extreme beauty is the saddest of things. I don't know why. And I don't wonder about it. I just watch my friend and feel grateful for the fact that I can see this world clear enough to break my heart.

This can't be the creek Chuck was talking about.

Maybe not. Let's just keep walking. The trail has to cross it sometime.

We leave the meadow and duck back into the tree line. The trail is clear as day and maintained. Here and there, the turns are lined with stones fit together by hand. Stone steps. Bridges. Proof that it is a busy wilderness, but proof also that among those people are a few caretakers. It eases my jealousy. The forest begins to fall away and the trail steps up onto a sandy rise. We head for the granite expanse. The air introduces itself. We breathe in and put our heads down and our weight into the hike. The trail shows itself readily enough and we gain elevation. Boulders, sand, the occasional gnarled pine. More boulders. Rocks. Tiny patch of wildflowers. In the distance: pass after pass of boulders, granite, sand and lone pines. We keep walking.

I begin to feel a little silly way up on this barren mountain carrying a fly-rod. It's evident that we missed the creek. It's most likely dried up and we just walked right past it. But it feels right to keep hiking and it never feels right to put the rods down so we just keep going — two dusty, ragged fishermen walking through a waterless high-country. We'd been saying all week that what we really needed was some good hiking. All the streams we'd been to, the bars, the places, just didn't take much gettin'-to to get to, and our laziness was nipping at the heels of our moral code, flexible as that is.

Well, we've been saying all week we needed to hike.

Yeah, good thing we listen to us. Even if it is subconscious.

Glory replies with a shrug.

No shit. We asked for this, didn't we?

Um hm.

God, it's beautiful, though. "Desolation." Makes you really think about that word, huh? Like, all of a sudden, I'm not sure I know what it means.

It doesn't mean what we thought it did, anyway.

Exactly. It's not *nothing*. You know?

It sure isn't. It's just the opposite. Feels like everything. Feels like we're dead. Feels like we're ghosts walking through these hills.

Yes it do.

We might a died a hundred years ago, and we're just figuring it out. Took a hike in Desolation to see ourselves.

Well, we're retarded then. Did I go through all this heartbreak for nothing?

No. We just walked in here and got dead for a second. I hope this is where I really go, though. These mountains, fly-rod in hand. This empty everything and the space. The space is so... so... Damn.

I wonder if people can see us right now.

Probably not. But if they can, they're going to wonder what the hell they're lookin' at.

We're a strange sight, I guess. But we've been on a strange journey. What the fuck, man. What the fuck... I talked to Leo yesterday.

Oh honey.

Yeah.

What did he say?

He can't do it.

I'm sorry, Rose. Did he say why? We know why.

He had plenty of reasons.

Fuck.

Maybe he's right. Maybe it was impossible. Maybe I fell in love and being in love was enough. I stopped *seeing* it, and him, maybe.

You didn't do that.

No. I think I did. Maybe we both did. But this love still feels bigger than everything. Feels like the only thing. I'm not sure which one of us is the fool.

Fuck.

Yeah.

Leo. One conversation brought the end of possibility. I didn't know how I felt after that conversation until we walked up here. I feel Desolation. In my heart. My chest is filled with this expanse. Filled. Not empty. Not nothing. I breathe and there is no skin on me to keep the air in my lungs. The wind picks it up and blows it away from me. This is what it feels like to be a ghost. It feels like flat blue sky, northwest wind, grains of sand crawling. Not emotion. Not feeling. But not nothing.

We pull off our hats and run our fingers through our hair. Face the breeze. Wipe the sweat off our foreheads with our sleeves. Hikers walk past us but say nothing. They stop and check their map for the trail. Our trail does not exist yet. It is made by our own walking. We climb in silence toward granite crags that do not beckon. They don't care one way or another about us. In Desolation, you are alone. Everything here exists because it survives. The gnarled and twisted pines that live on wind and a few millimeters of sand grow from cracks, their bulbous trunks spilling over solid rock. They spend six hundred years growing four feet tall and ten feet around. Or they grow bent over and crawl, forced to the ground every winter by thousands of pounds of ice and snow. They live on nothing. They are strong and beautiful and they get space in exchange for their struggle. Living things do not crowd each other in Desolation. It's hard enough to live in this place, and that knowledge replaces pity with respect.

*I want my life to be like these trees* is all that I can think. I don't need much. I don't care if it's hard. I want to be shaped by my own struggle and be respected for it. No one should feel pity for a hard life. Or for loss. Even the trees that are dead are still standing. Bleached white ghosts. They spent hundreds of years growing and will take another hundred in falling down. The trees down on the valley floor in deep soil are standing one up against another and they don't live very long. They all look the same, save a few. They grow straight and tall. But up on this pass under towering storm clouds, they take impossible shapes. A clear record of their life. The toil of their existence is not just etched upon the surface like a sentimental photograph of a bum or some other rendered soul. No, they *are* their life. Every single turn of a branch or gash in a trunk is a map of the balance between its push to grow and the forces of nature against it. Growth and obstacle. Growth and denial. Growth and destruction. Some seasons, it lays new roots and some seasons it's uprooted, save a few. Maybe save only one. One little root with its tip barely turning the edge of a narrow crack, left to feed an entire mass of twisting half-petrified wood and needles. And it doesn't start all over. It just starts there.

*We've been starting all along.* It rings in my head. All the time, a beginning. My little root. And it is enough. Because even if I'm dead, I'll still be standing. There isn't much difference between the living and the dead in Desolation. And certainly no single moment when a thing dies. No line to cross. No conversation to have.

He had good reasons, Glory.

I know.

He said our relationship was a hot one, but not a warm one. That we loved each other but never cared for each other. But fuck, man, for me it felt like this place. Desolation is not nothing.

Nope.

It's just all there is.

All there is. All that needs to be, baby. All that needs to be.

# Under The Tree

*September 1*

Main Street is hot and bright, and it pursues me as I duck into The Hangman's Tree. I pause in the doorway for a moment until I can see. Vincent emerges, sleeves rolled up, cigarette on his lip as he polishes his reflection into the dull bar top. The place is empty. He looks me up and down, then gestures with a nod to the stool in front of him. Meeting his approval, I throw my keys on the bar and take a seat. He pops a cap off of a tall bottle and places it on the bar.

How's the writing coming, Rose-bud?

Well, there's plenty of it, but I'm starting to think the story's bad. Maybe I'll burn it.

Is this part of your creative process?

I'm serious.

Maybe you just don't like the turn the story has taken. Doesn't mean you shouldn't write about it.

I don't respond. Vincent puts two glasses on the bar. I watch him deftly fill both to the exact same level.

So what's this little meeting all about? Chicago wasn't making any fucking sense on the phone.

I ask as I slide my glass toward me.

I don't know. I try not to engage him directly if I think he's manic or got into the neighbor's drug cabinet. Where's Glory?

Should be here soon. She was helping Dad run the scales back at the sherry house. You got anything stronger than this? I've had a hell of a morning.

Why?

Leo moved the last of his stuff out. Let's just say it was, um, tense. That and I miss the kids so bad it hurts.

I know, little mama. But it's good that they're not here. Margaret Waters knows what she's doing.

Vincent grabs a bottle of Maker's Mark off the back shelf just as the door swings in and slams against the wall. It bounces back and wrestles with Chicago for a moment before he slams it back again. He storms in, more disheveled than usual: hair and a wild look in his eyes. He's sucking air like he ran all the way into town. He strides forward and drops a pile of stuff on the bar that scatters everywhere. Folders, envelopes, photos... and an old tin box.

Take it easy, Champ!

Vincent says, trying to keep the papers from falling behind the bar. Chicago ignores him and cranes his head searching the room.

Where's Glory?

She's not here yet.

What? We need her! Fuck!

He screeches to the ceiling. I've seen him a mess, and drunk and wild like an animal, but never out of control. I reach for his shoulder.

Settle down.

I will not settle the fuck down. We need her. She's the only one who can fucking explain this shit. I've been losing my goddamn mind. And you snatches just run off into the mountains! I'm serious right now. Deadly fucking serious!

Why don't you fill us in then?

Vincent says with some irritation as he pours a shot of Maker's and slides it in front of Chicago. Chicago looks at it, takes a deep breath and sighs. He looks exhausted. I imagine lines in his face that were not there before. As he picks up the shot glass, I notice his hand trembling. He tosses it back and bangs the glass down on the bar. Flicks it with the back of his fingers, sending it sliding back to Vincent. He props his elbows on the bar, drops his head into his hands.

Glory's dead.

He says, looking back up. Vincent leans into the bar and looks at Chicago hard.

The fuck you mean, "Glory's dead?"

I mean she's fucking dead. She's either dead or someone's gone through some FBI-style lengths to fuck with us. Look at this shit!

Chicago says, grabbing the folders and paper clippings. He spreads them across the bar.

I found these here in that tin box from the cliff at Mokelumne.

He slowly pushes one away from the other in a ragged line across the bar top. I pick up the photo closest to me. It's a picture of Glory under the arm of a handsome man, sitting on a tailgate in the sunshine. Vincent looks briefly at the photo.

So what? Just some guy with Glory.

Just keep lookin'.

Chicago says, nodding to the other stuff. There's some newspaper clippings, so I pick one up. "Double Drowning: Wanted Couple Found Dead, Mokelumne River." There's a big photo of the river and next to it, two small mug shots. Under one it says, "Jason Harding, 22." And under the other: "Gloria Ann Nolte, 27." It's a photo of Glory. My eyes scan up to the corner of the paper, where it says, "Mountain Democrat, September 7, 1982."

Chicago reaches into the tin box and pulls out a little leather pouch on long leather strings. Vincent touches the pouch as if he expects it to nip at his fingers. Then he opens it and turns it upside down. A stream of big speckled salt crystals pours out on top of the bar. He pulls the clipping out of my hand and carefully reads through it. He sets it back on the bar alongside the other items. We sit for a long while in silence, looking through everything, one after the other after the other.

And I don't know what the fuck these are about, but they were all stuffed in there with everything else.

Chicago tips the box over and a pile of fortune cookie fortunes spill out and expand across the bar top.

Crazy random shit is what it is.

Vincent says holding one up, then another, trying to decipher them. They are crinkled and I notice that most are scribbled with handwriting.

What are you guys doing in here, scrapbooking?

All three of us jump when we hear Glory's cheerful voice calling from behind us. We hadn't heard her come in. We turn toward her, but no one knows what to say, so no one says anything.

What's going on? What is all this?

She walks over, pointing to the mess on the bar. She slows as she nears it, then stops, going no further. Vincent hurries across the room to lock the front door. He comes back and stands behind Glory, his hands in fists at his side.

You need to explain this, Glory. What kind of joke is this?

Chicago interrupts before Glory can answer.

It's no joke! I—

Shut up, Chicago! Let her explain herself.

Vincent snaps at Chicago, stepping beside Glory. All eyes turn toward her. She looks from face to face, but says nothing. Chicago jumps off his stool, but Vincent pushes him back. Glory straightens her back and shrugs her shoulders defiantly.

I have no idea what you're talking about.

Vincent leans over and grabs the newspaper article.

What the fuck is this then?

Glory takes the article from him and stares long and hard at it. She offers no defense, no explanation. She appears as dumbfounded as we are. Vincent grabs a bunch of Chinese fortunes, clutching them in his shaking hand, waving them at her.

And these? What the fuck are these, Glory? Or is that even your name? How did you *make* all this shit? And why would you? Or are you just some sick girl who looks like a dead woman, and you wanted to fuck with people?

Glory hasn't taken her eyes from the article she's holding. Vincent shoves the handful of fortunes in her face.

What the fuck, Glory?

Vincent drops the fortunes like confetti across the photos and other papers. Chicago slaps his hand on the bar.

It's not her fault! She didn't make this shit up. I fucking checked it out, if you assholes would just listen to me for one second. Ok? Sit the fuck down.

Chicago says, nostrils flaring. Vincent sits down at a bar table, leans back abruptly, presses his hands to his temples and glares at the ceiling. Glory sinks onto a stool, laying the article on the bar in front of her with care. She spots the tin box and her eyes grow wide.

That's Jesse's box.

She says, unconsciously recoiling from it.

I unlocked this motherfucker two days ago and found these here things inside.

Chicago says, singling out the salt pouch, the photo, the article.

And these.

He sweeps the fortunes back into a pile.

That newspaper mug shot there is obviously Glory, there ain't no denying it. And that's her in the photo too. On the back, there's a stamp from the printer, it says 1980. That's over thirty years old. I don't know about you all but I'd say she ain't aged a bit. And these fortunes. They're just regular old Chinese fortune cookie fortunes, but each one has been written on. They all say "9-7" and then the year. They're all dated, man! There's one for every single year starting with '82. The most recent is from September 7th last year.

Vincent grumbles from his table.

They're obviously fake.

Chicago cricks his neck and visibly overcomes a look of irritation.

No. They ain't fake. I went down to the goddamn newspaper office and looked this shit up. That's the same article they printed. I saw the one in their files. Then I went down to the police station to see if I could get any old records.

He says as he pushes around the pile of papers and folders.

Now *I* don't believe you. No one would give *you* police files.

I say, losing faith in his story.

You know how much time I spend in the police department? They fucking love my ass down there. I keep 'em in business. They were more than happy to help me out with something besides testing out the drunk tank. Plus I got a little girlfriend who works in booking. But *how* I got 'em ain't the point.

Chicago huffs, then finds what he's looking for. He holds up a folder.

It's *what* I got that counts. Police reports and records on Glory, that there kid Jason and one other motherfucker.

Jesse.

Says Glory, soft and low. Chicago stops and looks at her.

Yeah, girl. Jesse. That is one bad motherfucking hombre, honey. I'm real sorry.

He fans out a stack of old photos and papers from a police folder. I catch a glimpse of a photo of what appears to be a bruised leg and mug shots. There's more but Chicago stacks them back together in a pile, then puts them back in the folder. He taps it twice on the bar before tossing it aside. He waves a dismissive hand over it.

244

But that shit don't matter. Glory here calls him Jesse, but what matters is the dude's real name is James Parker.

So what?

Vincent says, pretending to be bored. Chicago leans toward him and enunciates clearly:

James Parker. Or just "Parker."

Chicago pulls out the picture of Glory on the tailgate.

Recognize that rig?

Vincent takes the photo from him to get a closer look. He lets out a breath of air.

Motherfucker.

I look closer at the picture. It's a blue F100. I study the man's face and I recognize him from the photo in the first letter Glory got. The blond and bristled head, the eyes squinting against the glare. He's hard. And handsome. Glory looks happy under his arm. He looks like he'll protect her. Is protecting her. I look deeper and wonder when she realized how dangerous that kind of safety can be.

You think that old guy we've been seeing around is *this* guy? I ask.

Ain't no doubt.

Chicago says, proud of piecing it together. Vincent, still studying the photo, slowly nods his head in agreement.

At that, Glory stands up, tipping her stool over as she reaches over to pick the tin box up off the bar. She stands there, focusing all her attention on it for a moment. Chicago reaches out to touch her arm, but stops when she shuts her eyes tight and a low growl starts to grow in her throat. She squeezes the box 'til her fingers turn white and her growl explodes into a yell and then a deafening scream. We are all pinned in place, unable to react or even breathe.

She cocks her arm back and launches the box at the mirror behind the bar. Bottles of bright amber liquid burst into an explosion of glass shards. The mirror cracks and falls straight down in jagged plates, like a silver dress undone and dropped at the feet of an angry angel. Glory's legs buckle under her as she collapses against the bar, then slides to the floor.

In a flash, Vincent is at her side. He kneels down and threads his arms under hers. She buries her face in his shoulder, sobbing and heaving, as he lifts her up, holding her while Chicago rights her stool. Vincent sets her down, but she won't let go. He patiently peels her hands from his shirt. Tears roll down her cheeks. Her hands wipe her face, hide her eyes.

Chicago pulls his stool up next to hers, keeps a hand on her. Vincent steps behind the bar, glass crunching under his hard boots, bends and picks up the box.

But... but I'm real.

Glory says, looking at Chicago with tear-streaked eyes. His hand squeezes her flesh, as if to reassure them both.

No one said you ain't real, honey. You're just dead. I guess there's a difference.

No one speaks. A silence creeps in from the ceiling and the doorwells and through the remaining bottles glowing in the low light of the remains of the back bar. It wraps around us a comforting blanket, taking each one in and sealing us together in its lonely embrace. We ease back into it. Pull it up around our shoulders and under our chins. Shapes pass by and darken the etched and foggy window that faces Main Street, but they do not pause. The Hangman's Tree is not open for business. At least no business but ours.

Chicago takes the papers and folders from the bar top and stacks them all together. Then with a huff, he stands and tosses them to the far end of the bar. It breaks the silence, turning us loose. I let out a breath, unsure of how to proceed.

I just can't understand it. How can it be?

Chicago clears his throat and with some animation, gestures for us to lean in and listen.

Well, I been workin' through it day and night. I think what happened is she fell through a worm-hole.

Aw hell!

Vincent slams the bar top with a fist and turns to the back bar. He opens the icebox and yanks out six bottles of beer and sets them on the bar. Then he turns around and fishes out six more. He pops the caps off half a dozen in a row. Pop, pop, pop, pop, pop, *pop*! Foam flows over the bottle necks, but he ignores it.

You're fucking crazy. What the fuck do you know about worm-holes? You've been stealing too much cable!

Vincent snorts, glaring at Chicago.

What the hell is a worm-hole?

I ask, dumbfounded.

It's a spot where the fabric of space and time kind of folds over on itself and then, well, them two time spots is real close. Or the same even, and stuff can slip through. Or be in both at once. It makes sense to me. And scientists say it's possible, for your information, Vincent!

Chicago says, snatching a beer off the counter and downing half its contents.

Maybe it's God.

Glory says, still shaken.

God's a dick.

Says Vincent, downing a beer of his own. Chicago is undeterred.

Or it could be a re-incarnation thing. Like, she has to keep comin' back 'til she does it right or something.

Maybe we're the ones who slipped through the worm-hole.

I say, looking suspiciously around the bar. Chicago slaps his head.

Shit! I hadn't thought a that!

He starts to stand up, but Glory grabs his arm and pulls him back into his seat.

No. You're in the right place, Chicago. You have outstanding warrants to prove it.

She cracks a small smile. Vincent glares at her in disbelief.

How can you laugh at a time like this?

What am I supposed to do? I'm dead. I'm not dead. What do you think it's been like for me the last half hour? I'm clicking my heels, but I'm not going anywhere. So fuck it. I'm not going to sit here and continue to cry about it. I don't know how it happened and I don't really care. Give me a beer.

Vincent pushes a bottle over to her, but as she grabs it, he holds on and looks her in the eyes.

We're going to figure this out, Glory.

I know.

She takes the beer and gives his hand a squeeze.

Let's make a plan.

I say, not knowing what else to do. This seems to ease Vincent's discomfort.

Yes, a plan. I'm a little worried about this September 7th thing, though. That's in one week. Obviously, that creep goes into Mokelumne every year and has himself a little ceremony.

That, or if it's like some science fiction thing, she might just disappear on that date! Or... or something else happens, like she turns into a soulless demon! Or maybe she fucks up the future if she doesn't reenact the past! Or something...

Chicago looks around wildly. Then swallows the rest of his beer. Glory waves her hands wearily and cuts everyone off.

Here's the plan. I'm going to go back to the sherry house now and help Frank with that last row of barrels. If he doesn't get that done today, he's gunna be pissed and I'll be out a home. Dead or alive, a girl needs a place to sleep and a cup of coffee in the morning.

She stands up, gives Chicago a kiss on the forehead, then walks over and gives me a tight hug.

Let's go to Blue Creek on Wednesday. It's supposed to be hoppin'.

She says as she puts on her faded jean jacket and heads for the door. Vincent follows her and puts his arm across the door as she tries to leave.

Wait! You're in denial, Glory. You have to do something about this. Don't you?

Do I? Right now, Vincent? How about this: I just had my entire reality chopped into a neat little pile of crazy. How about you let me think about that for just a little bit, ok? And maybe after the fact that I've already died sinks the fuck into my seemingly alive consciousness, then maybe I'll be able to know what to do. But for this moment, I've had quite enough. I love you, but I'm going home.

He drops his arm as she unbolts the door, pulls her sunglasses down and disappears into the bright light of Main Street.

# Flight

## Glory

*September 2*

Before the sun has pierced the gown of morning mist that lays draped between the vine-crowned hills to the east, Glory rises to my tip-tapping gently against her windowpane. She sees me and smiles. She pushes the window open and offers the edge of her hand and I hop on. She walks me over to the old cast iron bedpost and lets me perch there.

She didn't know what to do when she went to bed, but she knows now. She skips a shower, as the noise will wake the house. Stealthily, she packs her duffel bag with the only things she'll need. She hasn't accumulated much, even with the encouragement of comfort. She zips the bag.

She carries her boots and we slip upstairs silently to the kitchen. She looks at it a good long while. It's always a surprise what's actually hardest to let go of. This kitchen for instance. Margaret's old chopping block, worn and concave in the center from years of use. Some of those cuts are from Glory. She traces her finger along the many little grooves. She picks up a pad of paper, then hesitates.

I should leave a note. But what can I say?

I don't answer. She puts the notepad down. There is no way to say. We know this. No way to give thanks and no way to explain. But she needs to give him something. So he knows.

She reaches around and untethers the old tin coffee cup from her duffel strap. She examines it. White chipped porcelain and rusty dents lay connected in scratches and scuffs. Some from her. Some from others. She sets it next to the coffee machine with a faint clink upon the tile countertop. She goes into the cupboard and pulls down the bag of grounds. Measures it precisely into the filter. Eight scoops, just like he always has to have it. She sets the timer to brew in an hour.

You stay here, little bird.

She says as she shoulders her bag. And slips out the side door, closing it silently behind her.

# Harvest

## Frank

*September 2*


I pull the old army jeep to a dusty halt in the brisk morning light of fall. I open the door to the kitchen as Dad finishes the last of his coffee from the old white tin cup. The handle is still hot as he sets it down along with the morning paper.

It's the first day of harvest. Tanks are clean and empty and all the portals are open. Bins are counted, stacked and waiting. Men are gathering. Pulling on boots, waiting for orders, looking up to the hills, to the rows, to the work. The forklift blows black smoke as it stacks the old wooden bins three high and two deep onto the flatbed.

Dad hears the deep throttling of the tractor as it warms up in the brisk September air. He's needed, he knows. He looks again at the little tin mug and turns it slowly around in a circle. Looking at every angle. He leaves it settled on the front page, just to the side of the fold, and pulls on his felt hat as he stands up, pushing the chair back with a scraping across the wood floor.

Morning, Dad. Any more of that coffee left?

I ask, seeing the cup but saying nothing. He gestures off-handedly at the coffeemaker.

Plenty. Help yourself. But hurry up; we need to get to work.

He says, heading for the door. I get my coffee and catch up. We walk the road between the house and the winery, flanked on both sides with orderly rows of vines. His vineyards are measured and planned, as vineyards are. This is farming. The crossroads of expectation and faith. Of planning and hope. Vines are planted, watered, pruned, thinned, protected. And with this care comes the expectation of a crop and the faith that all your efforts will pay off. You plan for the worst and hope for the best. Hope for good weather because no amount of faith can waylay a spring storm. He waits for the right time. He has an instrument to tell him when to pick. It's a little scope that measures the sugar by refracting the light. You squeeze the juice from a grape onto the lens and look through it toward the sun. The sugar bends the light and is measured by degrees. It says, *I'm ready*. Or it says, *Not Yet*. Or it says, *Too Late*.

*She didn't plant any seeds with purpose and order*, I think to myself. *She hiked a trail. Rounded bends and in watching for sleeping snakes and rough ground, she found things growing. Wild vines, and she grew like them.* California Wild Grape. It thrives in the rugged canyons of the Sierra Nevadas, skirts the edges of trout streams and trains itself upon the limbs of the massive oaks that file along the valley floor. Its vines grow long and rampant, beautiful and green, but it bears no edible fruit. They will never be subjugated to rows and terraces. They're wild and resilient and that is their strength.

Grapes are gleaned from the vine today. Men in their boots walk their rows. Men in their boots race the heat and the ripening.

Harvest is nothing but timing.

Dad says this aloud, shaking his head and watching his feet walk the road. *Harvest is nothing but timing*, I repeat to myself. He tends the vines and fruit for months, an accumulation of seconds, one after another after another until the moment of picking. He watches the sugars as they climb the scale and the acids as they go down it. He waits. Waits for the balance between the two. When these oppositions meet, before they pass each other by, with one or the other, or both, going in the wrong direction. When opposition becomes balance, he picks. All things come to this moment. A reaping.

We pass by the old sherry house and see the door ajar. Dad stops to stare at it. He is the only one who bothers with this old place and the tedious process of it. He detours to the old building, pushes the door open, lighting the rows of barrels stacked three high. The youngest on top, the oldest on the bottom. He walks around the corner row and finds her sitting against a far barrel, just beyond the edge of morning light that casts a bright rectangle across the floor. Dad walks over and sits down next to her. I come quietly in and stand just inside the door.

I kind of thought you were leaving, Glory. He says.

I kind of was.

What happened? You didn't get very far.

I started down the road and then, I just didn't know where to go.

Are you afraid something's going to happen to you?

What I'm afraid of has already happened. Now I'm just trying to get away from it.

Dad looks up at the large and black-painted oak barrels stacked all around them.

You know what I like about the sherry process? I know everyone thinks I'm a fool for bothering with it. But it's the most beautiful wine and the most under-appreciated. The thing about it is that you're taking a little bit from this year and mixing it into last year's batch. Then you take a little of both of those mixed together and then you add it to the year before them. And so on. Until you get to the oldest row of barrels and they have that old wine, but they also have every other year up to the present mixed into it. So the past and the present get to be in the same spot and become the same thing. And any mistakes or flaws from bad years or bad weather get evened out and folded into the whole. They don't get tossed out; they just get integrated and tempered by the whole span of time and the process. Whatever bad happened in this old vintage down here at the bottom is still in there, but it's got all the good too and a little of the good and bad from all the rest of it. It's not like the wine we make up in the winery. That's one vintage at a time. You've got one shot. If it's a bad year, then it's a bad year forever and there's nothing you can do about it. No, I like this process. It's just so much more… reasonable.

Glory gets up and dusts off her pants.

I don't think you're a fool, Frank. And I don't want to be one, either.

Well, if you're not leaving just yet, can you help us take the samples this morning? I have to leave early; the doctor wants me to come back in for an emergency follow-up.

Sure I can, Frank. Is everything all right?

Dad, you were just in two days ago. What's the emergency?

I say, stepping into the room. He looks from me to Glory, a little bemused expression on his face.

They can't find my heart.

What do you mean, they can't find it?

Well, I mean, they went looking for my enlarged heart to check on the progress and everything, and it was gone. Just my normal heart now. Same size it used to be. I thought the doctor was going to have a heart attack himself.

He says as he shuffles around the cupboards gathering the sampling equipment and buckets. He hands me a bucket as I stand there dumbly blinking and trying to grasp what it means.

It's impossible! It's a permanent condition, isn't it? What happened?

Glory doesn't say anything, but she has a mysterious smile on her face. She hops up and takes the shears and gloves from the shelf. Dad just shrugs.

I don't know. It just shrank, I guess.

With a slight but satisfied grin, he picks up the buckets, kicks the door open with his foot and steps out into the engulfing light of day.

# I Want to Come Undone

## Rose

*September 5*

The landscape is dark and moving. We undo and undo and undo. *What's happening here?* Someone asks me. *Tell me the story.* I point to the old snag on the ridge. *Glory took off her hands.* I say. *And turned in her skin for a cloak of feathers and a set of talons. She sits at the western edge and waits.* I move to the center of the old room. I undo and undo until I'm nothing but a pile of strewn and loosely tangled ribbons blowing across the floor. The room is empty and the floor is bare and disappearing. The house is dismantled; the bricks are strewn across the hills. The weeds grow through the carpet and I sleep under a big oak tree and shoot cans off the remains of the fireplace. It is constant night and the big dipper sits on the eastern horizon. There's a red-tailed hawk and a dead tree full of buzzards on the ridge. They see me stumbling around below and when I finally give in, they land on my arms and my cheek, pluck the rings from my fingers and tear open my belly with their beaks. Rend my guts and fly off trailing ribbons and my blood and my life. They fly away as the world brightens. The sun wakes me. This landscape is home. The buzzards are laughing and I am laughing and Glory drives up in the jeep and her feathers are under her skin and she says: *Get the hell up out of the grass, dumb-ass!* She says: *We need gas.* Tells me I need to get the gear and tell Frank where we're fishing today so in case we don't come back he knows where to come looking.

The phone screams and rips me from this place. Eyes snap open to pillows, ceiling, room. The sun is barely up. I reach for the phone.

Hello?

Hi honey, it's Mom.

Hey. What's up? Damn, it's early.

It's time for us to come home. Are you ready?

Ready? No. But please come home. It's time.

Yes it is. We'll be back in a couple of days.

# Hope Valley

## Blue Creek

*September 6*

Chicago curses as the Scout drops its whole left front end into a deep rut, scraping sharply against the big granite rock he meant to keep the tire on.

Fuck's sake!

Snaps Vincent as his shoulder slams against the side door. Chicago lurches the Scout to the right.

Some things worth doin', take doin'.

Chicago replies as he hits the gas hard and pops the vehicle out of the hole. It ambles forward. We crawl along the impossibly narrow and boulder-studded trail, a determined steel turtle working its way begrudgingly forward, clanking its shell as it goes.

Blue Creek is protected by a tough little road and a bad reputation. It's small and brushy where it comes out of the lake. The lake is a temporary home for trailers, pop-up tents and fat kids in inner tubes. When the campers get bored of flailing the lake with their hook-dangled lures and power bait, they go to the outlet and flail their hardware across the tiny pools and channels. They do this for an eighth of a mile or so before tiring of the effort. Any fish they snag are small and too inexperienced to get out of the way of the ripping Castmaster in time.

A mile below the lake the creek opens up and the brush dissipates and so do the people, leaving only delicate white aspen and pine to politely mingle with the short and dense marshy grasses that border the water. The high-elevation, shallow valley is surrounded by red volcanic pinnacles and cones, dragon-shaped and alluring in the distance. The sky is blue. The granite here is a vibrant rust-stained red. The trout are all Brookies, and their red-streaked bodies, golden bellies and black-and-white dotted sides are invisible against the red cradle of stone beneath the water.

Chicago yanks the Scout to a halt on a bluff of dense pines overlooking the creek below. We get out and assemble the gear without comment and head for the creek. We separate almost immediately, taking more distance than etiquette requires. No one wants to bring it up. And so we don't. I leave the stream and climb high up on a red volcanic rock that sits perched and peering over the water. Chicago has skipped ahead and is standing out on a shorn stump in the middle of a channel. The toes of his boots are over the edge of the stump but he stands graceful, comfortably balanced on the edge. His shoulders are quiet, hands lazy on the dark handle of the old bamboo rod. He picks the line up and lays it back down in a peaceful, fluid movement.

I turn around and climb down from the rock, head upstream and walk far enough to buy me an hour alone. I depart from the creek and detour up one of the craggy volcanic ridges that jut from this range like red fins from a massive sea-creature. Gaining the peak I look down at Hope Valley sprawling below. This area is unlike the rest of the Sierras. Volcanic forms rest amidst sweeping barren slopes that slide into an endless series of lush green meadows and fingerling streams. I don't come here often; it is a powerful place. But I will, someday. When I am old and wise enough to understand it.

I head back down toward the stream. I come to a broad cliff over which the creek delicately cascades in fine and discordant drops. The pool is round and blue below. The rocks are smooth and warm. I lie down and force myself to nap. It's all I can do. The hour wanes as the water murmurs past. The grasses at my head shush me and the sun makes shapes behind my lids.

Then the sun is blocked. I open my eyes to find Chicago's face two inches from mine and his legs straddling me.

Ah, dang! I was just about to kiss you, Sleeping Beauty!

I push him off with some effort.

Get off me, Rumplestiltskin. You need to find a better way to get women than ambushing them.

Why? It's perfectly effective.

He stands up, offering me a hand. Glory and Vincent are settling in by the waterfall. Glory takes a seat on a rock at the water's edge. She sits there quietly looking at the stream as it goes by. Vincent puts his large format camera on the tripod and turns it toward her. He looks through it for a long moment. Then he stands back, holding the cable and trigger.

You look beautiful, Glory.

As she turns to look at him, he clicks the shutter. Chicago jumps between them, waving his arms. When no one laughs, he throws his hands up in defeat.

> Goddamn it. I can't wait anymore. We have to talk about tomorrow. What the hell are we going to do?

Glory turns back to the water, not answering him. I try and offer some solution.

> I don't know. I just... I'm at a loss. Maybe we just do nothing and see what happens.

This sets Chicago off. He whirls around to confront me.

> Do nothing? How can we do nothing? How about we go in there and intercept that shit-bag? How about that? We know he's gunna be there.

> I don't think you've thought that through.

Vincent says, moving his camera equipment a little further away. This just works Chicago up more.

> Oh you don't? Well, I've thought that and about twenty other plans through. What have you been doing, huh? I haven't heard one single suggestion from you!

> It's all I've been thinking about since you threw that shit on my bar, Chicago. So you better just check yourself right now.

Vincent says, his tone dropping low and threatening. Chicago spits on the ground.

Bullshit. You've just been your usual silent self. Well, actin' tough ain't helping anyone. If you really love her, like I think you do, then you'll do something. Or did she turn out to be just another pretty girl for you to study, like all the rest of 'em?

Vincent takes two long strides, closing the distance between them, and throws a hard, fast punch into Chicago's face. Chicago falls backwards over the rock behind him, landing hard in the dirt.

He puts his hands under his shoulders and pushes himself slowly up, blood streaming from his nose into the sand. He wipes at it, sees the red streak across his hand. Then he leaps up faster than anyone can register and rushes Vincent.

Throwing his shoulder into Vincent's belly, he tackles him to the ground. They wrestle in a rising cloud of dust, the thud of punches landing punctuated by grunts and curses.

I run over to try to pull them apart.

Stop! Fucking stop!

I scream and force myself between them. I kick one off as I lay on the other. They register that it's me and slowly let go of each other. Chicago stands up and kicks a rock violently across the river and then goes and slumps down against a tree. Vincent rips his arm away from me and gets up to put his equipment away. I stay in the dirt, shaking my head in the hopelessness of it.

I'm going into Mokelumne tomorrow.

Glory says, getting up from her rock and walking to the edge of the stream. We're all stunned for a moment. Chicago finally breaks the silence.

Good! I told you guys that was what we should do. We'll go in there and fix that motherfucker.

Glory squats on her heels by the water and dips her hands in. She scoops it up and gently lowers her face in her hands. The water washes down her cheeks. She runs a wet hand behind her neck while the other drips water back into the river.

Alone.

She says without turning around.

What? No, you can't do that. He'll kill you!

I say, half-rising from the dirt and the dust. She turns to face me, a resolved look in her eye.

So what? He already has.

# We Have To Be Brave

The ring clinks irritatingly against the steering wheel. I tap, tap, tap it. Turn it with my thumb round and round, but it finds no comfortable rest. I turn it some more. Emigrant Road is climbing. The moss glows electric green on the north face of the trees. *It's so you don't get lost*, I remind myself. *You can always check the trees and know. Because the sun just don't shine everywhere or all the time.* I turn the ring. Turn the wheel. I brace the wheel with my palms and work the ring free with my other hand and throw it into the center console. It plinks. Glory looks down at it.

I was wondering when you were going to take that off.

The midmorning light is hard and bare. The sky is a relentless blue. The trees are straight and green and nothing else. The haze of summer is gone, but fall refuses to show itself. The range is naked and unconcerned as we drive steadily across the cut-off to Mokelumne country. I adjust the rearview, peeking behind us.

Haven't seen the Scout yet.

They'll be there.

You don't have to do this, Glory.

I know. But I want to.

Aren't you scared?

I should be, I guess. I remember everything, Rose. He pushed me in. I begged him not to. I grabbed on to him. I screamed. I tried to get a foothold on the sandy rock, but I kept slipping and he just looked at me and let me go. I think the last thing I said was, "No."

I can't take this.

Glory looks out the window, away from me.

I don't think the last word a person says should be "no."

She says, looking out the window.

And I want to see him.

But why?

I ask, feeling sick and desperate. She turns back to me, picks up my ring and turns it around. She holds it up to me.

Because I love him. Remember? You should understand that by now. Love doesn't give a shit what's right or wrong or what you want. It's not just for good people or bad ones. Oh, he was bad. I know it and I knew it. I remember driving on the freeway one night. I was in the middle of the backseat between Jesse and this woman. She'd helped some guys rip off one of Jesse's Rock Creek operations. She wasn't even all there. She had a little mental disability or something. She was a bitch and a criminal, but she was also just kind of dim-witted. He reached over me and opened her door and held me against the seat while he pushed her out. Just pushed her right out onto the highway. Then he pulled the door closed and didn't say a word.

Jesus.

Glory carefully puts the ring back into the console with the coins and bobby pins.

Rose, I didn't know it was so bad until you reminded me what good was. And I can't thank you enough for that. I'm not claiming I was blind. I know just how wrong and fucked up everything was. But I loved him and I thought that was going to make some difference.

Love isn't enough, I guess.

It's not. You're fucking lucky, Rose. Your marriage? Your husband? That ain't shit compared to what you had to begin with.

I know. But it doesn't make it feel better right now. I love you and I'd trade anything to stop this from happening.

You know better than that, baby.

She says, smiling. We cover the rest of the miles in silence. The way, familiar. I strain my eyes toward the granite half-domes of Mokelumne, still and paramount on the horizon. They are strong and waiting. If there is some beauty to be had in this landscape today, it doesn't show itself. No glint of insects hovering, no flowers creeping from under the strewn rocks, no fool's gold billowing through the water, viscous and shimmering. No, there is none of this. Not today. Today it all just sits back and waits.

We pull up into the dirt parking area. Chicago and Vincent lean against the Scout in the bright noon sun. They straighten up to face us as we pull up next to them. They look, as they always look. Chicago has his "Fuck You" hat propped high on his forehead, his dirt-blond hair objecting from behind his ears. His button-up shirt is sun-faded and half-tucked into his dirty jeans. Vincent stands straight and squared, as usual. He watches Glory as she gets out of the Landcruiser and walks over to them.

You boys gunna do some fishin'?

She says, kicking dirt over their boots.

Fuck you, Glory.

Chicago says. I can see him flex his jaw, holding back expression. Glory doesn't notice or pretends not to. She walks around to open the Landcruiser tailgate and shuffles through the gear.

> Well, suit yourself. But I am. I don't really know what's going to happen up there today. Maybe nothing. If that's the case, I'll sure feel stupid hiking all the way in there without my fishing gear.

Vincent catches his breath audibly and turns away, pinching his hand between his eyes. He braces himself against the rack of the scout. I walk over to Glory and put my hand on hers as she pulls her old and battered fishing rod out of the back. I take it from her and put it back amongst the gear. I pull my Sage out from the back and hand it to her.

> If you go in there and it's just fishing, you better make it count.

No, Rose. This is yours. I can't…

> You can. You need it. You deserve it. Catch a big one in there, ok, Glory? Promise me.

I will.

She takes the rod and draws me close. I bury my face in her hair and we both take a long breath in. And out. I put my forehead against hers.

I know.

She says, then steps back, tucking the rod under her arm. Chicago takes his hat off and walks up, turning it nervously in his hands. He stands right up close in front of her, then takes the hat and puts it snugly on her head. He tweaks the brim down low as his hands slip down over her ears. He cups her face and gives her a long and steady kiss. He drops his hands. He says nothing as he walks back and leans against the driver's side of the Scout.

I look over to Vincent; he is leaning with both hands propped against the roof, staring hard at the ground. He's shaking his head. He kicks the tire; rocks and dust cloud around his boot. He makes a fist and hits the roof hard, once.

Damn!

He straightens his shoulders and takes a deep breath, looking up into the sky. He breathes out and then turns to give a long and beautiful look to Glory. He saunters over, reaching around to his back hip. He unsnaps the leather strap that holds his bowie knife and sheath. He slides it through his belt loops and hands it and the knife to Glory.

I don't need that.

She says, looking from the knife to his face. He takes a step closer, grabs her side and pulls her close. He wraps his arms around her, threading the leather straps through her jeans. He slides the sheath and knife on and snaps it tight. He checks it with two quick tugs. Not letting go, he says:

> You come back, Glory. You hear me? You fucking come back. Whatever it takes.

He steps back. Glory looks around the circle at each of us in turn. Then she shrugs, picks up her gear and pulls her hat down tight.

> Well, as Frank would say: If I'm gunna get there, I might as well start.

And with that she turns away and heads up the short granite slope that borders the dam. In seconds, she disappears into the shrubby green entrance of lake trail. We sit silently, watching the expanse of the reservoir as the wind begins to pick the waves up off the surface. We watch the north shore and know we won't see her through the thick and selfish canopy of black oak and scrub brush. Chicago looks at me.

> Just say the word, Rose.

I nod my head.

> You better follow her.

> You sure you guys shouldn't come?

> She made us swear. She wants to, needs to, do this alone. It's her fate and we have to respect her wishes. The only reason you're going in there is to be a witness. Just in case, just in case... oh, I don't know.

> I know, Rose. I get it.

He jumps up and grabs a small pack from the back seat and leaps up the first rise of rocks. He pauses on the top rock and looks back.

Don't let her see you! I shout. No matter what happens up there. It's her life, you got it? You let it be.

I got it, girl.

Chicago says, eyes straight and clear. Before he turns away, Vincent takes a few steps toward him.

Hey! Don't forget what we talked about.

Oh, I won't, brother.

With that Chicago quickly turns and jumps off the rock and slips into the green.

What did you talk about?

I say, turning to Vincent. He gives me a quick look, but says nothing. Then he gets in the driver's seat of the Landcruiser, leans over and opens the passenger door.

Get in.

Without another look back, I walk to the side, step dusty boots onto the old rubber mat, pull the heavy metal door closed with a slam and sink into the rumble of the engine as Vincent swings us up and onto the broad river road. We gain some distance in silence.

Why didn't you tell her? I ask.

Tell her what?

That you love her.

He shakes his head and grips the wheel.

Fuck, Rose! You better just stop.

I won't. You could love her.

I can't.

But you already do. What are you so afraid of?

He waits a long time to answer.

Everything I've ever loved turned into something vile and
disgusting. I don't want to do that to her.

He looks me straight in the eye.

I've got bad blood.

You're not cursed.

I say and then say no more. We make our way along the valley floor,
following the river, and then slowly begin the climb up the immense
canyon wall. The mantra of miles roll steadily under our tires. The blur of
trees in their procession past my window lulls me as exhaustion pins me
heavy to my seat. The 'Cruiser lifts and floats just above the road,
occasionally swinging wide and drifting out over the sliding slope of the

canyon. Vincent brings it back with a gentle turn of the wheel. A thrumming vibration from the chassis distracts me, shaking my feet and then my legs. Its vibration becomes a sound, low and dark, and then it rises, pitching and screaming, until my eardrums inflate into a black expanse, like bat wings, which then snap tightly around my head, cutting off the sound and sealing me in darkness.

Blackness and nothing but the sound of wings beating. Faster, I beat them. Going toward it, the faintest smell of pine. A breeze. The water. I burst upon the flash of light and all below me speeding by. Water. Trees. Rocks. Forest. In strobes the trail appears below me. And I find him. I swing past him and up the trail to a dead snag at the place where the trail splits. I watch him come.

The wind blows steady reassurance to my black and thudding breast as Chicago moves fast along the trail that undulates through the cavernous shade of the black oak forest.

He makes only the slightest of sounds, dipping under low branches and hopping washes and fallen trees without breaking stride. He must set the right pace. Quick enough to get close, then head up into the crags they call the Mokelumne Tetons where he can see the lay of the land. The lake blinks blue occasionally from the side when there is a break in the trees. He does not look at this or anything other than the trail as it unfolds before him. He sees the trail in his mind the moment before it appears. As he always has, and he never loses it. I ascend from my perch and follow him, skimming the treetops as he runs below. One mile. Two. And he hops off the trail and up a moss-covered knoll that slides from the base of a steep and shattered mountain face. Through these cracks he climbs quick as a cat. I circle above.

Sweat breaks his brow and darkens his shirt. He crests the first tooth in the jaw of the mountain and walks with hard breaths to the edge with all of the river glistening below. The wind is cool and eases his efforts. The belly of Mokelumne lies full and sultry a quarter-mile below. The hard mounds of the granite headwater ease into the creases of green forest cut by the raging river that stops only occasionally to gather in deep black pools before the whole of it spills full and finally into the wide arms of the lake below.

He watches for Glory and then he sees her. And from my height I see her too. The bright red of her hair a moving dot along the trail just beyond the inlet. We look closer and see, all in and among the trees and brush flanking her: the ancestors. They're following. There are maybe twenty. Maybe more.

This is ok.

Chicago says to himself. He looks up the trail toward the Blue Hole cliff; no one's there. He shakes his head and drapes his shoulders in relief. He stands to go.

Hey, where you going? You don't see something funny down there?

A voice says with a laugh. On a rock behind Chicago sits a man. He is weathered and smiling to himself. He wears an old red blouse faded to pink, deerskin pants and good boots. He laughs again, grabbing his knee. I

278

fly down to the shrub behind the rock and land. The old man looks at me and laughs again. Then he stops.

Magpie! You are funny too.

He says then stands up and leans on Chicago as he points over his shoulder to the trail below.

Look, little half-boy!

Chicago follows the direction of his finger and squints to see a man, seated just above the Blue Hole cliff, waiting.

Well, fuck me. I almost missed that.

Chicago says, peering closer. The man lets go of Chicago and sits back upon his rock. His shirt is blue now. Upon his head, a foam-fronted trucker hat with a picture of a leaping bass that says "Fuck You" in black pen. Chicago lurches forward.

Hey! That's my hat!

This hat? Yes! It is a very good hat. Very funny.

The old man says, laughing and rocking on his seat. Chicago reaches toward him and the man stops dead still.

No.

Says the man, shaking his head and looking down into his lap. In his lap he is holding a knife. Vincent's knife, and he moves it as if he's cutting slices off of an apple. But there is no apple. Only his hand. He turns his wrist and each time a finger falls to the dirt with a soft plunk. Three, four fingers, and he pauses. Then he laughs again, shaking his head.

It's funny.

He says as he stands up and climbs into the rock he was sitting on and disappears.

No!

Yells Chicago as he turns back toward the river. He scrambles to the edge and looks down. Glory is making her way to the clearing where, waiting for her, is a man.

Jesse. Fuck!

Chicago scrambles as quick and as quiet as he can down the escarpment until he is close enough to hear the sound of her voice. He crouches down behind two rocks on the ledge above them.

I fly down and circle the man. I land on a branch near his head and look hard at his profile. In the clear and bulbous orb of his eye, the sun shines through. On the surface of his lens, the lake sits, reflected. On the inside, another reflection moves and flickers. The picture plays upon his side of the lens. He is there, in his room. In his bed. He gently brushes the long red trailing curls from her breast. He wants to see them bare as she lies on her side next to him. He runs his finger along the curve of her hip as he buries his face in her neck. He shuts his eyes hard. Opens them and all that shines in his eye is the sun as he watches the trail.

He stands up from the stump he's been waiting on, pulls a bandana from his back pocket and wipes the sweat from his brow. It's time. He senses her coming so he makes his way to the spot. The smell of her memory grows strong and pungent as she draws near. He hears her footfalls. He takes his seat on a nondescript rock along the edge of the clearing. She comes around the bend in the trail and walks to the center of the space. She drops her pack at her feet and looks at him. Neither of them speaks for a long moment.

Hello, Jesse.

She finally says, resigned.

You want some water, babe?

He draws a canteen from behind his hip and proffers it to her. She walks over and takes it. She takes a long drink, keeping her eyes on his. She screws the lid back on and hands it back. They regard each other. He stands up, towering over her.

I knew you'd come. I don't know how on earth you're here, but I knew you'd come. Once I saw you.

She looks at him without reply. He spreads his hands wide.

Say something.

What do you want me to say, Jess?

He shakes his head.

I don't know. Maybe nothin'. Maybe it's just me that needs to say something. I can't tell you I'm sorry; it's just too little for what I've done to you and I know that. There's not a day that goes by that I don't think about you. Every single part of you has become a map in my mind. And I go through it, every bit, every day, relentlessly. I've pictured every hair on your head, spent a day on each one. Every moment since the moment I killed you has been a living hell. That's all I can give you, I guess, to make up for it.

Nothing makes up for it.

I know. I can't make any excuses, babe. There's something wrong in me. And I never cared to fix it and quite frankly I don't care to now. I don't give a damn about all those people I hurt. I don't regret any of it. Some of us are just here to hash it out with some others. But with you, it's different. It's because I loved you.

You always had trouble showing your affection.

She steps close to him and puts her hand on his cheek. He closes his eyes and pushes his face against her palm. She lets her hand drop, and then walks out toward the edge of the clearing. She looks down at the river, calm and peaceful. Jesse moves behind her, wrapping his arms around her waist. He lowers his chin into the back of her neck and talks low into her ear.

You're here now. By some miracle. I don't even care how it's possible. Part of me thinks it must be so we can do it right this time. You're going to come back to me.

Yes.

She turns to face him.

Good, honey.

282

He says. Moving back to look at her in his arms.

We're here to do it right this time.

As she says this, she steps back and off the edge of the cliff. She slips down quickly, their arms still locked. She drags him to his knees, her feet dangling over the churning blue water below. He shouts, tightening his grip on her.

Glory! No!

Yes.

She says. She looks him in the eyes and lets go.

# Still Waters

*September 8*

Chicago sits on a corner of the Water's hearth reciting the story. He runs his fingers through his hair, pressing hard. Margaret sits next to me at the table and sips a cup of tea. Frank stands by the window with his hands in his back pockets, watching the children running in the pastures below. Vincent sits on the couch stiffly, watching his friend and listening to the words, one by one, as they come.

It's 10:38 in the morning and through the bay windows of the living room, the sun caresses every surface in its most gentle and nurturing light. The breeze outside is measured by the slight and rhythmic quaking of leaves and the nodding of the dandelion seeds as their glowing orbs sway heavy on tall stalks. It is the sweetest hour of the day. When things are good. The time of day when you begin to think of what might be nice for dinner. The time of day when a second cup of coffee is much enjoyed. A time for good things.

It's not a time for stories like this one. And so it doesn't quite make sense. And the time of day is just as good a reason as any — a very good reason, in fact — to not accept it.

Frank looks out the window at his grandchildren as they run swatting dandelion seeds along their path. The whole field around them rises in an undulating wave of tiny sunlit spirits lifting weightlessly off the ground as if, for them, gravity has ceased to exist. *Gravity does not drag upon small things as it does upon big ones*, I think as the weight of this story fills the room.

The story is over. I look at my mother and I can see. She is not surprised.

How did you know?

I ask her. She looks at me with some kindness.

People see what they want. Instead of what is.

She stands up to clear the cups from the table. The sunlight through the window incrementally brightens, catching on the wet rings left upon the glass where it circles and shines, golden and unbroken.

# Last Call

*September 8*

I whoo and turn my head all the way around to look behind me. Ruffle the white downy feathers of my chest. I spin my head back around as Vincent leans against the dark alley wall and lights another cigarette. He looks at me through eyes narrowed and lit by the bright and burning ember.

You want one?

He asks Chicago. Chicago shakes his head. It's almost time. The neons are turned off and the lights of street-side cars pan the brick wall as people go home for the night. Chicago steps back from the old truck he was leaning on and back into the shadow next to Vincent.

A figure ambles up the sidewalk and turns into the alley and around the back of the truck. The old man deftly fishes the keys from his pocket and lumbers into the front seat. Vincent puts his hand on the door before it closes and scoots in beside the man, pushing him to the center. Chicago slides in from the other side. The sound of two metal doors shutting echo down the street and disturb no one.

What do you want from me?

The old man demands.

Everything.

Chicago says as he brings the butt of a hand-club down hard at the base of the old man's skull.

And then some.

He clarifies as the man slumps over into the dashboard. Vincent quietly pulls the truck out into the street and onto the eastbound freeway, settling in for one more long and familiar ride.

Mokelumne Canyon, even today, is a remote and hard-to-reach place. A hundred years ago, it was ever more so. At the turn of the century, there was a man named Wolfe who had finally had enough. He and the law, he and the townsfolk, he and most people, just couldn't seem to see eye to eye. He was oft blamed for things that went missing from people's yards and houses. Sometimes he took them, sometimes he did not. But stealing is a matter of perspective. In some cultures, if someone needs something and someone else has it and doesn't use it, then it belongs to the one who needs it. Wolfe was a sufficient man and a small-statured man, but gifted with ox-like strength and a quick and unapologetic attitude. The deputy in Jackson found this out when he tried to harass and embarrass Wolfe on the street and was instead disarmed and ended up looking down the barrel of his own gun. This put Wolfe at irreconcilable odds with the authorities.

So he packed up some things, including an entire cast-iron stove, put them all on his back and hiked deep into Mokelumne Canyon. Because he was strong and because he could. And he cared not for the rest of it anymore. Way up into the middle he went, the farthest point from any town in any direction. There by the river, in a dense patch of forest, he built himself a cabin. A church of devotion to solitude set within a cathedral of nature where the chorus of running water lilts a hymn that echoes around and up the spires of pines as they reach toward the heavens. Here he stayed, and here he died, and all in between was a paradise.

Good men and bad men are a matter of perspective, too. Sometimes it's not the man who needs to change, but the place.

The old man awakes to the smell of smoke. Chicago sits prodding the charred and crackled logs in the stove with an old tire iron, the end of which glows red and throbbing amidst the licking flames.

I found this in the back of your truck.

Chicago says to the man who strains to say something through the duct-tape across his mouth.

Yeah, I know. I've always been real lucky that way. When I need something, I just find it. Just like that!

Chicago says with a whistle, admiring the iron in his hand. The old man struggles against his binds, causing the chair to creak and scratch muted upon the soft dirt floor of the cabin.

Settle down there, old man. Vincent's not quite ready yet. Are you ready yet, Vincent? I think Jesse's gettin' impatient.

Vincent squares the lens of the large-format camera up to the man in the chair, adjusting one leg of the tripod and then another. He takes his time because it's important. It's important when you take a person's portrait that it truly reflect him. That it be as accurate as possible. And to really capture this, you can't just get the look he wears on his face when he knows he's being studied. That's an illusion, one that Vincent knows how to dispel. So he waits. A person will look at the camera and set his face in expectation. And here, he waits. But the click of the camera never comes and then the person can't hold it anymore because illusions are hard to sustain, and so that face falls away. For just a moment it's gone, but before the person can generate it again, the camera clicks. In the in-between. In the moment that is real.

Vincent makes a final adjustment to the camera so that everything that needs to be in the frame is in it and nothing that does not. Then he stands to the side, letting the thin black cord to the trigger fall out of his hand to the floor with a dull thud. He looks at his subject and knows he will not have to wait for the illusion to drop. The man is bulging against his ties and glaring, ferocious and strong, back at the camera. This is the face of a man who knows and is not hiding.

Should we let him say somethin'? Chicago asks.

Is there anything he *could* say?

Vincent kneels down in front of the man and looks him in the eye, taking his time.

You deserve it and you know it. You want it. You're grateful even. Every day you walked the earth after killing Glory the first time was a living hell, but every day you've been alive since she did it for you has been worse. You are such a lucky man, Jesse. She loved you. She never took her love away. But all you wanted was her power. And now she's taken that back. So there is nothing left for you. Isn't that right?

290

The man settles down a little in his chair, matching Vincent's gaze with his.

I think he agrees!

Says Chicago. Tapping the end of the tire iron jauntily against the hearthstone, knocking ash into a delicate pattern on the floor. Vincent steps back behind his camera.

Five white owls crisscross in front of the moon, periodically interrupting the light that foams in a gentle, pulsing column through the windows of the cabin. One of the owls is me, and I see. I watch, as I always have, what happens in these places. Our paradise of tradition and illusion and love. Our Mokelumne. Sometimes it takes. Sometimes, you give it up. And peace is knowing when to do either.

High up in Mokelumne Canyon sits an old cabin built long ago by a lone and stubborn renegade. If he ever loved anyone, no one knows. His cabin is a destination for a few, often curious, and sometimes desperate people. Sometimes they make it there. Sometimes they don't. Tonight the moon hangs suspended over the head of a soon-to-be dead man, hanging on its chain and casting waves of irregular light as it dangles above. Tied to his chair, we must wonder if he found what he was looking for or if, in fact, he ever knew what it was he wanted. It doesn't really matter to us. It only matters to him. Outside the cabin, trees are lit in the periodic flash of a camera bulb and the dull thuds of flesh and groans of man are mingled and composed in the harmony of wind and the rushing water of a fisherman's river.

# The Ground Floor of Promise

*October sometime*

The room is covered in dust, strewn and dismembered. Shelves that once held neat rows of books and records are sparsely adorned with bits of broken toys and old apple cores. The books and records lay streaked across the floor, a cargo plane's worth of debris from a wrecked marriage. The bodies are going to be hard to identify.

Time to search the wreckage. Begin to clear the debris. Of course I'm standing here alone with my broom. Did I think anyone would be here with me for this? No. In fact, I didn't think about this much at all. This is a dark place, a half-underground room on the ground floor of my foreclosed house. Leo built it to use as his studio but it never took. Then he built it as a family movie room but that never took either. Then he built it as a playroom for the kids and it sort of took, but it became a place for them to escape to where they could become wild creatures in a dark cave dancing on records and playing house with the blown German glass Christmas ornaments that we got for our wedding. A whole set. A bride and groom, a shiny glittering wedding cake and a whole host of delicate blown glass hearts in pink, red and silver. A tiny red heart with two raised gold rings. Lyla was always trying to sneak into the Christmas ornament box because she's a crow. She likes everything that shines and sparkles. But German glass is thin as butterfly wings and delicate.

Holding my broom and dustpan, I interrupt the light through the doorway, a miner bewildered by the bright glints of treasure reflecting and embedded in my memory. So many tiny broken pieces. They run through the cracks of the wreckage, are lodged between the braids of my grandmother's rug. I don't look to see if I can find the bride's head or a broken heart with the rings split in half or something else poetic like that. I know Lyla has them already. Has them hidden away somewhere safe. Or has lost them, which is just as safe as anything.

At this point, it's just me and my broom. And do I want anyone else here? No. And of course it's this room that's the biggest disaster. The one I've been putting off, the one that got so trashed. Leo built this room; he built a lot of this place, but this room especially. The floors are black planks, the walls are grey, the shelves are perfect, the wine cellar is subtle and elegant.

There was a giant movie screen in this room, with red velvet curtains at the sides. It was brilliant and it reminds me of him. He tried; he did. I tried too. It's not that we didn't take; it's just that we didn't hold.

I walk back and forth across the wooden planks, bending to pick up the books and records. Pick up the braided rug and shake out a tinselly song of promises. And where are you, Leo? No, I would never ask him to come help with this. He has hauled away his share of the disaster. He left enough here to remind me, though. An anniversary gift. A select record or two. A guitar pick. I had no idea how heavy a guitar pick could be. I put it back down. Do I want him here, not to help, but maybe to... to... to what? I look at the plank I'm standing on, bouncing gently over waves of dark expanse. The blank stare of my own future looking back at me. No. No, I don't want him here now. Sweep the thought away with my broom.

You made the right choice, Leo, of course you did. It just wasn't possible. Love has nothing to do with what's possible. It just sometimes makes you try to do impossible things. I don't know how big this one was, but I'm done now with speculating. You sure had some quiet ways. And in them there was great promise. Sweeping up this mess, I'm struck by the vast and heartbreaking difference between promise and promises. Never to be confused again. Promise is potential. Promises are wagers made on a future not one of us can ever know.

And where is Glory? She's gone and left me with this real life. Where are the hawks? I stare at my broom and wait for the feathers to fan out from the bottom. Nothing. Do I want her here anyway? No. No, all I want here right now is me and my broom. All of this, all of this breaking down and unraveling and upturning has been so I can stand here alone on the shards of my own promises at the ground floor of my life and pick it up by myself. I'm the only person I can safely say I'm going to be with for the rest of my life. I belong to no one. I love everyone. And I don't want any of them here.

On my knees, I stack books and cry. Tears fall between the planks and fall away to a sea of no one's making. I'm not drifting and I'm not forging in any direction. I'm putting records back into their sleeves. I'm putting the records next to the books in a box. I'm sweeping up beautiful glittering dust and rolling up my grandmother's rug. The rug, the books, the records and everything, I stack neatly in the cellar for another day. Today I cleaned it up. Taking it away will have to wait just a little bit longer. A few of those records are worth keeping. That guitar pick will have to be moved somewhere. And maybe someday Lyla will find a little dusty box in her drawer full of books and open it up to find a delicate blown glass bride's face, some glittering shards and an almost intact heart. A salvaged collection of beautiful things, given for love, and fragile in their potential.